"With a powerful story ... ...nce worth swooning over, *Saving June* is a fresh, fun and poignant book that I couldn't tear myself away from."

–Kody Keplinger, *New York Times* bestselling author of *The DUFF*

"The strength of Harrington's writing is that it leaves no point of view unturned. She portrays the far-reaching pain caused by all types of bullying, and more important, stresses the strength a teenager gains when they are bold enough to go against the crowd."

–*Booklist* on *Speechless*

"*Saving June* should become a movie some day—it even includes its own soundtrack."

–*VOYA*

"Harrington has created a powerful, strong-willed character, portraying her with true-to-life complexity. Even at her most unlikable, Chelsea never ceases to be fascinating."

–*Publishers Weekly* on *Speechless*

"*Saving June* is an incredible debut. Like the best of songs, it brings tears to your eyes and makes you smile. Like the best of road trip stories, it takes you on a vivid jou... ... ...uthor of *Ballads of Suburbia*

**Also available from Hannah Harrington
and Harlequin TEEN**

SPEECHLESS

HANNAH HARRINGTON

Saving June

H HARLEQUIN®TEEN™

Recycling programs
for this product may
not exist in your area.

ISBN-13: 978-0-373-21202-6

Saving June

Printed in U.S.A.

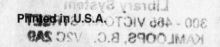

For Judith St. King,
my second mother.

one

According to the puppy-of-the-month calendar hanging next to the phone in the kitchen, my sister June died on a Thursday, exactly nine days before her high school graduation. May's breed is the golden retriever—pictured is a whole litter of them, nestled side by side in a red wagon amid a blooming spring garden. The word *Graduation!!* is written in red inside the white square, complete with an extra exclamation point. If she'd waited less than two weeks, she would be June who died in June, but I guess she never took that into account.

The only reason I'm in the kitchen in the first place is because somehow, somewhere, someone got the idea in their head that the best way to comfort a mourning family is to present them with plated foods. Everyone has been dropping off stupid casseroles, which is totally useless, because nobody's eating anything anyway. We already have a refrigerator stocked with not only casseroles, but lasagnas, jams, homemade breads, cakes and more. Add to that the lemon meringue pie I'm holding and the Scott family could open up a restaurant out of our own kitchen. Or at the very least a well-stocked deli.

I slide the pie on top of a dish of apricot tart, then shut the refrigerator door and lean against it. One moment. All I want is one moment to myself.

"Harper?"

Not that that will be happening anytime soon.

It's weird to see Tyler in a suit. It's black, the lines of it clean and sharp, the knot of the silk tie pressed tight to his throat, uncomfortably formal.

"You look…nice," he says, finally, after what has to be the most awkward silence in all of documented history.

Part of me wants to strangle him with his dumb tie, and at the same time, I feel a little sorry for him. Which is ridiculous, considering the circumstances, but even with a year in age and nearly a foot in height on me, he looks impossibly young. A little boy playing dress-up in Daddy's clothes.

"Can I help you with something?" I say shortly. After a day of constant platitudes, a steady stream of thank-you-for-your-concern and we're-doing-our-best and it-was-a-shock-to-us-too, my patience is shot. It definitely isn't going to be extended to the guy who broke my sister's heart a few months ago.

Tyler fidgets with his tie with both hands. I always did make him nervous. I guess it's because when your girlfriend's the homecoming queen, and your girlfriend's sister is—well, me, it's hard to find common ground.

"I wanted to give you this," he says. He steps forward and presses something small and hard into my hand. "Do you know what it is?"

I glance down into my open palm. Of course I know: June's promise ring. The familiar sapphire stone embedded in white gold gleams under the kitchen light.

The first time June showed it to me, around six months ago, she was at the stove, cooking something spicy smelling in a pan while I grabbed orange juice from the fridge. She was always doing that, cooking elaborate meals, even though I almost never saw her eat any of them.

She extended her hand in a showy gesture as she said, "It belonged to his grandmother. Isn't it beautiful?" And when she just about swooned, it was all I could do not to roll my eyes so hard they fell out of my head.

"I think it's stupid," I told her. "You really want to spend the rest of your life with that jerk-off?"

"Tyler is not a jerk-off. He's sweet. He wants us to move to California together after we graduate. Maybe rent an apartment by the beach."

California. June was always talking about California and having a house by the ocean. I didn't know why she was so obsessed with someplace she'd never even been.

"Seriously, you're barely eighteen," I reminded her. "Why would you even *think* about marriage?"

June gave me a look that made it clear the age difference between us might as well be ten years instead of less than two. "You'll understand when you're older," she said. "When you fall in love."

I rolled my eyes as I drank straight from the jug, then wiped my mouth off with my sleeve. "Yeah, I'm so sure."

"What, you don't believe in true love?"

"You've met our parents, haven't you?"

Two months later, June caught her precious Tyler macking on some skanky freshman cheerleader at a car wash fundraiser meant to raise money for the band geeks. The only thing really raised was the bar for most indiscreet and stupidest way to get caught cheating on your girlfriend. Tyler was quite the class act.

A month after *that* disaster, our parents' divorce was finalized.

June and I never really talked about either of those things. It wasn't like when we were kids; we weren't best friends anymore. Hadn't been in years.

Now, even looking at the ring makes me want to throw up. I all but fling it at Tyler in my haste to not have it in my possession. "No. I don't want it. It's yours."

"It should've been hers," he insists, snatching my hand to try and force it back. "We would've gotten back together. I know we would have. It should've been hers. Keep it."

What is he doing? I want to scream, or kick him in the stomach, or something. Anything to get him away from me.

"I don't want it." My voice arches into near hysteria. What makes him think this is appropriate? It is not appropriate. It is so far from appropriate. "Okay? I don't want it. I don't."

Our reverse tug-of-war is interrupted by the approach of a stout, so-gray-it's-blue-haired woman, who pushes in front of Tyler and tugs me to her chest in a smothering embrace. She has that weird smell all old ladies seem to possess, must and cat litter and pungent perfume, and when she releases me from her death grip, holding me at arm's length, my eyes focus enough for a better look. Her clown-red lipstick and pink blush contrast sharply with her papery white skin. It's like a department store makeup counter threw up on her face.

I have no idea who she is, but I'm not surprised. An event like this in a town as small as ours has all kinds of people coming out of the woodwork. This isn't the first time today I've been cornered and accosted by someone I've never met acting like we're old friends.

"It's such a tragedy," the woman is saying now. "She was so young."

"Yes," I agree. I feel suddenly dizzy, the blood between my temples pounding at a dull roar.

"So gifted!"

"Yes," I say again.

"She was a lovely girl. You would never think…" As she trails off, the wrinkles around her mouth deepen. "The Lord does work in mysterious ways. My deepest sympathies, sweetheart."

The edges of my vision go white. "Thank you."

I can't do this. I can't do this. It feels like there's an elephant sitting on my chest.

"*There* you are."

I expect to see another stranger making a beeline for me, but instead it's my best friend, Laney. She has on a dress I've never seen before, black with a severe pencil skirt, paired with skinny heels and a silver necklace that dips low into her cleavage. Her thick blond hair, which usually hangs to the middle of her back, is twisted and pinned to the back of her head. I wonder how she managed to take so much hair and cram it into such a neat bun.

She strides forward, her heels clicking on the linoleum, and only meets my eyes briefly before turning her attention to Tyler.

"Your mom's looking for you," she says, her hand on his arm. From the outside it would look like a friendly gesture, unless you knew, like I do, that Laney can't stand Tyler, that she thinks he's an insufferable dick.

"She is?" Tyler glances from me to Laney uncertainly, like he's weighing the odds of whether it'd be a more productive use of time to find his mother or to stay here and see if he can convince me to take the stupid ring as some token of his atonement, or whatever he thinks such an exchange would mean.

"Of course she is," Laney says glibly, drawing him toward the doorway to the dining room. She's definitely lying; I can tell by the mannered, lofty tilt in her speech. That's the voice she uses with her father—one that takes extra care to be as articulate and practiced as possible. It's completely different from her normal tone.

As soon as Laney and Tyler disappear from sight, the woman, whom I still can't place, starts up her nattering again with renewed vigor. "Tell me, how is the family coping? Oh, your *poor* mother—"

And just like that, Laney's back, sans Tyler. She sets a hand on the woman's elbow, steers her toward the doorway.

"You should go talk to her," she suggests with a feigned earnestness most Emmy winners can only dream of.

The woman considers. "Do you think?"

"Absolutely. She'd *love* to see you. In fact, I'll come with you."

This is why I love Laney: she always has my back. We've been best friends since we were alphabetically seated next to each other in second grade. Scott and Sterling. She's the coolest person I know; she wears vintage clothes all the time and can quote lines from old fifties-era screwball romantic comedies and just about any rap song by heart, and she doesn't care what anyone thinks. The best thing about her is that she thinks I'm awesome, too. It's harder than you think to find someone who truly believes in your unequivocal, unconditional awesomeness, especially when you're like me: unspectacular in every way.

As they walk away arm in arm, Laney glances over her shoulder at me, and I shoot her the most grateful look I can manage. She returns it with a strained smile and hurries herself and the woman into the crowded dining room, where I hear muted conversation and the clatter of dinnerware. If I follow, I'll be mobbed by scores of relatives and acquaintances and total strangers, all pressing to exchange pleasantries and share their condolences. And I'll have to look them in the eye and say thank you and silently wonder how many of them blame me for not seeing the signs.

"The signs." It makes it sound like June walked around with the words I Am Going to Kill Myself written over her head in bright buzzing neon. If only. Maybe then—

No. I cut off that train of thought before it can go any further. Another wave of panic rises in my chest, so I lean my hands heavily against the kitchen counter to stop it, press into the edge until it cuts angry red lines into my palms. If I can just get through this hour, this afternoon, this horrible, horrible day, then maybe…maybe I can fall apart then. Later. But not now.

Air. What I need is air. This house, all of these people, they're suffocating. Before anyone else can come into the kitchen and trap me in another conversation, I slip out the back door leading to the yard and close it behind me as quietly as possible.

I sit down on the porch steps, my black dress tangling around my legs, and drop my head into my hands. I've never felt so exhausted in my life, which I suppose isn't such a shock considering I can't have slept more than ten hours in the past five days. I close my eyes and take a deep breath, and then another, and then hold the next one until my chest burns so badly I think it might burst.

When I inhale again, I breathe in the humid early-summer air, dirt and dew and—something else. A hint of smoke. My eyes open, and when I turn my head slightly to my left, I see someone, a boy, standing against the side of the house.

Apparently getting a moment to myself just isn't in the cards today.

I scratch at my itchy calves as I give him a cool once-over. He's taller than me by a good half a head, and he looks lean and hard. Compact. His messy, light brown hair sticks out in all directions, like he's hacked at it on his own with a pair of scissors. In the dark. He's got a lit cigarette in one hand and the other stuck in the front pocket of his baggy black jeans. Unlike every other male I've seen today, he's not wearing a suit—just the jeans and a button-down, sleeves rolled up to his elbows, and a crooked tie in a shade of black that doesn't quite match his shirt.

I notice his eyes, partly because they're a startling green, and partly because he's staring at me intently. He seems familiar, like someone I've maybe seen around at school. It's hard to be sure. All of the faces I've seen over the past few days have swirled into an unrecognizable blur.

"So you're the little sister," he says. It's more of a sneer than anything else.

"That would be me." I watch as he brings the cigarette to his lips. "Can I bum one?"

The request must catch him off guard, because for a few seconds he just blinks at me in surprise, but then he digs into his back pocket and shakes a cigarette out of the pack. He slides it into his mouth and lights it before extending it toward me. When I walk over and take it from him by the tip, I hold it between my index finger and middle finger, like a normal person, while the boy pinches his between his index finger and thumb, the way you would hold a joint. Not that I've ever smoked a joint, but I've seen enough people do it to know how it's done.

When I first draw the smoke into my lungs, I cough hard as the boy watches me struggle to breathe. I look away, embarrassed, and inhale on the cigarette a few more times until it goes down smoother.

We smoke in silence, the only sound the scraping of his thumb across the edge of the lighter, flicking the flame on and off, on and off. The boy stares at me, and I stare at his shoes. He has on beat-up Chucks. Who wears sneakers to a wake? There's writing on them, too, across the white toes, but I can't read it upside down. He also happens to be standing on what had at one point in time been my mother's garden. She used to plant daisies every spring, but I can't remember the last time she's done that. It's been years, probably. His shoes only crush overgrown weeds that have sprouted up from the ground.

I meet his eyes again. He still stares; it's a little unnerving. His gaze is like a vacuum. Intense.

"Do you cut your own hair?" I ask.

He tilts his head to the side. "Talk about your non sequitur."

"Because it looks like you do," I continue. He looks at me for a long time, and when I realize he isn't going to say anything, I take another pull off the cigarette and say, "It looks ridiculous, by the way."

"Don't you want to know what I'm doing out here?" He sounds a little confused, and a lot annoyed.

I blow out smoke, watching it float away, and shrug. "Not really."

The boy's stare has turned unquestionably into a glare. I'm a little surprised, and weirdly…relieved, or something. It's better than the pity I've seen on people's faces all day. I don't know what to do with pity. Pissed off, I can handle. At the same time, I don't want to be around anyone right now. At all.

I should be inside, comforting my mother. The last time I saw her, she was sitting on the couch, halfway through what had to have been her fourth glass of wine in the past hour. If

I was a good daughter, I'd be at her side. But I'm not used to being the good one. That was always June's role. Mine is to be the disappointment, the one who doesn't try hard enough and gets in too much trouble and could be something if I only applied myself.

Now I don't know what I'm supposed to be.

I toe into the garden a little, drop the cigarette butt and scrape dirt over to cover the hole. At this point I have two options: face the throng of people inside, or stay out here. It's like a no-win coin toss. Option number one won't be pretty, but I might as well get it over with, since I don't really want to stand outside being glared at for no reason by some stranger, either. Even if he does share his cigarettes.

"Well, it's been fun," I say drlly. "We should do this again sometime. Really."

I teeter across the uneven yard in my stupid shoes, aware that one misstep will send me sprawling. I've got one foot on the porch stairs when he calls out, "Hey," in a sharp voice.

I turn. The boy steps away from the white siding, out of the garden. He pauses, his mouth open like he's going to say something more, but then he closes it again like he's changed his mind and flicks the last inch of his cigarette onto the grass.

"You tore your...leg...thing," he says.

I bend my leg up to examine it—sure enough, there's a tear in the tights, running from my ankle to my shin. When I glance back up at him, he's disappearing around the corner. What the hell? Does he think that makes him, like, an impressive badass or something, having the last word and mysterious exit? Because it doesn't. It just makes him kind of a jackass.

The back door opens—it's Laney.

"Harper?" she says, looking confused. "Are you okay?"

"I'm fine," I say automatically, even though really, nothing could be further from the truth. I smooth my dress down and carefully make my way up the porch steps. "Thanks for rescuing me earlier. I needed that. I was getting a little—" I stop because I don't really know what word I'm searching for.

Laney shrugs like it was nothing. "Don't mention it." She holds something out to me—a covered dish. Of course. Her face is apologetic. "It's quiche, courtesy of my *dear* mother."

Back in the kitchen, I try to rearrange the refrigerator shelves to make space, but despite my valiant efforts, the quiche won't fit. Eventually I give up and leave it out on the counter. The whole time Laney watches me cautiously, like she's afraid at any moment I'll collapse on the kitchen floor in tears. Everyone has been looking at me that way all day. Maybe because I didn't cry during the memorial service, even when my mother stood at the podium sobbing and sobbing until my aunt Helen gently led her away.

I don't know what's wrong with me. June was my sister. I should be a mess right now. Inconsolable. Not walking around, dry-eyed, completely hollow.

"I saw your dad out there," Laney says. "He looks—"

"Uncomfortable?" I supply.

She makes a strangled sound, something close to a laugh. "I see he left the Tart at home. Thank God for *that,* right?"

The Tart is Laney's nickname for my father's girlfriend. Her actual name is Melinda; she's ten years younger than he is and waitresses for a catering company. That's how she met my father—the previous April, she'd worked the big party his accounting firm threw every year to celebrate the end of tax season. The party was held on a riverboat, and during her breaks, they stood out on the deck, talking and joking about the salmon filet. Or so the story goes.

Dad maintains to this day nothing happened between them until after the separation. I have my doubts.

The truth is, I don't actually hold any personal grudge against Melinda. She's nice enough, even if her button nose seems too small for her face and she has these moist eyes that make it look like she could cry at any moment, and she wears pastels and high heels all of the time, even when she's doing some mundane chore like cleaning dishes or folding laundry. And sure, she can't hold a decent conversation to save her life, but it's not like I blame *her* for my family being so screwed up. She just happened to be a catalyst, speeding up the inevitable implosion.

"You look really tired," Laney says. "I mean, no offense." She winces. "I'm sorry. That was so the wrong thing to say."

She says it like there's a right thing to say. There really, really isn't.

"I'm just ready to be...done." I rub at my eyes. "I'm sick of talking."

"Well, then don't! Talk anymore, I mean," she says. "You shouldn't if you don't want to. Here, come on. Let's go upstairs and blow off the circus."

It's easy to get from the kitchen to the bottom of the staircase with Laney acting as my buffer, diverting the attention of those who approach with skilled ease and whisking me to the haven of the second floor in a matter of seconds. In the upstairs hallway, there are two framed photos on the wall: the first is of June, her senior portrait, and the second is my school picture from earlier this year. Some people say June and I look alike, but I don't see much resemblance. We both have the same brown hair, but hers is thicker, wavier, while mine falls flat and straight. Where her eyes are a clear blue, mine are a dim gray. Her features are softer and prettier, more delicate; maybe I'm not ugly, but in comparison I'm nothing remarkable.

There used to be a third picture on the wall, an old family portrait. For their tenth wedding anniversary, my parents rented this giant tent, and they hosted a festive dinner with a buffet and music and all of our family and friends. June and I spent the evening running around with plastic cups, screaming with laughter, making poor attempts to capture fireflies, while my parents danced under the stars to their song—Frank Sinatra's "The Way You Look Tonight."

Toward the end of the night, someone gathered the four of us together and took a snapshot. June and I were giggling, heads bent close together, our parents standing above us in an embrace, gazing at each other instead of the camera. It always struck me in the years after how bizarre it was, how two people could look at one another with such tenderness and complete love, and how quickly that could dissolve into nothing but bitterness.

That photo hung on our wall for years and years, staying the same even as June's and mine were switched out to reflect our progressing ages. Now it's gone, just an empty space, and June's will remain the same forever. Only mine will ever change.

I stare at June's photo and think: *This is it. I'll never see her face again.* I'll never see the little crinkle in her nose when she was lost in thought, or her eyebrows knitting together as she frowned, or the way she'd press her lips together so hard they'd almost disappear while she tried not to laugh at some vulgar joke I'd made, because she didn't want to let me know she thought it was funny. All I have left are photos of her with this smile, frozen in time. Bright and blinding and happy. A complete lie.

It hurts to look, but I don't want to stop. I want to soak in everything about my sister. I want to braid it into my DNA, make it part of me. Maybe then I'll be able to figure out how this happened. How she could do this. People are looking to me for answers, because I'm the one tied the closest to June, by name and blood and memory, and it's wrong that I'm as clueless as everyone else. I need to know.

"Come on," says Laney gently, taking my hand and squeezing it, leading me toward my bedroom.

I drag my feet and shake her off. "No. No, wait."

I veer off toward June's room. The door is closed; I place my hand on the brass knob and keep it there for a moment. I haven't been inside since she died. I try thinking back to the last time I was in there, but racing through my memory, I can't pinpoint it. It seems unfair, the fact that I can't remember.

Laney stands next to me, shifting from foot to foot. "Harper…"

I ignore her and push the door open. The room looks exactly the same as it always has. Of course it does—what did I expect? Laney flicks on the light and waits.

"It doesn't feel real," she says softly. "Does it feel real to you?"

"No." Six days. It's already been six days. It's *only* been six days. Time is doing weird things, speeding up and slowing down.

June's room has always been the opposite of mine—mine is constantly messy, dirty clothes and books littering the floor. Hers is meticulously clean. I can't tell if that's supposed to mean something. She'd always been organized, her room spotless in comparison to the disaster area that is mine, but I wonder if she'd cleaned it right before, on purpose. Like she didn't want to leave behind any messes.

Well, she'd left behind plenty of messes. Just not physical ones.

"Do you know what they're going to do with—with the ashes?" Laney asks.

The lump that's been lodged in my throat all day grows bigger. The ashes. I can't believe that's how we're referring to her now. Though I guess what was left was never really June. Just a body.

Thinking about the body makes me think about that morning, six days ago in the garage, and I really don't want that in my head. I look up at Laney and say, "They're going to split them once my dad picks out his own urn."

"Seriously?"

"Yeah."

"That's—"

"I know."

Screwed up, is what she wanted to say. It makes my stomach turn, like it did when Aunt Helen decorated the mantel above our fireplace, spread out a deep blue silk scarf, and set up two candleholders and two silver-framed black-and-white photos of June on each side, leaving space for the urn in the middle.

"It should be balanced," she'd said, hands fisted on her hips, head tipped to the side as she studied her arrangement, like she was scrutinizing a new art piece instead of the vase holding the remains of a once living, breathing person. My sister.

Laney hooks her chin over my shoulder, her arm around my stomach. I don't really want to be touched, my skin is crawling, but I let her anyway. For her sake.

"There wasn't a note?" she asks, soft and sad. I shake my head. I don't know why she's asking. She already knows.

No note. No nothing. Just my sister, curled in the backseat of her car, an empty bottle of pills in her hand, the motor still running.

I know that because I'm the one who found her.

I slip away from Laney's grasp. She hasn't asked me for the details of what happened that morning, and I'm pretty sure she knows the last thing I want to do is talk about it, but I don't want to give her an opening.

Everything has changed and everything is the same. Everything in this room, anyway. The only addition since June's death is a few plastic bags placed side by side on the desk, filled with all of the valuables salvaged from her car—a creased notepad, a beaded bracelet with a broken clasp, the fuzzy pink dice that had hung around her rearview mirror. The last bag contains a bunch of pens, a tube of lip gloss and a silver disc. I pick it up to examine it when I notice the desk drawer isn't shut all of the way.

I draw it open and poke around. There are some papers inside, National Honor Society forms and a discarded photo of her and Tyler that she'd taken off the corner of her dresser mirror and stashed away after their breakup. And on top of everything, a blank envelope. I pull out the letter inside and unfold it. It's her acceptance to Berkeley, taken from the bulky acceptance package and stored away here for some reason I'll never know. Tucked in the folds is also a postcard, bent at the edges. The front of it shows a golden beach dotted with beach-goers, strolling along the edge of a calm blue-green sea, above them an endless sky with *California* written in bubbly cursive.

The only time I ever heard my sister raise her voice with Mom was the fight they had when Mom insisted June accept the full scholarship she'd received to State. Mom said we couldn't afford the costs. It would've been different before the divorce, but there was just no way to fund the tuition now, not when Dad had his own rent to pay, and the money that had been set aside was used to pay their lawyers. Besides, she reasoned, June should stay close to home. There was no reason for her to go all the way across the country when she could get a fine, free-ride education right here.

When June was informed of this, she and Mom had screamed at each other, no-holds-barred, for over an hour, until they were too exhausted to argue anymore and June had finally, in defeat, retreated to her room. She didn't speak to our mother for an entire week, but she accepted the scholarship and admission to State and never mentioned Berkeley to us again.

I turn the postcard over, and it's like all of the air has been sucked out of the room.

Laney notices, because she lifts her head and says, "Harper? What is it? *Harper*."

I'm too busy staring at the back of the card to answer. Written there are the words, *California, I'm coming home,* in June's handwriting. Nothing more.

Laney pulls it from my hands and reads it over and over again, her eyes flitting back and forth. She looks at me. "What do you think it means?"

It could mean nothing. But it could mean something. It was at the top of the drawer, after all. Maybe she meant for it to be found.

California was her dream. She wanted out of this town more than anything. She must have been suffocating, too, and we'd drifted so far apart that I never noticed. I never took it seriously. No one did. And now she's dead.

"It's not right," I say.

Laney frowns. "What's not right?"

"Everything." I snatch back the postcard and wave it in the air. "*This* is what she wanted. Not to be stuck in this house, on display like—like some *trophy*. She *hated* it here, didn't she? I mean, isn't that why she—"

I can't finish; I throw the postcard and envelope back into the drawer and slam it shut with more force than necessary, causing the desk to rattle. I am so angry I am shaking with it. It's an abstract kind of anger, directionless but overwhelming.

Laney folds her arms across her chest and bows her head.

"I don't know," she says quietly. "I don't know."

"How did things get so bad?" I whisper. Laney doesn't answer, and I know it's because she, like me, has no way to make sense of this completely senseless act. Girls like June are not supposed to do this. Girls who have their whole lives ahead of them.

We stand next to each other, my hands still on the drawer handles, when the thought comes to me. It's just a spark at first, a flicker of a notion.

"We should take her ashes to California."

I don't even mean to blurt it out loud, but once it's out there, it's out—no taking it back. And as the idea begins to take root in my mind, I decide maybe…maybe that isn't such a bad thing.

"Harper." Laney's using that voice again, that controlled voice, and it makes me want to hit her. She's not supposed to use that voice. Not on me. "Don't you think that's kind of a stretch? Just because of a postcard?"

"It's not just because of a postcard."

It's more than that. It's about what she wanted for herself but didn't think she'd ever have, for whatever reason. It's about how there is so much I didn't know about my sister, and this is as much as I'll ever have of her. College acceptance letters and postcards. Reminders of her unfulfilled dreams.

"Your mom would totally flip," Laney points out, but she sounds more entertained by the prospect than worried. "Not to mention your aunt."

I don't want to think about Aunt Helen. She's just like everyone else downstairs, seeing in June only what they wanted to see—a perfect daughter, perfect friend, perfect student, perfect girl. They're all grieving over artificial memories, some two-dimensional, idealized version of my sister they've built up in their heads because it's too scary to face reality. That June had something in her that was broken.

And if someone like June—so loving, kind, full of goodness and light and promise—could implode that way, what hope is there for the rest of us?

"Who cares about Aunt Helen?" I snap.

Laney hesitates, but I see something in her eyes change, like a car shifting gears. Like she's realizing how serious I am about this. "How would we even get there?"

"We can drive. You have a car." Not much of a car, but more than what I have, which is nothing. Laney's dad is loaded but has this weird selective code of ethics, where he believes strongly in teaching her the lesson of accountability and made her pay half for her own car, and so after some months of bagging groceries, she'd saved up enough to put half down on a beat-up old Gremlin.

"My Gremlin is on its last leg. Wheel. Whatever. There is no way it'd make it from Michigan to California."

"Yeah, but still—" I'm growing more convinced by the second. "That's what she wanted, right? California, the ocean?"

Laney just stares at me, and I wonder if this is how it will be from now on, if I am always going to be looked at like that by everyone, even my best friend.

I don't care. She can stare at me all day and it won't change my mind. There were so many things I'd done wrong in my relationship with my sister, but this. I could do this. I owe her that much.

"I'm going to do this," I tell her. "With you or without you. I'd rather it be with."

I expect Laney to say, "It would be impossible," or, "I know you don't mean it," or, "Don't you think you should go lie down?"

Instead, she glances down at the postcard, brow furrowed like if she stares hard enough it'll reveal something more.

When she looks back up, her mouth has edged into a half smile. "So California, huh? That's gonna be a long drive."

two

Aunt Helen is the last to leave that night. Laney leaves because her mother forces her, and even then I have to all but shove her out the door.

"I can stay," she says. She has her arms around me, clinging to me like a life preserver. I'm getting the idea that she needs to give me comfort way more than I need to be receiving it. "For as long you want. I don't want you to be alone."

It would be nice to have her here, but I know this is something I'm going to have to handle on my own. Better get used to it now.

I eventually pry her off and try to force a smile, but it's like my lips have forgotten how. I sigh. "Go home. Seriously, it's fine. I promise."

I know she's not convinced, but she squeezes me once more, kisses my cheek and lets her mother drag her out the door.

Before Laney it was my father, who hadn't spoken at great length to any of us all day, but as he left, he grabbed me in a stiff-armed hug. In that second I had this feeling, the kind that grabs you by the throat, a desperate desire for him to stay, because he knows Mom so much better than I do, because he might know how to fix this.

When he pulled back, he ruffled my hair the way he did when I was a kid. Except now the gesture felt unnatural, like he was out of practice. And I knew he couldn't fix anything in our family. Not anymore.

"I'll be in touch, kiddo," he promised, but promises from my father never meant anything before, and I don't expect them to mean anything now.

As always, Aunt Helen can't leave without making a fuss, telling my mother to get some rest, and that she'll be over later the next morning, and gushing about how beautiful the service was.

"I know she was looking down on us," she sniffs, dabbing her eyes with the wrinkled tissue she's been clutching in her hand for hours. "She would have been *so* touched."

It's pretty much the most clichéd thing anyone could possibly say, not to mention the most untrue, but apparently it's enough to start her waterworks again, which in turn makes my mother cry. Aunt Helen reaches for me, and I brace myself for another hug, but she stops halfway, her hand awkwardly wound around my shoulder. The way she's looking at me is the kindest it's been in days.

We've never gotten along. Aunt Helen is really into church and prayer and Jesus; she doesn't approve of my black hoodies and black nail polish and my admitted penchant for excessive swearing. And ever since I announced in the middle of last Easter's family brunch that I'm not sure I believe in God at all, she's treated me like I'm some kind of heathen. Maybe it wasn't the best timing on my part, but I did get a kick out of the horrified look on her face.

Of course, back then, questions of God and the afterlife weren't really relevant to my life like they are now. I think

Aunt Helen is hoping I'm going to have this moment of revelation where I'll declare myself a born-again Christian who
sees the light of Jesus's love. But June dying hasn't given me any
spiritual clarity. It's just made everything even more confusing.

"Take care of your mother, okay?" she says to me now.
"She needs you."

I nod. "I know. I will."

"I'll be over tomorrow to help with things. Feel free to call
if you need me." She pauses and sniffles a little before giving my shoulder an awkward squeeze. "I love you, sweetie."

My eyes snap up to hers in surprise. I can't remember the
last time she said that to me. The confusion must show on my
face, because she clears her throat awkwardly and takes her
hand off my shoulder.

"All right then." She nods quickly and hurries to the front
door before I can fully react. With her back to me, she says,
"Remember—this too shall pass."

I don't know if she is saying it to me, or to my mother, or
to herself. As the door closes behind her, I figure it doesn't
really matter.

In some ways I admire Aunt Helen's unwavering certainty
in God's divine plan. It must be comforting, to have faith like
that. To believe so concretely that there's someone—something—out there watching guard, keeping us safe, testing us
only with what we can handle. I've never believed in anything
the way Aunt Helen believes in God.

I don't really know what's supposed to happen now that
everyone's gone. I'm pretty sure my mother doesn't know, either, because we look at each other for a long time in silence.

"Well," she says after a while. Her mouth hangs open like
she's mid-sentence, but she doesn't finish whatever thought
was on her mind. She just turns and wanders into the living
room. I'm pretty sure she's still a little drunk. The last time

she drank this much was right after Dad left. I hope this isn't going to be a repeat of those days.

I follow her and watch as she drops onto the couch and slides off her heels. Flowers and cards are everywhere. I step over a heart-shaped wreath, scrunch in at the other end of the couch, and turn on the television to some formulaic sitcom. The sudden wave of canned studio laughter is startling to my ears. A few minutes later I turn it back off. Mom doesn't seem to notice.

"Do you need anything?" I ask. I keep my voice low, like I'll scare her if I talk too loud.

"No." She doesn't move. "Did you eat?"

"A little." All I've had today is an apple from this morning, but I can't stomach the thought of eating anything more.

"You should eat."

"I will." I stand. "You're sure I can't get you something?"

After a moment, she shakes her head. I hesitate, wondering if I should press, and then give up and go to the kitchen. Dirty plates and silverware are stacked on the counter, so I rinse them off and stick them in the dishwasher. The methodical process of sponging the dishes off and stacking them is a nice distraction. I like having something to do with my hands, kind of like how it was when I smoked in the garden earlier with that weird boy.

And really, what was *that* about? What was he even doing here? Did he know June? Probably he was just someone in her grade. Most of the graduating class attended the service, but only her closest friends came to the wake. June was friends with everyone, always had invites on the weekends for movies and shopping and parties, but she didn't really have one single best friend. Not like how I have Laney, and only Laney.

Still, there was something off about that boy. He wouldn't have been there if he was just some passing acquaintance. It bothers me, the idea that he might have had some role in her life and I didn't know about it. I can't stop thinking about the look on his face. That open display of hostility. All of June's other friends either kept their distance or wanted to cry on my shoulder. At least this guy didn't bother hiding his true feelings. It was sort of refreshing, really.

When I'm done with the dishes, I go back to the living room, only to find Mom fast asleep. The sight of her curled up in her dress, eyes closed and lipsticked mouth parted, makes me ache. She's been falling apart ever since it happened. I have to admit, I'm glad Aunt Helen has been around to help, even if her control-freak ways grate on my nerves. I am so not equipped for this. I've never been good at the emotional stuff. Except anger. Anger, I'm good at.

Not too long ago, June told me I had the thickest skin of anyone she knew. "Nothing ever gets to you," she said, like it was a compliment. "You're like a rock. An island."

I told her to shut it with the poetic crap. What I didn't point out was how completely wrong she was. Things get to me all the time—I just don't see the point in making a big deal out of it. I learned pretty early on that no one, aside from Laney, is interested in hearing about my stupid teenage angst. Venting to her is enough of an outlet for me.

I never knew what June's coping methods were, if she had any to begin with; I never even thought about it, really. Her life seemed so perfect from the outside—what could she possibly have to be upset about? Sometimes I'd catch her standing in front of the mirror in her room, just staring, like she was looking for imaginary imperfections. I used to think it was pure vanity, but I slowly came to realize it wasn't that. It was insecurity.

It didn't make sense to me. How could she be insecure, when everyone—our parents, her friends, her teachers, Tyler—

always told her how perfect she was? It pissed me off, if anything. As soon as I learned, early on in life, that I could never measure up to June, I'd made it a point to be her polar opposite. June was unfailingly polite; I'm brash and don't go out of my way to be nice to people I don't like, ever. June spent crazy amounts of time and energy on her appearance, the right clothes and the right hair style; my default look includes hoodies, jeans, a ponytail and excessive eyeliner. June made honor roll every semester; I flirt the line between average and below average, cut class on a regular basis and there's basically a revolving door to the detention room designed specifically for me.

When I was a little kid and used to get in trouble, Mom always used to say, "Why can't you be more like your sister?" But I wasn't interested in being like June, and I definitely didn't want to live in June's shadow. Even if mine was less impressive, at least it was my own.

I take an afghan off the ottoman and drape it over my mother, who now has one dead daughter and one delinquent. June's unmatchable goodness and my unmatchable knack for constantly disappointing my parents used to even each other out, but now the scale is tipped, unbalanced, spotlighting my own failures more than ever. No wonder Mom's such a mess. I tuck the afghan in around her shoulders and place a pillow under her head. She doesn't stir at all, just keeps on snoring. She always snores after she's been drinking.

That night, I lie in bed, miles from sleep. Closing my eyes, I think about how tomorrow will be the first day June is gone, *really* gone. Life will keep going and everyone will return to their usual routines, and it'll be the first real day of living without my sister. My life is now divided into two periods: With June and After June. I can't wrap my mind around the idea of it.

Laney's right; it doesn't feel real. Nothing does.

Sometime between gazing at the ceiling and thinking, I must drift off, because when my eyes open again, it's not as dark outside anymore. Also, there's an insistent beeping coming from downstairs. When it doesn't go away, I sit up and listen harder. It sounds like the smoke detector. I scramble into the hall and down the stairs two at a time.

"Mom?" I call out as I make my way into the kitchen. Okay, I don't see fire yet, but I can smell acrid smoke. My heart leaps in my chest. "Mom? What's going on?"

I find her sitting at the wooden table with an open bottle in front of her. At the stove, dark smoke curls up off a flat pan. I rush over and grab the pan handle, shove the whole thing into the sink and turn on the tap. Whatever was cooking has burnt to an indistinguishable black crisp. I drag a chair under the smoke detector and wave a dish towel until the blaring of the alarm silences.

"Mom, are you okay?" I ask. The adrenaline's still pumping, leaving my mouth completely dry.

Her eyes are glassy and dull, and she doesn't look at me. "I was making eggs."

"Oh." I return the chair to the table and eye the mostly empty wine bottle. "Mom…how long have you been up?"

She shrugs off the question, her slender fingers picking idly at the label. "It's just us now," she says. "The two of us." Finally she drags her gaze off the bottle and looks me in the eye; she looks as tired as I feel.

I know what she wants me to do. She wants me to come over and put my arms around her and tell her it'll be all right, but I can't. I can't because I don't know if it will. I can't because the thought of touching anyone right now makes me sick inside. Why is it so hard?

Eventually I say, "Yeah. I guess so."

Her throat works as she takes a long swallow of wine. When she sets the bottle back down, I wrap my fingers around the neck and gently pry it away from her.

"You should get some sleep," I say. I walk around the table to help her stand. "Here. Come on, let's go."

She doesn't fight me on it. With my arm around her waist, I lead her to her bedroom, peel back the covers and carefully roll her onto the mattress. She makes a soft sound as I pull the comforter over her, blinking up at me, already half-asleep.

"Harper," she says, voice slightly slurred. "I'm sorry about the eggs. I wanted you to have something to eat."

It's sweet, really, that she almost burned down the house in a drunken stupor for the sake of my appetite. Fucked up, but sweet. I hope this doesn't become a habit, though. She drank a lot after Dad left. I thought we were done with that.

"Go to sleep, Mom," I say softly. Her eyes flutter, her gaze vacant again, and a minute later I hear her breathing deep and even, so I know she's out.

The house is eerily quiet. All this time I thought silence would be a welcome reprieve, but it's less comforting than I imagined. The house feels so much bigger and colder than it ever has. I consider going downstairs to clean up my mother's mess, but the thought alone leaves me drained, so I start for my room, only to end up in front of June's. It's like I've stepped into wet cement; my feet stay rooted in place.

I stand outside the door for a while, until I feel stupid enough for being scared of a freaking door to force myself to open it and go inside.

This time I look for the last signs of life. One of her pillows is askew; a gray sweater is draped over the back of her desk chair. Other than that, nothing. I go to her desk and pick up one of the plastic bags. Again I notice the blank CD. There's no case for it, just the disc. As I slip it out of the bag, I realize that it must've been playing in the car stereo when I found her.

I turn the CD over in my hands. It's a normal blank disc, silver, with the words *Nolite te bastardes carborundorum* scratched across the bottom in black marker. I don't recognize the phrase—Latin, maybe?—or the handwriting. It's definitely not June's, which was round and loopy and girlish. I wonder if it's a mix Tyler had given her, back when they'd dated, but that's doubtful. Tyler's not bright enough to quote another language, and promise rings aside, his romantic gestures don't usually go beyond big talk. His idea of chivalry is coming to the door to pick a girl up for a date rather than honking from the driveway.

I switch on June's stereo, slide the disc into the tray and flip it to the first track. There are a few seconds of silence, and of all the things I expect to hear from those speakers, it most definitely is not the startling guitar riff that comes blaring out. A backbeat chimes in, an echoing bass, accompanied by a man's voice—rough around the edges and with a certain swagger to it.

I turn the volume up a few notches and stretch out on the floor, my back on the carpet, and feel the bass thrumming through me, vibrating. *You make a grown man cry.* This is not June's music. When we were younger, she plastered posters of manufactured boy bands on her walls, bought the albums of teen pop princesses. As a teen she listened to girls with guitars who didn't really know how to play, mainstream hip-hop hits, whatever generic pop medley was currently in high rotation on the Top 40 station.

The rock song ends and another by a different band comes on, slower, sort of bluesy. The singer is almost mournful, talking about a girl who had nothing at all.

I stay on the floor and listen to one song blend into the next.

Some I can place—after all, everyone knows "Stairway to Heaven," and Laney had a Billie Holiday phase that lasted long enough for me to recognize her distinctive velvety croon—but most of them I don't recognize. Each one is different, ranging from amped-up rock to jazz refrains, strung together in a way that feels like it should be schizophrenic, but somehow the transitions work. It's not jarring. The music rises and falls in the way a conventional story is supposed to, building up and hitting the climax and then easing into the conclusion.

I close my eyes and try to feel whatever my sister had felt in this. Which song was playing when she carefully, purposefully, popped sleeping pill after sleeping pill, those last moments of awareness before she slid into dark, permanent nothingness? More important, who made it in the first place? And what did *they* mean by it?

Did anything mean anything?

Aunt Helen comes over the next morning, as promised. She and Mom sort through the crazy amount of flowers and cards covering every spare inch of our living room. I stay in my bedroom, listening to June's CD on the neglected Discman I recovered from the depths of my closet. I can't stop thinking about it.

This isn't June's kind of music, and it's not my kind, either. My iPod is loaded with recommendations from Laney, all of the underground rap she likes, and some of my favorite indie artists, like the Decemberists and Cat Power and Sufjan Stevens. The songs on this CD sound more like something my parents would've listened to when they were my age.

I listen to the music and stare at my walls. They're covered in pictures I've taken ever since I got my Nikon SLR for Christmas and started taking photography more seriously. The only blank wall is the one nearest to my bed. I've been saving it for something special, but I don't know what.

I'm still staring at the empty white space when Aunt Helen comes up to my room with a sandwich and a glass of milk. I take out my headphones and sit up when she enters. She doesn't knock or anything, of course. Just barges right in and looks at me a little suspiciously. I think she does this because she wants to catch me in the middle of something. She probably thinks I sit up here carving emo poetry into my wrists with a razor blade. It's like I'm on suicide watch, by mere association.

"I made this for you," she says, thrusting the plate into my hands. "You should eat something."

I look down at the peanut butter and jelly sandwich. I hate jelly. I also hate when people come into my room without knocking.

"Thanks," I mumble. She stares at me, frowning, until I take a bite. God, with the way everyone's carrying on, you'd think I'm anorexic or something. I know I'm on the scrawny side, but seriously, this is getting ridiculous.

Satisfied, she takes a step back and surveys my room. Her frown deepens when her eyes land on the *Reservoir Dogs* film poster tacked up over my dresser. Jesus probably wouldn't approve, so of course, by proxy, Aunt Helen doesn't, either.

She tears her gaze away from the poster and looks at me again. "I know this is a difficult time," she says. "It's going to be an adjustment for all of us."

An adjustment. Talk about your understatement. I put down the sandwich and take a drink of milk, waiting to see where she's going with this.

"Your mother and I are worried about how you're coping," she continues. "She says you haven't…been very emotional."

It's true. I can't deny it. I haven't cried at all, not once. Even when I try to summon tears, it's like the well inside of me is bone-dry. There's just…nothing.

I glance away and shrug. "Maybe my mom should be worried about how *she's* coping. I'm not the one getting drunk off my ass, am I?"

"Don't take that tone with me," Aunt Helen snaps. "Your mother is doing her best. She only cares about you." She sighs, the tension easing from her shoulders. "Listen, Harper. I realize how hard this is for you."

A flash of anger heats up in my chest. She doesn't understand. She can't. If she did, she'd leave me alone instead of trying to force me to talk about this.

"You just have to take comfort in the fact June is with God now," she tells me.

I stare at her coldly. "Don't Christians believe people who kill themselves go to hell?" I ask.

Her eyes widen. "I don't think—"

"Get out. Please."

"Harper—"

"Just go, okay?"

Once she's left the room, shutting the door hard behind her, I lie down on my side. I hate Aunt Helen. I hate her stupid *your-sister's-in-a-better-place* crap. Like she could somehow know that. The anger bubbles up again, white-hot, and I lash out one closed fist and punch the wall. It doesn't make me feel any better, just hurts the hell out of my knuckles. My eyes burn like maybe I'm going to cry, but no tears come. Dammit.

Neither Aunt Helen nor Mom bother me for the rest of the night; I don't know if I should be upset about that or not. Instead of thinking about that, or my weird, inexplicable inability to cry, I choose to focus on the CD and what it might mean.

So June liked classic rock. It should be an inconsequential detail. It's not like it *matters*. But part of me feels like if I listen hard enough, I'll decode some secret message, put together the pieces of a puzzle that will shed light on some aspect of my sister's life I have no insight into. If I was in the dark about something as simple as her musical taste, what else was she hiding?

Examining that thought keeps me up all night. After hours of obsessing over it, I finally crack. I set the disc player aside and reach for my cell phone on the nightstand. Even in the dark, I can punch in Laney's number by memory. It rings about six times before she picks up.

"Hrrrmph?" I figure that's her version of hello at this hour.

"It's me." My voice comes out just above a whisper, too tight, and I don't know why my heart is beating so fast.

"Harper?" she says. There's a pause and the rustle of bed sheets. "What's wrong?"

Of course she would think something is wrong. Nobody ever calls in the middle of the night with good news.

"Nothing," I assure her hastily. "Nothing's wrong. I… Sorry, were you sleeping?"

"It's two in the morning. What do you think?" She yawns, and I can hear her shifting around like she's settling back against the pillows. "So what's up? You're sure everything's okay?"

I tell her about finding June's CD, how it had been playing in the car when I found her, how I know the handwriting on the disc isn't June's, and it isn't Tyler's, either. Laney goes quiet for a long time, and I start to wonder if she's fallen asleep somewhere in the midst of my rambling when she speaks.

"What does it say on the CD?" she asks.

"*Nolite te bastardes carborundorum.*" I recite it from memory. "I think it's Latin or something."

"Huh."

"You ever heard of it?"

"I don't think so. But that's what the internet is for, right?" I can practically hear her grinning on the other end of the line. "I'll come over tomorrow after school—we need to talk about how the hell we're going to pull off this California thing anyway, so we can look into it then. Unless you want me to come over right now."

"You don't have to."

"Yeah, I don't have to, but I will. If you need me to. Just give me five minutes—"

If I know Laney at all, the muffled noises I'm hearing are probably the sound of her getting dressed and grabbing her car keys. That's the kind of person she is.

I quickly say, "No. Don't. If you fail your exams due to sleep deprivation, your parents will never forgive me. It can wait."

I don't have to worry about exams this year. Two days after June and the garage and the pills, an emergency phone conference was conducted between my parents, the superintendent, the principal, the assistant principal and the guidance counselor, who all came to the conclusion that it would be best for all involved to allow me to skip the remainder of the school year and leave my grades as is.

As far as silver linings go, this one is really inadequate.

It turns out I was right: *Nolite te bastardes carborundorum* is, in fact, Latin.

"Well, not exactly," Laney corrects me. "I guess it's, like, bastardized Latin? Kind of like a joke. It translates roughly to 'Don't let the bastards grind you down.'"

I raise my eyebrows. "All this from the internet?"

"Google is *so* my bitch."

We're in June's room, on Laney's insistence that there might be more clues to the identity of the mastermind behind the mix CD. She drapes herself across June's bed, hanging off the edge upside down, her long wavy hair dangling to the floor. I feel sort of weird about her making herself comfortable on my dead sister's furniture, but it's not like everything can stay perfectly preserved in here forever.

I open one of June's desk drawers and ask, "How were your exams?"

"Precalc can just fuck right off," she moans, flinging an arm over her eyes.

"It went that bad, huh?" I wince sympathetically, then shoot her a sideways look. "So, um. What's it like?"

"What's what like? Precalculus?"

"No. You know. School."

School is a subject neither of us has broached. Mostly I haven't even bothered to consider the situation at Grand Lake High since everything went down, but now a sort of morbid curiosity gnaws at me. Laney pulls herself back onto the bed, sits with her knees under her and her hands in her lap, hiding behind a shroud of blond hair.

"It's…really weird." She clears her throat and glances at me nervously. "There was this assembly, for the whole school. All these girls crying who didn't even know her. I swear I wanted to kick them in the face. Oh, and they postponed graduation by a week. The guidance counselors made everyone quote, unquote 'close to the situation' have, like, an hour-long *debriefing* on our *feelings*. The administration is totally freaked out."

"Really?"

"I think they're afraid it's contagious, and one day they'll walk in and find the whole school drank cyanide-laced Kool-Aid or something," she says. She studies me carefully for a moment. "Are you okay? Like, generally speaking? I feel a little weird talking to you about this."

I look away and shrug. "You shouldn't. I wanted to know."

"Yeah, but…" Laney looks ready to say more, but she just sighs again and lets it drop, much to my relief.

I open the next drawer, pawing through the mess of papers there. It's more of the same—old homework assignments, class notes, a flimsy old binder project now falling apart. Nothing of importance. I wonder what my mother is going to want to do with all of this stuff. Throw it away? Or keep the room intact out of sentimentality, like some kind of shrine dedicated to June's memory?

Okay, that would be totally creepy.

"Hey," says Laney. She's leaning over and digging stuff out from under the bed. "I think I found something."

She resurfaces with a brown paper bag in hand. I sit on the bed next to her as she dumps its contents out onto the bedspread. Two CD cases tumble out. The first case cover has a painting of a man with a cigarette in his mouth, standing in the night under a neon sign, a woman in a fancy dress to the side gazing straight at him. The second cover has a man's head in black-and-white, overlapped by a series of squares and diamonds and circles, the lettering done in a light blue.

"Tom Waits," Laney reads off of the first CD's front, picking it up to examine it more closely. "Hmm. Never heard of the dude."

"What about the Kinks?" I question. I pass her the other CD.

"Actually, I've heard of them. Do you remember that guy? Colin Spangler?"

"Didn't you date him a few months ago?"

"Yeah, if by *date* you mean 'made out with in the back of his mom's minivan that one time.' Anyway, he was really into them. They had this one song about, like, a transvestite or something? I'm pretty sure Colin was super-gay. I mean, I'm not judging. But. Definitely gay."

Did my sister really listen to this stuff? I keep trying to make it fit with the image I have of her in my head, and it doesn't make sense.

"Where'd she even get these?" Laney asks, shaking the bag like there will magically be an answer inside. Nothing but a receipt flutters out. She smoothes creases from the bag with her hands, and then stops abruptly. I follow her gaze to the black logo emblazoned on the side.

"The Oleo Strut," I read aloud. "Where is that place?"

"It's way off on Kilgore," she explains. "By Stowey's Pizza. I drive past it all the time, I just never knew what it was."

She picks up the receipt as I scan the back of the Tom Waits album.

"A clue!" she shrieks, so loud I nearly topple off the bed, then springs to her feet frantically. "Harper, where's the CD?"

"It's on top of the stereo," I say. I watch as she practically dives to snatch it off the desk. "And what kind of a clue?"

"A handwriting sample!" she exclaims. She jumps back onto the bed and hands me the receipt. "Look on the back. That *T* is *unmistakable*."

"You've been watching way too much *CSI*." I roll my eyes, but flip the receipt over anyway. There's a note scribbled on the back in faded blue ink.

J.—
Hope you like my picks. Let me know what you think.
—Your Favorite Person in the Universe

It's the initial that bothers me most. That single letter. No one has ever shortened June's name like that. And the tone of the note, the signature—it suggests an inside joke, some kind of casual closeness. I crumple the receipt in my fist and toss the balled-up wad over my shoulder.

"You know what we should do?" Laney springs off the bed again, bouncing on her toes. "We should go to this Oleo place!"

"What for?"

"Uh, hello? To see if they might know who bought these? Don't you watch television? You always start at the scene of the crime."

"Last time I checked, buying music is not a crime," I point out. "Actually, they kind of encourage that, with all the illegal downloading these days—"

"Work with me here, Harper." She rolls her eyes. "I mean, aren't you curious? This could really lead to something."

Of course I'm curious. It's driving me crazy, not knowing. It's why I called Laney in the first place. I don't even have to say anything and she can see it, written all over my face.

"Go put on your shoes," she says, pushing me off the bed, "because we're totally going, right now."

Grand Lake is a town split into two sections, with the namesake lake as the epicenter. There's the east side of Grand Lake, where Laney and I live, primarily consisting of well-kept houses in quiet suburbs, and then there's the west side, generally considered lower income and populated with more apartment complexes. The east and west sides have two elementary schools and one middle school each, and after that, the kids are shuttled into the town's sole, centrally located high school.

The whole town centers around the lake. "Grand" is something of a misnomer, since it's pretty small, and the only stretch of beach is the man-made one behind the iron gates of the Grand Lake Yacht Club, where the town's upper crust keep sailboats and pontoon boats and have a dining hall for club dinners. The area by the lake was an amusement park in the fifties, with a Ferris wheel and roller coaster and everything, but they tore it down long before I was even born. Now there's just the park and a few businesses and restaurants, including the waterfront Sterling's Steakhouse. Laney's father, Richard Sterling, owns the joint, but we never eat there because Laney doesn't eat meat, much to her family's chagrin.

To get to the west side, you have to drive past the lake and through this strip called Windermere Village. Windermere is a shopping area, purposefully kept antiquated with a cobblestone road, the streets lined with gaslights and outdoor sculptures. There's an old-fashioned ice cream parlor called Duncan's, a bunch of old family businesses and other little shops. It's the kind of place where mothers amble with their baby strollers and golden retrievers, and older women wearing fluorescent headbands power walk in pairs.

I don't usually have much reason to go west past Windermere. As we speed by in Laney's piece-of-crap car, I watch the newer housing areas give way to dated apartment buildings. She turns down a side road, passing a gas station and a liquor store, and continues down to a two-story building made out of dusty red brick. That's when I see the sign, lit up in neon-green over the doorway of a store on the bottom level: the Oleo Strut.

A bell above the door chimes as we walk in. There's a guy behind the counter, looking like he's in his twenties, sporting Buddy Holly frames and an eyebrow ring. His brown hair is short and spiky. He scrawls something onto a notepad at rapid-fire pace, pausing every so often to fiddle with a calculator—it's one of those old-fashioned ones, with a ribbon of receipt paper churning out with each button pushed.

"Can I help you?" the guy asks, distracted. He punches a few more numbers into the calculator and scratches the top of his head.

Laney looks at me expectantly, but I'm not sure how to even begin, so she jumps in without missing a beat.

"This is going to sound *so* weird," she starts, "but we're trying to find out the identity of someone who made a purchase from you a few months ago. We know what was bought, but that's it. Maybe if we gave you the date, you could, like, look back through security tapes or something?"

Now he looks at us, bemused, tapping the pen cap against the countertop. "Yeah, we don't keep track of that."

"Well, you look like the type who has an *amazing* photographic memory." She pushes herself up against the counter, bending so far over I'm sure her boobs will spill out of her top, and gives her most charming smile. I roll my eyes behind her back. "The Kinks? Tom Waits? Any of that ring a bell?"

"Sorry, kid, my memory is for shit," he says with a grin, and I'm impressed with the fact he doesn't even give her chest area so much as a second glance. He jabs the pen in our direction in mock seriousness. "That's why you should stay away from drugs."

As he starts to walk toward the back room, Laney throws her hands up in frustration.

"A walking PSA," she mutters under her breath. "How helpful."

Suddenly he turns to face us again. "Hey, you know, you might have better luck with my brother. He works the register sometimes and he's good with faces."

"And where would he be?" I ask.

He nods his chin in the direction of the back of the store. "Stocking. I think he's doing vinyl."

With that, he disappears. Laney and I exchange glances.

I shrug. "Worth a shot."

The store is so crammed with music that it's difficult to squeeze through the aisles. Everywhere are carts filled with

CDs and cassettes, handwritten signs plastered on the walls categorizing them by genre, and even those have subcategories. The rock section is split into classic rock, garage rock, glam rock, soft rock, psychedelia, alt-rock and indie rock. Punk contains anarcho-punk, garage punk, hardcore and riot grrrl. New Wave has an entire cart to itself.

We're turning a corner when Laney says, "That must be him."

I look in the direction where she's pointing, and suddenly I can't breathe.

"Oh my God," I gasp. I grab her arm, haul her around the corner and safely out of sight.

It's the boy. The boy from the wake, who leaned up against my house and smoked cigarettes and glared a lot. The boy who obviously had *some* connection to my sister, but at the time I'd been too preoccupied to even consider his, like, existence, never mind what that connection could be.

Well. Now I know. Sort of, anyway.

"Hey," Laney says. Her eyes widen. "I know him!"

"You—you do?"

"I mean, I don't *know* him, but I know of him. His name's Jacob. Jake Tolan." She frowns. "He looks way different without blue hair."

"Blue hair?" I sneak a furtive glance around the shelf. He has one of those sticker guns in his hand, is labeling a stack of vinyl records and putting them away in alphabetical order.

I *have* seen him before. Blue-haired boys stand out at Grand Lake High. And then something clicks—Tolan. I know that name. It was on one of those forms I discovered while rifling through June's drawers. Her National Honor Society papers, the ones she filled out to log her tutoring hours.

"That's him," I realize. "He's the one who gave June those CDs."

"Wait, seriously?" Laney peers around behind me, scrambling to get a second look. "How do you know?"

"I'll explain later." At her skeptical look, I add, "I promise. Just—go look around or something. I want to talk to him alone for a second."

She raises her eyebrows, but then she nods and goes to browse the shelves. I step out from around the corner and begin to peruse as nonchalantly as possible. I thumb through the D's, watching Jake out of the corner of my eye before sliding out a record at random.

"That's a good pick."

I jump a little when I realize he's at my shoulder, still wielding the sticker gun. If he recognizes me, he masks it well.

When I just stare at him blankly, he leans over and taps the cover with one finger. "Miles Davis. *Kind of Blue*. Circa 1959, I believe. It's one of the most definitive jazz albums of all time. You listen to a lot of jazz?"

"Yes," I lie. I pause. "No. I mean. I'm just looking." Feeling bolder, I say, "Any recommendations?"

He thinks for a moment. "John Coltrane is a must, and you've gotta listen to Charlie Parker. Oh, and Thelonious Monk. That man could play the hell out of a piano."

"When you put it so eloquently..." I pop the Miles Davis back into its rightful place and turn to him again. "What about Tom Waits?"

Jake looks confused. "What about him?"

"I've heard he's good. Any recommendations?"

"Tom Waits isn't really jazz. I mean, he is, but he isn't. There is *one* album—" He stops mid-sentence and stares at me, and I swear I can actually see him working out the connection, how he gave the same one to June. Which means he knows that I know. Abruptly he turns his back on me and returns to the stack of records, stabbing the sticker gun against them with vicious concentration. "I'm busy. You can look for it yourself."

"Right. Well, take it easy, Jake," I say. I make sure to pause for effect before adding, "Don't let the bastards grind you down."

Not the smoothest hint drop ever, but it gets my point across. This time his head snaps around so fast it's a wonder it doesn't come flying clean off his neck. I know I've struck a chord with that one, even if I'm not exactly sure what it means. His mouth opens, but if he says anything, I don't hear it because I'm already halfway down the aisle.

Jacob Tolan can suck it. He's not the only one around here who can make a mysterious exit.

three

"That is so weird," Laney says.

I glance at the column of people ahead of us and nod. "I know."

"No, I mean, that is so *weird*," she stresses. "Like—I cannot even!"

We're waiting in line at Windermere's local coffee shop, The Windermere Coffee Co. Creative name, I know. Our repeat business here is not due to customer loyalty but because somehow Grand Lake manages to be so obsolete that even the all-seeing Starbucks corporate machine has skipped over the town entirely.

"So what are you going to do about it?" Laney asks.

"What can I do? He knows I know. I don't even know *what* I know, but I'm pretty sure I know *something*. You know?"

This line of thinking is confusing to follow even for me, but because Laney is my best friend, she nods and says, "Oh, yeah, I *so* know."

Laney orders a soy *venti* latte with, like, five shots of three different flavored syrups, hazelnut and mint and vanilla. It sounds gross. I like to keep it simple: skinny chocolate mocha, extra whip. After the bored-looking girl behind the counter takes my order, I look around the crowded shop, hugging my arms around my middle. It feels weird, being out in the real world again. Around people just living their lives like normal. Their presence is oppressive. The very fact that the world is going on as usual, like nothing ever happened, makes me want to scream. I know it's irrational to expect everything to grind to a halt because of June, but still. A wave of anxiety builds in my chest, my head pounding so loud it drowns out the noise of people talking and tapping away on their laptops.

The snap of the cashier's chewing gum brings me back down to reality.

"That'll be two dollars and ninety-five cents," she says.

Before I can reach for my wallet, Laney hands over a ten-dollar bill, covering for the both of us. I'm about to insist on buying my own when I catch the eye of two guys, both college age. One is tall, kind of slick looking and gives off major smarminess vibes. The other is pudgy and acne ridden, like one of those guys from the "before" shots in commercials for Proactiv. They're huddled at a nearby table, whispering and sneaking long looks our way.

"Hey, princess, is that you?" the tall one suddenly calls out.

Laney turns, and the moment she makes eye contact with the guy, all of the color drains from her face. Her eyes dart from him to the door, like she's going to bolt, but then she smoothes out her expression and walks over to them, fists balled at her sides. I have no idea what is going on. I take the change from the cashier and trail behind her, juggling both of our drinks.

"I love a girl who *comes* when she's called." The tall one leers, and the greasy fatty bumps his fist into the guy's shoulder and laughs, saying, *"Nice,"* like that was some display of razor-sharp wit instead of being totally gross.

I expect Laney to punch him in the face, or at the very least tell them off, but she does neither.

"What do you want, Kyle?" she asks stiffly.

Kyle? I glance at her, surprised. She knows this guy?

"What, we can't share a friendly hello?" The guy—Kyle, apparently—grins, and I notice how bright his teeth are. "Last I knew you had no problem sharing more than *that*."

His gaze travels up and down her body lazily and lingers. The whole leering thing is giving me major creeps. Laney's face scrunches up funny; I wait for her to lay the smack down, the way she always does when some loser hits on her, but she just stands there, speechless. Finally I nudge her elbow and hand her the latte.

"We should go. I've got that—thing," I say lamely.

Acne Guy snickers. "Oh, right. Wouldn't want to miss that *thing*."

Laney spins on her heel and rushes out the door. I'm so shocked that all I can do is level my iciest glare at Acne Guy before hustling out of the store after her, bumping into an entering patron on the way. No time for snappy comebacks when my best friend is making a mad dash.

Outside, Laney's already inside the car. I can't run while carrying steaming coffee, and she has the keys in the ignition by the time I manage to climb into the passenger seat. She doesn't even wait for me to buckle in before peeling out of the parking lot, tires screeching.

"Gah!" I yelp as a bit of hot coffee sloshes over the cup and lands on my hand. "Will you stop for a second? Jesus!"

We pass another block or so before she bothers to slow down. She white-knuckles the steering wheel, staring straight ahead and ignoring me.

"Who was that?" I demand. "Why are you—"

"Just give me a minute, okay? Please."

I fall silent. I've never seen her like this before. So shaken up. It's really freaking me out.

Laney calms down enough to take a sip of her latte, then hits the turn signal and pulls into an empty parking lot. She shuts the car off, tosses the keys on top of the dashboard and slumps against the seat, head rolling back. I stare at her and wait.

"That was Kyle," she finally says.

"I gathered that much." I take a long drink of my mocha, watching her.

"We had sex."

I almost do a spit-take. Laney looks over at me as I choke and cough, wiping the coffee and whipped cream off my chin.

"You—what?" I'm still sputtering. *"When?"*

"Almost a week ago. He was behind me in line at the gas station, and we just started talking...."

"So that's your prerequisite for sex now? Standing behind you in line at the Gas-N-Go?"

It comes out harsher than I intend, but between the scalding coffee on my tongue and this little revelation, I'm more than a little off my game. Call me a prude, but this whole casual sex thing is so weird to me. I can't imagine sleeping with some guy I've only known for a few hours. I know Laney tends to be...more forward than I am, and it's not unheard of for her to mess around with guys she hasn't known that long, but a random hookup like this? Really?

Laney gives me an offended look. "God, Harper, no! It's more complicated than *that*." She sets her coffee down in the cup holder and exhales loudly. "It was right after...after June, and I was really upset, I wasn't even thinking. We talked a little, and he invited me to this party. And I got, like, seriously wasted. I don't even know how it happened. Next thing I know..."

I study her for a long moment. "Laney. Did he—"

"No!" she says quickly. She hesitates. "It's not like he *assaulted* me, okay? I didn't exactly say no."

"But did you say *yes*?"

"Yeah. I mean. I think so. Maybe. I must've, right?" Her eyes glisten wetly. "It was so stupid. *I'm* so stupid."

The look on her face guts me. I should've been there. I'm the one who watches her back, the same way she watches mine. I wouldn't have let this happen.

"You're *not* stupid," I tell her. I take a deep breath, trying to gather my thoughts. This is way too much to absorb in one sitting. "Look. Laney. It's not your fault that that Kyle guy is a sleaze. You could've told me earlier. I would've—"

"Would've what?" she says sharply. She shrugs and lowers her eyes to her coffee cup. "It happened. Whatever. It's over now, and it's not like I'm going to do it again. I thought about telling you. I was going to, but with—well, everything—" She swallows hard. "It seemed kind of unimportant. You have enough to deal with right now."

Laney's not the blushing virgin type; she had sex for the first time with short-stint boyfriend Dustin Matthews after sophomore year homecoming and spared me no detail in recounting the event. And from the stories she's shared, I know it wasn't her last time hooking up, either. Every time I looked remotely scandalized by her tales, she'd roll her eyes and say, "Sex is, like, not *even* a big deal, *trust* me," which maybe was true for those who were having it—not that I would know—but in my experience was a huge deal for those who weren't.

By the time we've finished our coffee, Laney seems to be feeling more like herself again. She slides on her oversize pink-tinted sunglasses and grabs the keys.

"We should get going," she says, and goes to start up the Gremlin.

Except it doesn't start.

The engine revs like a skipping record, then putters out. She curses and twists the keys again. This time the engine barely makes a noise at all. So she tries again.

And again.

"So I think we're stuck," she says to me, five minutes later when the engine has failed to start.

"Yeah, looks like."

She groans. "Today sucks."

"Do I need to call my mom?" I think about the inebriated state I found her in the other morning. "I think she might be busy...." Aunt Helen would probably come out, but the last thing I want to do is ask her for a favor.

Laney waves one hand. "No, it's cool. I'll call mine. I'm sure she'll be *so* pleased to tear herself away from *Days of Our Lives* in order to help out her only daughter."

She digs into her purse and whips out her cell phone. First she calls for a tow, and then she calls her mother. The towing guys come out first. We stand next to the curb as they hook the car up to the truck.

"Long live the Gremlin," Laney says somberly, pouring what little is left of her latte onto the pavement in commemoration as the mechanic's truck tows her piece of junk out of the lot. She lowers herself onto the curb and I sit down next to her, kicking at a stray pebble.

"Maybe it's just the battery?" I say hopefully. "Or the water pump. It could be the water pump."

"Whatever it is, there's, like, no way I can afford to fix it," she says. "I can barely manage to keep the tank filled these days. Even if I could swing it, it would wipe out all the money that could get us to California."

The idea of running away to California is like a silver strand of hope, this tiny, fragile thread tying me to the world, giving me a reason to have been left behind by June. Giving me

a purpose. And now that thread is thinning with every passing moment, worn down by the brutal scrape of reality grating away at it, bit by bit. It was probably a stupid idea in the
first place. And an increasingly impossible one.

But then I think of June's postcard, her words, that perfect, idyllic beach, and something in me resurges, clings to
that thread even more tightly. I'm not letting this go without a fight.

"Besides," Laney says, "the repairs will probably cost as
much as the stupid piece of crap is worth."

"Can't your dad pay for it?" I ask.

"You know how he is—for a guy who makes as much
money as he does, he's a total tightwad."

"But you get an allowance, right?" I press. "Don't you have
some of it saved?"

Laney looks at me incredulously. "Harper. I'm spending
four dollars a day on sugared caffeine. What do you think?"
She rolls her eyes. "And willing though my mom may be to
update my wardrobe, no way will she help me out with this.
Let's face it. It's a lost cause."

I'm not ready to give up yet. "There are other ways of getting to California," I point out.

"Like what? By plane? I think they're going to say something when your carry-on is a freaking *urn*."

Laney's uncharacteristically reasoned logic could not come
at a worse time. She's supposed to be the optimist, not me.

"What about a bus?"

"I am so not taking a bus. Have you heard how unsafe
those things are? We'd probably get mugged or murdered.
Or worse."

Now, that sounds more like the overly dramatic Laney I
know.

I sigh and look down at her feet. She has on black sandals

with a cork heel, and her toes are painted dark red—obviously she had them done recently. Her mom's idea of mother-daughter bonding time is getting pedicures together; a conundrum for Laney, who loves pedicures, but hates spending more time with her mother than strictly necessary.

"I think," Laney says, "we are at an *impose*."

"You mean an impasse?"

"Right, that. If the universe wants us to go to California, things will work out on their own."

"Don't say that," I snap. It always bothers me when Laney starts espousing this particular brand of fatalism. "This isn't about leaving shit up to fate. This isn't a game!"

"I wasn't trying to say that," she says, confused and a little hurt.

"I have to do this." My voice rises, almost cracking. I have to make her understand. This isn't just a joke or something I'm talking about for kicks. This has to happen. "I need your help. Please. I'm not just messing around here. I am so, completely dead serious, you don't even know. I *have* to do this. For June. I have to, or—" Or I'll never be able to live with myself. I can't bring myself to actually say it. I don't need to. Laney knows.

"Okay," she soothes, "okay, we'll find a way, okay? I promise. Just breathe."

I look at her and nod. I believe her. Laney never makes promises she can't keep.

Mrs. Sterling picks us up a few minutes later in her white SUV. During the drive back, she makes a lot of *tsk*-ing sounds with her tongue and keeps saying, "Laney, your father is *not* going to be happy about this," like Laney's to blame for her junky car breaking down. Her mouth looks weird, like she's trying to frown, except the Botox makes it impossible, and from the backseat I catch her glancing in the rearview mirror to brush her peroxide-blond hair away from her alarmingly orange fake-baked face.

When she pulls into my driveway, she twists around in her seat, smiles tightly and asks if my mother enjoyed the quiche.

"It was great," I lie, and open the door. "My mom says thanks."

"I'll call you," Laney says as I climb out. I wave, and she blows a kiss through the window.

The house is empty again. I think about eating, but I'm not really hungry, and besides, after tossing out the gross foods we'd been given, the refrigerator is bare; there's a bottle of wine on the bottom shelf, mostly empty. I dump what's left into the sink and tuck the bottle under some trash in the bin.

Someone left the television on in the living room—an infomercial advertising weight supplements flickers on the screen. A now slim woman holds an old picture of herself, thick and round, and tearfully proclaims that the product transformed her life, that her husband now loves to touch her and her children are no longer ashamed to introduce her to their friends, her life is now pretty and shiny and perfect, blah blah blah. How can this woman stand to listen to herself?

I'm flipping through channels when Aunt Helen and my mother come in, carrying brown grocery bags. Mom's hair is bushy and unbrushed, and she has on zero makeup. She's like the opposite of Mrs. Sterling. Usually she's the opposite of Mrs. Sterling in that she looks put-together without being overdone, classy without trying too hard, but now she just looks sad.

Mom withdraws an egg carton from the bag, sets it on the counter and just stares at it until Aunt Helen reaches over and puts it inside the refrigerator.

"Harper," calls Aunt Helen, "would you come in here for a moment? I need to speak with you."

This can only be bad. These types of "discussions" never seem to work out in my favor. I mute the television—I've landed on some documentary special about Area 51—and obediently trudge into the kitchen. Aunt Helen purses her thin lips as she leans against the refrigerator door, fingering the large bronze cross that always hangs around her neck.

"We've been discussing the...current situation," she says. Current situation. What is with all of these euphemisms? *Adjustments. Current situation.* No one can just outright say the ugly truth: *Your sister is dead, your mother is unraveling at the seams, your father is a regular Houdini who has once again pulled his well-honed disappearing act and you have the emotional capacity of a cinder block.* "Your mother feels it would be best—and I agree—for me to come and stay with you both for a short while," Aunt Helen continues. "Just to look after things."

The idea of Aunt Helen living here is enough to make my skin crawl. It's not that I don't appreciate what she's doing, especially for my mother, but I also know what I can and can't handle. Aunt Helen around twenty-four seven, hovering over me, shoving her religious-guidance crap down my throat, falls distinctly into the latter category.

"Okay," I say slowly. "Do you really think that's necessary?"

"*Someone* needs to be here for your mother, since you seem to be having no qualms about gallivanting around with your friends and leaving her to fend for herself," she says reproachfully. "Do you really think that's what your sister would have wanted?" Her accusatory tone cuts through me like a knife.

My eyes shift from her to my mother, shocked, but Mom won't even look at me. I can't believe I'm being ambushed. I mean, I know Aunt Helen's never liked me. I get it. June was always the golden child while I'm the rotten egg. I never even had to do anything to make myself look bad except be average in comparison to her saintly self. This is nothing new.

June wouldn't be so selfish. June wouldn't be so cold. June wouldn't abandon her daughterly duties. Except that she did, permanently, leaving me to take the reins of a role I cannot possibly fill. But no one wants to think about that.

My sister is dead and I'm still being measured up against her ghost. I'm not even surprised.

So why does it still hurt?

The hurt winds its way through me and curls my fists at my sides. My blood buzzes in my head so loud I can't think. I'm pretty sure if she says another word I'm going to throw something, possibly at *her*. So instead of doing something I know I'll regret, I storm out of the kitchen and don't stop until I'm up the stairs and in my room. I take the disc out of my Discman and throw it at the wall as hard as I can. It doesn't make much of a sound, just bounces off and rolls onto the floor, sitting there in one piece, mocking me. After some pacing back and forth, I put the disc back in the player and turn the volume up as loud as it will go.

For the rest of the night, no one comes to knock on my door and apologize, or see if I'm okay, or even to try and coax me down for dinner. It's so stupid, because all I've wanted is space, and now that I have it, there's this part of me that is just so achingly lonely I could die.

The idea of California tugs at me again. It's not even a mere wish anymore, it's just…necessary. I have to find a way to get there. Not just for June's sake, but for mine. I have to get out of this place before I suffocate. A second after that thought crosses my mind, I'm struck with the realization that maybe this is exactly how June felt, too, all of that time.

I wish she was here so I could ask. I wish she was here at all, sitting on my bed, recounting some stupid argument she had with Tyler, or complaining about how I've used up the last of the hair conditioner or sitting out on the roof with me as I sneak one of Mom's stolen cigarettes. We used to do that, sometimes. The first time June caught me smoking I thought for sure she'd rat me out, but she never did.

I wish she was here, but she isn't, she never will be, and I have to get used to that.

I wait until I know Aunt Helen and Mom have both gone to bed before I creep into the kitchen, make myself a peanut butter sandwich in the dark and go back upstairs. Sometime after midnight I fall asleep, listening to the CD on a loop. When I wake up, the sheets are caught in a sweaty tangle around my legs, the batteries in my Discman are dead and it's bright outside. A glance at my alarm informs me it's past noon.

Aunt Helen and my mom are gone. Again. Apparently I'm the only one expected to be under voluntary house arrest. I check the answering machine—no messages. My father hasn't called since the wake. Go figure. He's probably too busy with Melinda, the most important person in his life.

I don't know why I'm so annoyed; it's not like I want to talk to him. I almost feel like I wouldn't care if I never talked to him again. June is gone, and where is he? I don't care how hard it is for him. I don't care if he's uncomfortable in this house. I *needed* him, and if he couldn't be there for me over something so important, what good is he at all?

It's quickly becoming clear that the only person I can lean on at all these days is Laney.

I consider calling her when I remember she's elbow-deep in an AP English exam and unavailable for another two hours. Nothing good is on daytime television, and really, it makes me anxious to sit in the living room for too long with June's urn planted on the fireplace mantel, staring me down. There's nothing to do but roam the deserted house.

Mom started smoking again after she and Dad split. She thinks she's good at hiding it, like I don't know she keeps a stash of cigarettes hidden in her jewelry box. Sure enough, there's a pack of Camel Lights stowed away under a mess of necklaces, along with a plastic lighter. I nab both and retreat back into my own room.

There were times, before the divorce, when our parents would fight. Mostly it was Mom who would yell, while Dad sat silent, a stony wall to her barrage of shouts and accusations. I know she thought he was messing around on the side, during his late nights at the office, and hiding money from her. I have no idea how much of that was actually true—if any of it—but Mom would get so worked up, she must've really believed what she said. She'd just go on a total rampage, annihilating everything in her path. The best coping method was total avoidance, and so sometimes during their arguments, June would come to my room, near tears, and we'd climb out my window and onto the roof and just sit. Sometimes I'd smoke, sometimes we'd talk, and sometimes we'd just sit there in mutual silence. During our conversations, we never acknowledged the obvious: our parents' marriage was vaporizing before our eyes.

Maybe we thought if we didn't mention it, it would go away on its own. Maybe we just didn't know how to talk to each other the way we used to, when we were little kids and best friends who shared everything.

Now I wrench the window up and slowly slide my legs outside, climbing out just enough to sit on the ledge with my bare feet flat on the slanted roof, already warmed by the high sun. I shake a single cigarette from the pack at my side and stick it in my mouth. It takes only two tries to strike up a flame, which is quite impressive considering how hard my hands are shaking. I wonder if it'll always be this hard, to think about June, if I'll ever be able to separate the good memories from bad, or if they'll always be intrinsically tied together.

I light the end of the cigarette, inhaling deeply. The air is hot and still, the breeze nonexistent, the sun beating down in an otherwise clear sky. From my perch I can spot some kids a few doors down, skipping rope on the street and chanting in unison. *Christopher Columbus sailed the ocean blue, in nineteen hundred and forty-two. The waves got higher, and higher...*

If I close my eyes it's almost like June's beside me, the way she used to be. I can see her perfectly in my mind—those slim arms wrapped around her knees as she pulls her long legs in close to her chest. She used to sit like that all the time, like she was trying to make herself as small as possible.

Maybe she was always trying to disappear.

I'm sitting there, breathing in the mingled smells of smoke and cut grass and tar from the shingles, trying to remember, when suddenly a voice cuts through my meandering thoughts.

"Hey!" My eyes fly open to see Jacob Tolan, standing on the edge of my front yard, shielding his eyes from the intense sun with one hand and squinting up at me. *"Enjoying your moment of faux teenage rebellion?"*

The unexpected intrusion nearly sends me plummeting off the roof and to an early death. At the very least, a few broken ribs. Flustered, I quickly right myself and glare down at his figure. The first thing I notice is that he's wearing a black leather jacket open over a long-sleeved red flannel shirt, even though it's about a billion degrees outside, and black jeans, again. Possibly the same pair. What is this, the nineties?

"Get off my lawn," I shout, holding the cigarette away from my face.

"Oooh, tough words from the girl who smokes—let me guess—Virginia Slims?"

Who the hell does he think he is, coming here and accusing me of smoking girly cigarettes?

"Camel Lights, actually, dickwad." I take another long,

harsh drag, just to prove a point. Unfortunately, the effect is diminished when I start coughing up half a lung.

Jake extracts his own pack from his jeans pocket, tilting it up for me to see. "What do you know. Same brand. Got a light?"

I reel my arm back and chuck my lighter at him, hard. My aim is decent enough, but Jake dodges out of the way just in time; the flimsy thing barely clips him in the shoulder, and he shoots me a long, even look as he leans down and fishes it from the grass at his feet.

I keep on glaring as he straightens and lights his cigarette. "What do you want?"

He says, "We need to talk," and glances around conspicuously. "Preferably in, you know, private."

"Like...*private*, private?" I ask. Does he seriously think anyone would bother to listen in on this conversation?

He scowls and does that annoying squinty thing again. "Is there any other kind?"

Part of me wants to tell him to go screw himself; the other part of me is curious to know what possible reason he could have for coming around and wanting to talk. Curiosity wins out in the end. I stub the cigarette out, making sure to roll my eyes and blow out an exaggerated sigh so he won't think I'm, like, really wanting to *know* what he's doing in my front yard.

"Fine, whatever," I tell him coolly. "Give me a minute."

I scoot back through the window, carefully wedging it down, and then hurry downstairs. It seems like a good idea to make him wait for a while, just so he doesn't think I'm dying to hear whatever it is he has to say. Even if I kind of am.

I stand at the front door and count to thirty before I open it. Jake is still standing in the same spot, stomping out his cigarette, and instead of approaching me, he just cocks his head to the side until I march over.

"What do you want?" I huff.

I want to know what's going on, but if he keeps this up, forget it. I've never been the kind of girl to beg. I'm definitely not about to start now.

He grabs my arm and hauls me behind the towering oak tree at the edge of the lawn. "Let's talk in there," he says, jerking his chin toward the van parked right on the curb.

I glance around to see if anyone is in earshot. Our old neighbor Mr. Jones is mowing his lawn, and some woman pushes a stroller down the sidewalk. When the woman passes, she gives us a strange look, but then the baby starts wailing and diverts her attention.

I stare at Jake blankly. "Yeah, that's not happening."

"What? Why not?"

"Sketchy black van? Weird stalking of my house? What are you going to do next, offer me some candy?" I scoff. "Sorry, I saw that *Dateline* special, thank you very much. Besides, anything you need to say to me, you can say behind this tree."

He makes this annoyed growling sound in the back of his throat, then takes a deep breath. "Listen. I know what you and Laney are planning on doing."

Well, that is not what I expected. I look at him closely. He can't know. Can he?

"Uh, okay," I say. Best to play dumb. "I don't know what you're talking about."

"What, like I'd come all the way over here just to bullshit you? Do you think I'm an idiot?" He pauses. "Don't answer that."

Not a problem, as I'm sort of at a loss for words at the moment. All I can do is look at him. Up close, I get a better view; there's no denying the fact he is really, really good-looking, in this rakish, edgy, badass, *I-just-rolled-out-of-bed-and-screw-you-I-don't-need-a-mirror* kind of way. He has these piercing, unbelievably green eyes that are as gorgeous and sharp as the rest of him; it's like they can see straight through me. But I don't want to be seen. I just want answers.

Realizing his hand is still on my arm, I shake it off. He shoves his hands in his jean pockets and waits.

"How much do you know?" I ask cautiously.

"You, her. June—the urn." He pauses. "California."

"How did you—"

"You're not as discreet as you think," he says. His grin is so smug I want to punch him in the face.

"You spied on us, didn't you?" I don't even try to hide the amount of disgust in my tone. The thought of him listening in on our conversation by the door the whole time like some kind of creepster leaves me feeling horrified and violated and pissed off, all at the same time. I cross my arms over my chest. "Okay, so you know. Congratulations. Would you like a cookie?"

Jake looks me in the eyes intently. "I'm going with you."

"No."

"Yes," he insists. He steps forward, once again violating my personal-space bubble, and lowers his voice. "You take me with you, or I swear I'll tell your mother. I bet she'd love to hear what you're planning to do with her dearly departed daughter's remains. Or I could talk to your lovely aunt, who I had the pleasure of meeting the other day. She seems like the kind of person who'd be really on board with that plan."

My heart starts racing a little faster. If Mom found out… if Aunt Helen found out…it'd be over, no question. I'd be under permanent house arrest and twenty-four-hour surveillance. And they'd probably call Dad and tell him to speed up the urn selection process, and if they split the ashes before I can figure out how the hell to get to California, that's it. I'll have failed before I even started.

Jake *has* to be bluffing.

But what if he's not?

"Like she'd believe you," I say sarcastically, but I'm less sure now, and he can tell.

"Like she's not paranoid enough right now to listen to me?" He snorts. "I don't think so."

Damn. He has me on that one. "So now I'm being black-mailed by a tattletale?"

"Put it however you want," he says. He heaves a long-suffering sigh, like even having this conversation is a total pain. "Look, I've got a van—"

"That—" I wave a hand toward the contraption parked on the curb "—is not a van. *That* is a death trap."

"Leave Joplin out of this," he retorts, and I blink in surprise. His van has a name? Before I can whip up a snarky comment, he plows on. "*And* I have some money, and no one who'll even notice I'm gone. You're talking about two minors traveling across the country. If you take a car, or a bus, you'll never make it. The cops'll track you down in a second."

That—that is actually all really convincing. But I'm not ready to concede to his common sense, not yet. Everything about this is too weird. Too...*wrong*.

"Why do you even care?" I ask. "So my sister tutored you a few times for padding on her college apps. Big deal. You hardly knew her. Right?"

Jake doesn't seem to know how to respond to that one. At least five different emotions flicker over his face, none of which I can pinpoint. There's more to it—to him and June—than he's letting on. I know it.

"That's what I thought." I start heading back to the door.

Good. Now I have the upper hand. Now he's the one who'll have to beg.

"'Don't let the bastards grind you down,'" he calls out to my receding back. I stop, but I don't turn around until he breaks into a half jog to catch up to me. "Where did you hear that?"

I ignore him. "You're hiding something. I want to know why you're doing this."

"I have my reasons."

I shake my head. "That's not good enough." I need to know why he'd volunteer for this, why he cares about my sister at all.

"Yeah, well, too bad!" he shouts. "I told you the deal!"

Maybe my strategy isn't working as well as I thought. I called his bluff, but he doesn't look ready to budge. He looks me up and down and then abruptly turns away.

As he walks toward his van, he looks over his shoulder and says, "Your move, Scott."

four

Laney thinks Jake's offer is fantastic. "It's fate," she gushes.

"There is no fate," I say. "There's what you do and what you don't do."

I don't want to have this argument again. Though it would make sense, in a twisted way, for Jake's proposition to be a sign from God. Just more proof that if He indeed exists, He hates my guts.

Laney isn't having it. "Don't even," she chides. "This is nothing short of divine intervention and you know it."

"Whatever." I pull the phone away from my ear and double-check that my door is shut all of the way. The last thing I need is Aunt Helen eavesdropping on this particular conversation. "There has to be another way."

That's what I said last time, I know. But the idea of driving cross-country in a van with a boy I don't know is too crazy. Even for me.

"Hang on a second…" Laney pauses, working it out in her head. "You didn't tell him we'd do it?"

"Of course not. We can't drive to California with him. We don't even *know* him."

"Are you kidding? This is perfect! This is exactly what we've been hoping for! He has everything we need."

Okay, I'll admit. Turning it down does feel a little like kicking God in the balls.

I sigh. "It's too easy."

"You know I love you, Harper, but seriously? That's a really lame excuse."

The worst is that Laney's right; this is potentially kind of completely perfect. Minus the fact that Jake refused to answer any of my questions, no matter how hard I pushed, and he apparently holds a grudge against me for no reason I can figure out. But what other choice do I have? No good one. And I totally believed him when he threatened to blab to Aunt Helen.

Rock, meet hard place.

"All right, all right. I'll talk to Jake." I sigh in defeat. "I guess we need to start planning. Figure out when we should leave."

"Do you have a target date?"

"As soon as possible. Preferably."

She laughs. "I hear you. Exams are over, thank God, and Mom and Dad are going on a weekend trip to visit some friends in Pittsburgh—so maybe we should leave then? If it's okay with Jake."

"Oh, I'll *make* sure it's okay with him."

"What are you going to do? Threaten bodily harm?"

"I'll think of something." I pause. Outside the door, I can hear the sound of someone coming up the stairs. "Hey, Laney, let me call you back."

There's a knock at the door. It's Mom—it has to be. Aunt Helen doesn't knock. Clearly she does not understand both the symbolic and literal implications of a closed door. What if she caught me smoking? Or undressing? Or, like, *masturbating* or something? Not that I really do that, ever—but it's the principle of the thing. If she caught me doing *that*, she'd probably have a coronary.

I make a mental note to ask Laney for tips on where to acquire a vibrator. Maybe I can stow it in my nightstand, because I'm pretty sure when I went out for coffee, Aunt Helen searched my room. Imagine if she found something like that. Heads would be rolling.

Ooh, or maybe condoms. Or birth control pills. Now *that* would really freak her out.

I sit down on the bed and put the phone down. "Come in."

Mom opens the door, standing with it halfway ajar. She doesn't make a move to fully enter, just stays there, looking. But I can tell she's not really *seeing* me, is lost somewhere in her own mind. We've barely spoken over the past few days— we exist parallel to each other.

"Hi," I say, drawing my knees up to my chest and wrapping my arms around them.

"Hi." Mom hovers in the doorway, her hand on the knob. She leans on it like it's the only thing keeping her upright. Maybe it is. "Helen invited me to her morning church service this Sunday. Not just me—you, too. She thinks it would be good, for the both of us."

"Helen *thinks*?" I bristle. "No, thanks."

"Harper." She pauses, breathing in and out through her nose a few times, one hand pressed to her temple as if to prevent the onslaught of a migraine. "I don't appreciate your hostile attitude. She's trying to *help*—"

"Well, maybe she's trying, but she's not helping."

"She's helping *me*!" she snaps. Her chin quivers with the threat of tears. "I need someone right now. It's not like your father has been of any help, if you've bothered to notice. Helen is the only one who's here for me. I can't do this on my own.

Do you not understand that? Does that not make any sense to you whatsoever?"

So that's how my mother sees it? That she's all alone, save for Aunt Helen? My presence means nothing. I'm invisible, or worse, a burden.

"Helen says I need to surrender," she continues. "That I need to let God in, let Him take control. And I think it might help you find some peace, too, if you came with me."

"Let me think about it," I lie, because I know already that I will never step foot inside that church, know that come Sunday I'll be long gone from this town.

Why should I stay? Aunt Helen hates me. Mom doesn't need me. I can't do anything right. Really, I'm in the way. This just makes my decision all that much easier.

Mom nods once and starts to close the door. For a second, I want nothing more than for her to come back, to cradle me in her arms like when I was a kid and had badly scraped a knee, to smooth her palm across my forehead as if checking for a fever, to do something—anything—to remind me of the days when knowing that she was my mother and that she was there was enough to make the bad things better.

It's weird because I don't really want her to comfort me; I just want her to *try*. But that yearning is only a dull ache in my chest, the kind of phantom pains amputees get where their missing limbs should be. It isn't anything real.

The next day I take the bus across town to the Oleo Strut. The bus stop is three blocks from the store, and even though I have on a T-shirt, it's another blistering day, and by the time I arrive in front of the brick building, the thin cotton is stuck to my back with sweat like a second skin. No one notices when I enter. Jake's brother—I don't know his name—is behind the counter, arguing with a man in his forties dressed in a skuzzy, spiky leather jacket and a pair of dirty corduroys.

"Punk is *not* dead," Jake's brother is insisting emphatically. "Look at—"

"Who? Green Day? Avril Lavigne?" the other man sneers. "That's just manufactured pop bullshit. You've got all these poser bands out there, cranked out of big-name labels, pretending to be part of the counterculture when they're just another cash cow for the capitalist, consumerist machine. It's a gimmick. Kids these days think they can go out and buy punk self-identification through mass-marketed band apparel from Hot Topic."

"Yeah, but there *is* still good stuff, *true* punk. It's out there, it's just not being played on the radio. Punk isn't just a look. It's not even just about *attitude*. If you have the aesthetics and the posturing, you better back it up with the politics."

"Bullshit. Johnny Ramone was an NRA-supporting, full-fledged Republican!" the guy protests.

Jake's brother leans farther over the counter. "Fuck Johnny Ramone. The U.K. had the right idea—look at Joe Strummer. Look at the Sex Pistols, and Crass and—"

"Whatever, man. The culture's still dead. Nothing like that exists anymore."

"You just have to know where to find it," Jake's brother says. He withdraws a neon-green flyer from underneath the counter. "The Revengers. They're hardcore, the real thing, and they're playing a few shows in state later this summer. You gotta check them out—they don't mess around. If after that you still think punk's dead, I'll give you any record in the store, half off. Hand to God."

He holds up one hand solemnly. The man only grunts in response—but he takes the flyer before he leaves.

"You make a compelling case on behalf of punk rock," I say as I approach the counter.

"Someone has to do it," he replies with a grin. "Need help finding something?"

"Yes. I'm looking for the latest Green Day album."

He laughs, surprised, and eyes me more closely. "Hey, I've seen you before. You were in here the other day, with the blond girl, right?"

"Yeah, that was me." I pause and clear my throat. "Is your brother around?"

"Jake?" He rubs his chin. "He's not working today. But I think he's at home."

"Oh," I say, deflated. Too bad I was an idiot and never got his phone number. I could've saved myself a pointless bus trip. "Um. Could you tell me where that is?"

His amused grin widens. "We live upstairs. Second level. There's a side entrance outside, but it's locked. Let me lend you my key."

"Really?" I watch as he scrounges around in his back pocket. "I mean, thanks."

"No problem. Just drop it back off before you go," he says, procuring a brass key. "And if he puts on Bowie's early stuff and starts sweet-talking, dammit, you run. You run as fast as you can."

He winks at me, and I blush as I realize what he's implying. Rather than try to explain myself, I push out the door and walk around to the side of the building. The door there has a lock that sticks a little, but I lean my shoulder against it until it pops open, and a narrow staircase leads up to another wooden door. I pause for a moment before knocking.

A minute passes—no answer. I knock again, more persistently. Footsteps pad toward the door, a lock turns and the door opens to reveal Jake. He's bleary-eyed, shirtless and holding an open jar of peanut butter, a spoon stuck in his mouth. Somehow, he still makes it look attractive. He blinks a few times and pulls out the spoon with a loud popping noise.

Okay, maybe not so attractive.

"That's disgusting," I say.

"Nice to see you, too," he says through a mouthful of peanut butter.

I lean to the left and try to peer around him. "Can I come in?"

He sticks the spoon back into the jar and sighs. "You're not going to go away until I say yes, are you?"

"Nope."

He turns and walks back into the apartment, but leaves the door open, which I take as my cue to follow. The apartment has dark walls and thick brown carpet. The furniture is sparse—a ratty couch, a coffee table and a television in one corner. Shelves are built into the wall, only one of them filled with books, the rest used to house vinyl records and CDs and cassettes.

Jake flops down on the scratchy sofa and props his bare feet up on the table. "So how'd you get in?" he asks.

"Your brother gave me a key," I explain, sidestepping the huge-ass stereo system stacked on the floor. "He seems cool."

"Eli? Yeah. He's not bad."

"It must be cool to live above his store."

"It's not his store," he says. "He *wishes.* He's just the manager. The guy who owns it, Don, retired a few years back. Lives in Petoskey now. Eli looks after the place for him, apartment included."

"Oh." I look around again. "It's. Um. Charming."

"It's a shithole," he says, "but I've lived in worse." He sets the peanut butter jar on the coffee table. "Is that what you're here for? To admire the decor? Or is it something else?"

Okay. Time to cut to the chase. "So...the answer is yes."

"Yes...what?" he asks.

"Yes, you can come with us to California."

"I'm honored." He looks skeptical. "You came all the way here to tell me that?"

"It's not like I have your phone number," I remind him. "Anyway, we want to leave on Friday."

"For California?"

"No, for the mall." I roll my eyes. Something about Jake incites a lot of eye-rolling on my part, I've noticed. "*Yes*, California. What else would I be talking about?"

"Friday." He rolls the word over on his tongue like he's testing it out. "Okay, I think that's doable."

Well, that was easier than I'd thought it'd be.

"Is Eli going to be okay with you just taking off?" I ask.

"I'll tell him I'm going to visit friends or something." He shrugs and scratches at his stomach—still shirtless. Still making things totally awkward. For me, anyway; Jake seems obliviously unaware of his half-naked state. "He doesn't ask too many questions. It's not like he can call the cops—I'm eighteen now."

I nod curtly. "Good."

"And you?"

"What about me?"

"Your parents. Are they gonna freak?"

"My mother might. I don't know what she'll do."

Have a meltdown, probably. But she'll be okay. Aunt Helen will be there. She's better at picking up the pieces than I'll ever be.

"Here's what you have to do," Jake says. "You have to write a note. Let her know you left on your own. Otherwise she'll probably assume you've been kidnapped or some shit. And if she *does* call the cops, they treat runaway cases way different than abductions. They have to wait at least twenty-four hours before releasing the hounds, anyway."

"Wow. Your precise and in-depth knowledge of the legal ramifications is very helpful. And somewhat unsettling."

We go over the specifics of Friday's departure: I'll write a note beforehand, lie and say I'm spending the night at Laney's. Mom and Aunt Helen already said they're going to be at some church knitting-slash-study-group thing, so the house will be clear. I'll meet Jake outside around seven o'clock. If something goes wrong, I'll call or text him to let him know. We'll swing over to Laney's, pick her up and hit the road. Easy enough—or so I hope.

As we outline the plans, the knot in my stomach winds tighter and tighter. This isn't some vague scheme anymore; it's becoming more and more concrete. We're going to do this.

"I can't believe this is actually happening," I say out loud. I don't mean just this—the trip to California—but everything that has changed in my life over the past two weeks. Automatically I feel stupid, knowing that Jake will probably scoff or whip up some cutting retort in return.

But instead he says, "Yeah, I know," in a quiet sort of voice. His expression changes. There's something there—definitely not pity. Not even sympathy, exactly. Understanding? Maybe.

The bus will be coming around again in a few minutes. I begin to pick my way over the clutter on the floor—books and old newspapers, empty beer cans and piles of discarded clothing—and toward the door, when Jake stops me.

"Harper."

It's the first time he's used my first name. I hadn't even been completely positive that he knew what it was. We've never exactly had a formal introduction—how would that have gone? *Hi, I'm Harper, the sister who didn't die. You must be Jake, the guy said dead sister tutored, the guy who burned her the mix CD she was listening to when she overdosed on Mom's sleeping pills, the guy who blackmailed his way into joining our road trip for reasons I am none too clear on. Nice to meet you.*

"Remember to give Eli back the key," he says. "And do me a favor. Try and pack light."

Packing. I haven't even considered that. There are the obvious necessities, of course: Clothes. Money. The problem is that I have no idea how long we'll be gone, so how much am I supposed to pack? How far away is California exactly, anyway?

I call Laney to ask and she looks it up online.

"A little less than two thousand, three hundred forty-five miles," she reports. "It will take approximately thirty-four hours and twenty-six minutes."

Of course, that's only if you drive straight through—not taking into account bathroom breaks, food breaks and sleep deprivation. It'll take us a few days, at least. To be on the safe side, I drag my canvas duffel out of the closet and stuff it to the brim with clothes and water bottles from the fridge. I decide to leave behind my cell phone; it might have one of those GPS tracking chips if Mom does end up calling the cops, and I'm sure Laney will insist on having hers. I also stuff my old Polaroid camera, the one I found at a yard sale last summer, and a bunch of film rolls into the bag. Maybe there'll be something worth documenting along the way.

After digging through the hall closet, I find an extra pocket-size flashlight, batteries, a pocket knife and a roll of duct tape. I have absolutely no idea what on earth I'll need duct tape for, but I shove it in my backpack anyway. It's better to be prepared, right?

And then there's the most important item of all: the urn. Of course, that will have to come last.

The rest of the week leading up until Friday is uneventful.

Every time someone says my name, I expect to be called out on my plans, but it usually turns out to be something only fractionally more preferable: the privilege of being on the receiving end of Aunt Helen's moral harangues. Things have been tense between us all week. More so than usual.

It's not that I think Aunt Helen is evil. It's just that she thinks she has all of the answers. To questions of God, the universe, life, everything. She's always been like this. Maybe it's why she and Uncle Randall divorced when I was nine. Maybe she thinks by running our lives she can ignore the mess she's made of hers. Mom told me a while back how Helen really wanted kids, but there were conception issues, and Randall didn't believe in adoption, so it never happened. And then he left her, and now she's almost fifty, childless and alone. She fills her life with Jesus and taking care of my mother because really, what else does she have?

I'm feeling sorry for her, almost, thinking about all of this on Friday night in the kitchen. She and Mom get ready to leave the house while I sit at the table, slowly eating a bowl of sugared cereal. The dinner of champions. I'm taking my time, and the milk has made the cereal all soggy and soft.

Aunt Helen comes in and stops in front of the refrigerator. When I look up, a spoonful of cereal in my mouth, I realize she's staring at a picture of June stuck there with a magnet. It's from last summer, taken by me with the Nikon, when she was tanning in the front yard. In the picture she's wearing this rockabilly style cherry-print bathing suit, with high-waisted bottoms and a top that tied in front. A pair of Jackie O sunglasses cover her eyes. She's lying on her side in the green grass, long legs stretched out with one knee bent, propped up on an elbow as she rests her head of sun-gleamed brown hair on her hand. Her Mona Lisa smile is small, almost secretive, and the suit and the glasses make her look like a 1950s movie star.

I'm still staring at the photo when Aunt Helen turns around to face me.

"Harper." It's amazing the amount of sheer disdain that woman can squeeze into two syllables. She says my name like it's something dirty she wants to spit out of her mouth. "You know, you could come along to our knitting group if you'd like. They're lovely women from the church, and I'm sure they have a lot to offer you. Some spiritual guidance, perhaps."

I look away from the photo, at her, and then down into my bowl, ignoring that last comment. "I already told you. I'm spending the night at Laney's."

Aunt Helen scowls. That's the I Am Silently Judging You look—I recognize it because it's the same expression Laney has when she sees people wearing black and blue together, or the look I myself have when people pontificate on the brilliance of Ayn Rand. Aunt Helen is currently wearing a navy cardigan and black slacks. Figures. I wonder what her feelings are on *The Fountainhead*.

She takes a deep breath as though she's preparing to launch a lecture that, if similar to the ones I've endured recently, will say many things, like how I need to Let Jesus Take the Wheel, and It Is Time to Be an Adult, Harper, and also, You Need to Surround Yourself With Positive Influences. That's her roundabout way of implying that Laney is a *bad* influence, and also a vapid slut. Aunt Helen thinks hair color is a telltale indicator of sexual promiscuity levels—it's her belief that brunettes are inherently more virtuous. It is *my* belief that she's out of her mind, but no news there, I suppose.

A look at her watch must persuade her otherwise, because she simply sighs and says, rather mournfully, "My words fall on deaf ears," and leaves it at that. They're out of the house before six-thirty, my mother, still silent, shuffling behind Aunt Helen like a zombie. I try to look on the bright side: At least she's not a drunken zombie. Apparently she's traded alcohol for Jesus.

I'm not even sure which one is worse.

Seven o'clock rolls around faster than I realize; Jake'll be here any minute. Everything is set. My duffel and backpack, both stuffed so full they barely zip all the way, sit in a pile at the door. Now I have to take the last step. I have to take down the urn.

Aunt Helen and my mother picked it out; I wanted nothing to do with that decision-making process. It's a black vase with fine white veining patterns branching out across the polished marble, sleek and smooth looking. I've never touched it before, and even at the memorial service, I gave the table it was displayed on (next to a large black-and-white portrait of June and thick layers of flower bouquets) a wide berth. Just looking at the thing makes me uncomfortable, knowing my sister, the girl I grew up with, lived with, shared blood with, was burned away into nothing but dust and sealed inside that vase.

The same vase I stand in front of now.

Carefully, I put my hands around the cool marble and lift it off of the mantel. It's a lot heavier than I expected. If I hadn't been holding on to the urn for dear life, I might have dropped it. I hold it close to my chest and make my way slowly, cautiously, to the front door.

Outside it's nearly pitch-black, the porch light emanating just enough light for me to make out shapes in the dark. At first I'm sure Jake hasn't shown up yet, but my eyes adjust, and I catch sight of the van, headlights off, idling curbside farther down the street. He must have wanted to make sure he wouldn't attract attention. Which is a good idea in theory, but not so good when I, not exactly the most graceful person ever, have to carry a fragile, heavy urn half a block without stumbling over a crack in the pavement or my own two feet.

"About damn time," Jake says when I finally inch my way down the sidewalk and reach him. He leans against the side of the van, eyeing me up and down. "Where's your stuff?"

"First things first." I look pointedly at the urn in my arms. "You mind—?"

"Oh. Right."

He opens the doors in back, hops in and drags forward an old trunk with scratched, peeling bumper stickers slapped all over the top of it. The lid pops up to reveal two thick blankets inside. When he reaches for the urn, he looks to me for permission first, and I relinquish it to him, carefully, watching as he swaddles it in blankets so it won't move around. Clearly he's given the storage of the urn some forethought.

I return to the house to grab the rest of my things. Suddenly, it hits me. The note. The all-important note. Somehow in all of my preparations, I forgot to write one. I rip a sheet off the notepad in the kitchen. The problem: I'm suddenly struck with a massive case of writer's block. I don't know what to write. Nothing seems adequate…but I guess I could try to be honest.

I'll be back in a while, I write. *I don't know how long. I'm okay. With Laney. I'll call you. Don't worry.*

Leaving it in the kitchen is a bad idea; it'll be discovered too soon. I tape it to the mirror in my bedroom instead, knowing it'll take longer for them to find it, that it'll buy me more time.

I need as much of a head start as I can get.

Jake's van is rickety and loud and smells like cigarettes and pine trees—the pine scent due to a cardboard freshener that hangs from his rearview mirror. When I climb into the passenger seat, I have to kick aside a heap of CDs scattered on the floor in order for my feet to have any room. He pulls out onto the road, and as he drives, I pop open the glove compartment. It's overflowing with more CDs and cassette tapes. Who in the world needs to store this much music in their car?

"What are you doing?" he snaps, irritated, eyes flicking over to me as I dig through his array of music.

"Geez, are you trying to open up a Sam Goody in here or what?"

"If you think that's a lot, you should see my bedroom."

Is he trying to make me blush? Because it's not going to work.

I click the compartment back shut. "You know, if you got an iPod, you could save some serious space," I point out.

He frowns. "I like having something to hold in my hands. Plus, they have artwork, liner notes. There's nothing exciting about getting music off the internet."

"If you say so." I don't really see how buying music is exciting in the first place. "Your collection is impressive. Benefits of working at the Oleo, I presume?"

"You could say that."

I direct him down Laney's street. As he approaches her house, he flips off the headlights, puts it in Neutral and coasts into her driveway. We sit waiting, Jake already reaching for a cigarette, and when he lights it, I notice some movement at the side of the house.

It's Laney, tossing a bag out of the upstairs window. And then another. And another. A second later, she eases through the window space and crawls down the trellis. She's had plenty of practice from nights of sneaking out. Even in her plaid skirt and sandals, it takes only a minute or so before she's scaled all the way down and drops the last few feet. She gathers up her two suitcases and extra bag and bustles into the van, breathless and grinning.

"Three suitcases?" Jake twists around in his seat to gape openmouthed at her. "Are you kidding me?"

"Um, no?" Laney shoves the luggage into the far back and looks over her shoulder at him. "What do you expect me to do, carry around one garbage bag? I'm not some hobo! I need my *things*." She pauses, nose wrinkling. "Ew, why does it smell like a forest fire in here? Are you *smoking*? Harper, you know I hate that."

Laney hates the stink of cigarettes. I don't really blame her for that, either. But hey, she has her rebellion—boys and beer—and this is mine. She can get over it.

"Get used to it," Jake says as he backs out of the driveway and blows a stream of smoke in her direction, just to be an ass. I punch him in the shoulder.

"Gross." She shudders. "Have fun with your lung cancer, emphysema, yellow teeth and perma-bad breath. The rest of us will be over here, enjoying our health and maintaining our good looks. But you wouldn't know much about that, would you?"

He rolls his eyes at her in the rearview mirror. "Oh, that's funny. You should be a comedian."

"What a coincidence. That's actually my backup plan, you know, in case the acting thing doesn't pan out."

"You want to act?"

She fluffs out her hair and says, "I'm going to be the next Marilyn."

Laney does, actually, sort of have that Marilyn Monroe, classic Hollywood look. She dresses the part in her thrift-store attire, and then there's her wavy, finger-combed golden curls, the generous curves, the long dark lashes. On top of that, Laney has something my mother would call *presence*. It sets her apart from the other girls at school, makes the boys turn their heads when she walks by them in the halls.

"Laney is obsessed with old movie stars who died tragically in the prime of life," I explain to Jake. She shoots me a concerned look as soon as the words slip out of my mouth, and I smile enough to let her know I'm not offended or anything. It does make me think, though, about that photo of June on our refrigerator, the one where she looks almost like Natalie Wood or something. The swimsuit came from Laney, something she'd bought that was too small for her and too revealing for me, and so she'd offered it to June.

I don't know how, exactly, Laney feels about June now. She has an older stepbrother from her father's first marriage in college on the East Coast, but her relationship with him was never like mine with June; they barely know each other. And as my best friend, she spent a fair amount of time around our house. She and June treated each other almost like siblings. Even though it can't be the same, I wonder if that's what it feels like to her. Like she lost a sister, too.

"Wasn't Marilyn Monroe a little past her prime when she died?" Jake asks. I punch him again, and he scowls. "Would you stop doing that? You're gonna run us off the road!"

I squint out the window as he turns onto the exit leading to the highway. "So what, exactly, is the game plan?"

"I have to make a stop in White Haven," he says. He switches on his blinker and merges into the highway lane. "One of my friends has something I need to pick up. He said we could spend the night if we want. I haven't been there but he said it's not out of the way, so don't worry."

White Haven is a beach town by Lake Michigan, less than an hour away. I've only been a few times. Laney's grandparents have a vacation cottage there. The water isn't as pretty as it gets up north, but it's a nice beach with some big dunes. Peaceful.

"Hey, maybe we can go to my grandparents' place later this summer," Laney says to me from the back. She must be thinking the same thing.

I nod. "Yeah, maybe." Too bad when I get back home, I'm going to be grounded for life.

I really don't want to think about it right now. Jake, probably bored by our conversation, flips the radio volume up a few notches. The song that blasts out is one I recognize.

"This is 'Thunder Road,' right?" I ask after a moment.

He looks at me. "You like Bruce Springsteen?" I like the note of surprise in his voice. The fact that there's something about me he, the eternal enigma, doesn't have all figured out.

"My father loves the Boss," I say. "He likes to delude himself into thinking he grew up in a mining town in Jersey instead of the Michigan suburbs."

"Your dad's got good taste then."

"Obviously you haven't met his girlfriend."

Jake's mouth quirks into a half grin. In the back, Laney wrestles with the seat belt, grunting as she yanks at the stubborn strap.

"What is with this thing?" she grouses.

"I've been meaning to get that fixed," says Jake. "You'll have to sit on the other side."

"Joplin's not so infallible after all, huh?" I smirk at him. "What's with that name, anyway?"

"She's named after—"

"Janis Joplin," Laney pipes up from the other seat. She's busy buckling herself in. "Right? Though I don't know why you'd name your van after *her*. Wasn't she ugly?"

"But she had the *music*," Jake says fervently, fist clenched and pumping the air. He sees my and Laney's matching bemused expressions and sighs. "Never mind. Harper, grab that CD off the floor. The one on top."

I double over and snatch the first CD case from the top of the pile—another mix. I hand it to Jake, who takes one hand off the steering wheel, ejects Bruce and slides in the new disc. Almost immediately I hear a woman's scratchy voice, caterwauling on and on about a man named Bobby McGee. It isn't pleasant, per se, but it's raw and growling and full of conviction.

I love it.

"That's Janis," he explains.

"Oh," is all I can say.

We drive on, and Janis's song fades to make way for another. I realize each song has a name in it: Bobby, Eileen, John, Stephanie, Daniel, Layla, even one about a boy named Sue. Johnny Cash, Jake tells me when I ask who the singer is. I like it and tell him as much.

"You'd have to have no soul to not like Johnny Cash," he says.

The next song is about a girl named Ruby Tuesday. At first all I can think about is the chain restaurant, but then a lightbulb goes on in my head. That voice—it's the same swaggering male voice from June's CD, the first track with that startling guitar riff.

"Who is this?" I ask.

Jake stares at me like I'm the stupidest person he's ever had the misfortune of coming into contact with. "The Rolling Stones. Mick Jagger. Only one of the most legendary front men ever. You seriously don't know who he is?"

Laney leans up from the back, propping her elbow against my headrest. "Some of us like to live in the now."

"Yeah, okay, Ms. Monroe."

"That's totally different. This stuff is, like, ancient. Don't you have *any* music from the past decade? Jay-Z? Snow Patrol? Kelly Clarkson? Something relevant?"

"Everything on the radio is crap," snaps Jake. "It's fast food for your ears. It doesn't make you think. It isn't even *about* anything—not anything real. Don't you think music should *say* something?"

"So people have different tastes. So what? You don't have to be a jackass about it. Just because pop music doesn't say what you want to hear doesn't mean it doesn't say anything," Laney says. She falls back against her seat with a groan. "God, you're like a douche-baggy hipster music snob with the tastes of a forty-year-old white guy."

"Douche-baggy? Is that even a word?"

"See!" Laney gesticulates emphatically toward Jake with one hand. "Snob!"

"Look," I interrupt, trying for my most diplomatic tone, "if we have to listen to your classic rock, can we at least listen to the Beatles?"

Jake relaxes his hands on the wheel. "You're in luck."

He flips a few tracks ahead, and a second later, "Hey Jude" comes pouring out of the speakers. Finally, something I know and love. I grew up with this music. My mom's a big fan of the Fab Four, owns all of the albums. She used to sing "Yellow Submarine" as a lullaby when I was a baby. I wonder what she's doing now, if she's come home yet, how she'll react when she discovers my note. The thought of it brings on a pang of guilt, heavy in my chest. I try my best to ignore it.

It's easier to do when I have music to fill the silence. Jake sings along around his cigarette, his voice surprisingly on-key, and after a little while, I join in too, unsurprisingly *off*-key. Even Laney quits pouting long enough to chime in with the *nah-nah-nah-nahs* at the end.

Joplin hurtles down the highway, each mile taking us farther from Grand Lake and carrying us closer and closer to California—and to my sister's last chance at salvation. Maybe it's my last chance, too.

five

The bungalow in White Haven is nestled on the side of a high dune, only two flights of wooden stairs away from the beach bordering Lake Michigan. Overgrown bushes in the small yard shroud the front of the house, and Jake drives past it twice before I point out the numbers on the mailbox and he realizes it's the right address. There are two cars parked in the narrow drive, another right on the curb.

"It's a sweet pad, isn't it?" boasts the boy who answers the door. He's young, not far from our age, with long, ratty dreads and a T-shirt that reads Free Palestine. "My grandpa left it to us when he kicked it a few months back. My dad's itching to sell the place, but I convinced him to let me have it for the summer. Better than having me around his house." He directs an affable grin at Laney and me. "I'm Seth, by the way."

"Harper," I reply, then motion to our bags. "Is there somewhere we should—?"

"Yeah, yeah. Sure. I'll show you the room."

Seth hefts two of Laney's suitcases and leads us down a hall to a guest room. It's more of a glorified closet, with only enough space for one frumpy twin bed to be squeezed in. That alone takes up three quarters of the room.

"Sorry it's kinda tight," Seth says.

Unfazed, Laney drops her suitcase and plops onto the bed, testing the mattress. "It's cool."

"I'd give you the bigger room, but Gwen's taken it over—"

"Gwen?" Jake snaps to attention. "Gwen is here?"

I look over at him quizzically. Who is Gwen? Obviously someone he knows, seeing as the muscles in his neck have gone rigid, his hands fisted at his sides.

"Yeah, man, I thought I told you," says Seth. "She's been here for a week. Danny and Anna are, too. I swear I said something—"

"I think I would've remembered that detail." Jake tosses his bag onto the floor and pushes a hand through his hair.

"Dude, chill," Seth says, clapping him on the shoulder heartily. His smile widens. "I've got something that'll cheer you up."

"I told you, I don't smoke pot anymore."

"Not that! Hang on, let me go get it."

Seth disappears from the room. As soon as he does, Laney grins at Jake and says, "So, pot, huh?"

"You handled the peer pressure well," I chime in. "Your DARE officers would be proud."

Jake scowls. "Shut up."

Before I can think of more ribbing, Seth reappears with a plastic crate. He leafs through it and removes a slim vinyl record.

"This," he says, presenting it with a flourish, "is for you."

Jake takes the record and glances down at it. When he looks up at Seth again, his eyes are wide with disbelief. "No way."

"Yes way," Seth says.

I peer over Jake's shoulder at the album cover. It's a Jimi Hendrix LP—and the cover is signed in black pen. *Love Always, Jimi.* A real autograph. The record itself is in pristine condition.

"Holy shit!" Laney says. "That is too awesome! Is it for real?"

"One hundred percent authentic. My grandpa left it to me," Seth explains. "He was cool. All about the Hendrix. I guess he went to this festival in Germany in '67, and one of his friends was an organizer, so he got backstage and met the man himself. I know you're a fan, so—"

Jake shakes his head and tries to shove the album back into Seth's hands. "Seth. No. I can't take this."

"Yeah, you can. I owe you." Seth turns to Laney and I. "Three months ago, I'm in Detroit protesting a free trade conference, right? Some pig shoves me, I go flying into another, next thing I know I'm on the ground with a Taser in my back. I get thrown in city jail, no money and one phone call. So I call Jake. You know what this fucker did? He dropped everything, drove up and bailed me out, no questions."

"Like I could just leave you," Jake says. "You're too pretty. You're a delicate flower. They would've ripped you apart in there."

"You were in *jail*?" Laney sounds both curious and titillated. "What was it like?"

"Boring. Dirty. Smelled like ass," Seth tells her, shuddering at the memory. He looks to Jake. "Keep it, man. My gift to you. Besides, it's not like it's Marley. In that case, it might be different."

Jake gazes down at the album in his hands reverently, like it's a rare religious relic. "Thanks."

Everyone else, Seth tells us, is down at the beach, having a bonfire.

"You might want to grab a jacket," he says. "It's windier by the lake."

He's right; it's cool outside, with the sun almost set and the stars coming out from behind the clouds. I hear the waves the moment we step onto the back deck. There are plastic fold-up chairs leaned against the side of the house, so we each pick one and make our way down the stairs, through the grassy weeds and onto the sloping beach. An orange fire roars from a pit a couple yards down. As we get closer, I overhear several people in the midst of a spirited debate.

"It's about privilege. You can't erase that."

"No, but it doesn't mean you can't be an ally to the oppressed. If the majority is incapable of empathy—or of support—then the whole world is screwed."

"But so many people don't admit their own privilege! You can't fight what isn't even acknowledged. We have to check ourselves, and then maybe—" A tiny Asian girl with a pixie haircut suddenly notices our approach and stops mid-sentence, bounding to her feet. "Jake! You made it!"

She all but leaps into his arms as Laney and I stand back, amused. Jake does not seem remotely like the affectionate type, so to see him on the receiving end of a giant bear hug from a pint-size girl is pretty amusing. He sees us biting back laughter and glares, patting the girl's back and awkwardly maneuvering away from her hold.

"Hey, Anna," he says. "How's it going?"

"Discussions of cultural appropriation aside, it's all good!" She spins to face Laney and me, and, without warning, throws both arms around us in a suffocating squeeze. Considering her size, her upper-body strength is impressive. "Hi! I'm Anna!

It's so great to meet you!" Everything she says sounds like an exclamation point.

This time it's Jake trying not to laugh. I shoot him daggers over Anna's shoulder.

"Long time, no see." Danny and Jake exchange some complicated handshake thing, the way guys do. He has on a pair of ultraskinny jeans that look a lot like the ones Laney is always buying, and his bangs are long and swept to one side. "When was the last time? That sit-in in March?"

The voice that answers isn't Jake's. "And look how much was accomplished on behalf of immigrant rights."

Another girl sits on Danny's other side. Her long legs are crossed, arms folded across her chest, and she has dark hair cut severely at the chin, emphasizing her strong jaw and thin mouth. That's Gwen—which I realize, not due to my amazing intuition, but because she straightens in her chair and says, "I'm Gwen." I assume that information is for the benefit of Laney and me, but it's hard to tell since she isn't even looking at us. Her gaze is solely focused on Jake.

"Hi," I say, opening my mouth to make the obligatory introduction when Jake sets down his chair, its metal legs striking the sand sharply.

"You look good," he says. The words come out through gritted teeth. "I see college is treating you well. Too bad you didn't get into Pratt, though. I hear their art program is top-notch."

The antagonism in his tone doesn't escape me. Neither does the way Gwen looks from him to me and back again. That is definitely the look of a possessive ex. After Laney dumped Dustin and started dating one of his friends, he had that same look all of the time.

"It's too bad you've decided not to pursue secondary education at all, Jay." Gwen has that affected, high-pitched baby voice that some girls at my high school like to adopt, thinking it's cutesy and endearing when it of course has the opposite effect. It makes me want to stab my eardrums. "It's really expanded my horizons. But I guess you're happy at the Oleo."

She bares her teeth in a smile that is anything but friendly. Jake makes a noncommittal noise in his throat, unfolding his chair and flopping down on it. I follow suit and search for Laney. She's across the circle, lounging comfortably on Seth's lap, laughing at something he's said.

Typical Laney, already making fast friends. She has a knack for effortlessly fitting into any crowd—the kind of girl who walks into a room and leaves an hour later with fifteen new people added to her cell phone's contact list. Usually half of them are potential make-out partners. Funny how we can be best friends, when she's so magnetic and outgoing, and I'm— well. Not.

"Did you go to the Diego Lopez show?" Jake is saying. "I heard he played on campus."

Gwen snorts. "Like I would listen to that dreck."

"I haven't seen him live, but I've heard his stuff. It's pretty good."

"Yeah, but you like crap music. I mean, you like the *Doors*," Gwen says with a hint of disgust, like this name drop explains everything. She loops her arm through his and looks at him pityingly. "You poor, unenlightened soul."

"Uh—" I clear my throat. "What's wrong with the Doors?"

She stares at me as if I've grown a second head. "Only *everything*! Jim Morrison was nothing but a junkie with an overblown sense of superiority. The only reason anyone still gives a crap about him at all is because he died young. Bee-eff-dee." Her arm untangles from Jake's, and she shakes her head at him. "Really, Jay, for as much as you claim to be so dedicated to worthwhile music, you do hold some seriously blasphemous opinions."

I make a sound, the start of a laugh, and she jerks her head around to look at me. I quickly shut my mouth. This girl is too ridiculous. How does she even exist? Maybe she's thinking the same thing about me, because when she rises from her chair, she shoots a parting dirty look my way before sauntering off to the other side of the circle, hips swinging. I wait until she's out of earshot before turning to Jake.

"Really, *Jay,* what are you *thinking,*" I mimic. "You poor soul!"

"'Unenlightened,' my ass!" he mutters under his breath. "She's the one who never stops verbally fellating the Smiths."

"'*Bee-eff-dee.*'" I stretch each syllable out so they sound even more ridiculous and cringe. "Who talks like that?"

"Gwen, apparently," he says. He stares after her as she leans on Danny's chair. "Forget her. She thinks everything and everyone is overrated."

"So, how long did you two date?" I ask casually.

Startled, he tears his gaze off of Gwen and turns it to me. "What? Who said—"

"Please, I'm not blind. The unnecessary touching, the excessive nickname usage, the death glare imposed on any female in your two-mile radius. All classic signs."

Gwen is certainly…interesting. Is that the kind of girl Jake is attracted to? Petulant and pretentious? She's pretty, I'll give her that, but none of her outer beauty could really be worth putting up with the constant bitchitude and baby voice. Unless Jake is ruled entirely by his dick—which is totally possible. Most guys are.

If that's the case, well, good for him. He probably deserves someone of her caliber.

"Six months, junior year," he admits. "She ends up dumping me for some guy in her art class at the community college. Says I'm not 'mature' enough for her, but she hopes we can still be friends. Woe is me, right?"

"She still dating the guy?"

"I think that relationship lasted all of three seconds." Jake grins like he can't help himself. "No, she goes to school in Ann Arbor now. She's just on break."

"That's a shame. Here I thought we were on a fast track to bee-eff-eff-dom."

He snickers, scoops a stick off the ground and pokes idly at a log in the embers. "Yeah, the two of you really hit it off."

I'm not surprised she doesn't like me. Most people don't. I guess because I don't hide the fact that I can't stand people like Gwen, who take themselves too seriously, or people who don't take themselves seriously enough. I'm not like Laney, the chameleon, fitting herself into every social situation seamlessly.

Like right now—Laney's already deep in conversation, perched on the arm of Seth's chair as she compares favorite current fashion trends with Anna and Danny. I suspect from Danny's passion for eyeliner and scarves that as far as make-out partners go, he would be as likely a candidate for me as, say, Gwen. Hell, even Anna would probably be more interested, if her constant giggling and hooded looks sent in Laney's direction are any indication. Seth keeps mostly to himself. After a while of observing the ongoing discussion, he slides a beat-up black case out from beside his chair, withdrawing an acoustic guitar. He sits back and strums it a few times clumsily.

"Jay, you should play something," Gwen suggests from across the crackling fire. Somehow from the way she says it, and the dark look Jake gives her in response, I can tell a gauntlet has been thrown. Maybe some *You Got Served*-style dance-off shenanigans will ensue. That would be—well, that would be pretty awesome, actually.

Jake frowns and shakes his head. "I don't think so."

"No, man, you should." Seth comes over to hand him the guitar. "You're way better than I am."

Jake accepts it hesitantly. I watch as he draws it into his lap, shifts the strap over his head and slides his fingers down the neck of the guitar. His expression is oddly subdued when he bends his head down, hair falling across his eyes.

Everyone goes quiet as he begins to play. His singing is strong and clear, fingers finding the right chords with ease, eyes fixed on his hands. Shadows thrown from the fire play across his face while he sings about the day the music died in this plaintive, striking voice. Watching him, I can see how connected to the music he is. The guitar is like an extension of himself.

As he launches into the livelier chorus, Laney springs off of Seth's lap, grabs his hand and starts skipping in a circle around the campfire, one arm waving over her head. Anna joins in, and Danny, too, all of them twirling and dancing and belting out the lyrics in a hilariously off-key chorus. Only Gwen, Jake and I remain seated. Jake watches the commotion with a big grin while Gwen stares at her nails, bored, a liquor bottle dangling in one hand.

I watch them as they run and dance and sing in the same way that little kids do, carefree and not at all self-conscious. Like you do before you're old enough to worry about how dumb you'll look to anyone else. I wish I could be like them. Able to let go that way. But instead I'm the girl who sits on the sidelines, unable to feel anything but anger, my heart all hollowed out, my insides closed off, iced over.

Listening to Jake, though… I'm thawing. A little. Not enough to get me to dance—seriously, that'll never happen—but enough to enjoy it. The dancing, the fire, the moon. His song.

Even though everyone else is singing, too, Jake's voice carries the loudest. I catch his eye across the circle, and his grin spreads wider across his face. I smile back, ignoring the stink-eye I know Gwen is giving me without even looking her way. My attention turns to the loop of crazy teenagers romping around the fire pit, wild and untamed in the flickering fire-light, like gypsies.

They all burst into spontaneous applause as soon as Jake strums the last chord. I clap my hands, too, as Jake just smiles and slips off the guitar. This is the first time I've ever seen him look downright sheepish.

"That was great," gushes Anna, after they've all calmed down enough to take their places around the fire again. "Seriously, Jake, you should—"

"A road trip, huh?" Gwen cuts in, raising her eyebrows at Jake. "Why California?"

So she doesn't know. Who did Jake tell? Anyone? I don't think he'd be that stupid, but then, I don't really know him, do I?

Before Jake can whip up an answer, Danny says, "You should go to L.A. Track down Paris Hilton. Throw a can of paint on her or something."

"You know, we're driving down to Chicago tomorrow to meet Devon. There's this huge antiwar demonstration at Union Park." Seth tucks his chin over Laney's shoulder, and she leans back into him. It's so weird to me how comfortable she can be with someone she's known for less than three hours. "Why don't you guys drive down with us?"

"Jay doesn't *do* protests," Gwen cuts in. Her tone is so icy I'm pretty sure the air temperature actually drops a few degrees when she opens her mouth. "Not anymore."

What is that supposed to mean? Jake's face reveals nothing. As usual.

Laney clasps her hands together. "We should totally go!" She looks over at me and does her best pout, the one she reserves for conning people into getting whatever she wants. It usually works, too. "Can we, Harper?"

"Um, I guess." I glance at Jake to see his mouth turned down. "I mean, Jake's the one driving, so—"

He shrugs. "I'm okay with it. It's just—you should know this isn't a let's-hold-hands-and-sing-kumbaya kind of deal. It can get…intense."

I can't believe it. Here's another person treating me like a little kid, like I'm too fragile to deal with anything. I'm not a child.

"I can handle myself." I stand up and snatch the bottle out of Gwen's hands. "Give me that."

I unscrew the top, take a long swig and promptly gag. Whatever is in the bottle is vile. I choke as I swallow it down, trying desperately not to spew, despite the fact that my throat is basically on fire.

"What is this?" I cough and squint at the bottle's label.

"Uh, tequila?" Gwen says, like it should be obvious.

"It tastes like lighter fluid." I grimace, but that doesn't stop me from taking another long pull, and then another. Still disgusting, but by the fourth drink, it goes down a little easier. What the hell. You only live once.

As I'm working on my fifth, Laney steals the bottle from

my hands, laughing, and says, "Didn't you ever learn how to share?"

"We should go swimming," Anna says, out of the blue, and then hiccups. She slaps a hand over her mouth, smothering a giggle.

Danny looks at her like she just suggested knocking over the closest liquor store. Which wouldn't be such a bad idea, on second thought, considering how fast Laney, Seth and Anna are working through the tequila bottle. "Uh, sure, if catching pneumonia's your idea of a fun time. I don't want to freeze my balls off. I'm rather attached to them. Literally *and* figuratively."

Laney springs to her feet. "I'm game!" Of course she is.

"You don't have a suit," I remind her. Why do my words sound funny? Oh, okay. Maybe I *am* a little tipsy. I can't feel my toes.

"So?" She directs a coy grin at Seth. "I don't need one."

"A bunch of drunk kids skinny-dipping in the middle of the night. That'll end well," Jake comments with an eye roll, but Laney, Anna and Seth don't hear, or don't care, as they're already racing to the beach, peeling off their clothes as they run.

"They can be so juvenile." Gwen scowls. "I'm going to go inside and work on my project."

"Is this the one with the high heels?" Danny asks. He looks over at us from underneath his artfully arranged fringe. "She created this papier-mâché Jesus—except it's Jesus as a woman—and there are high heels instead of nails through the hands. And there's a tampon stuffed in Jesus's mouth." He shakes his head. "That is some fucked-up shit right there."

"It's supposed to represent the oppression women face due to traditionally gendered beauty standards driven into us by the patriarchy," Gwen says defensively. "I don't know why I bother trying to explain these things to you. Are you coming in or not?"

"Like I'd go swimming?" Danny scoffs. "Lake water is killer on my hair."

As the two of them trudge back to the house, Jake pats the pockets of his leather jacket. "I'm going for a smoke," he says.

"Like I care," I shoot back, but by the time the words come out, he's already out of earshot. My reaction time? Not so stellar at the moment.

I hear the sound of splashing and shrieking as Anna, Seth and Laney plunge into the water. I'm not *that* wasted, seeing as I have no desire to follow—it's either that, or else no amount of alcohol can lure me into unleashing my inner exhibitionist, apparently. I slip off my flip-flops and walk down the beach by myself, padding barefoot over soft and cool sand.

A ways down, I stop, roll up my jeans over my knees and wade into the water. It's cold—cold enough to make my feet go numb after only a few minutes. I don't care, though, because the alcohol makes me feel warm and loose and heavy, and I'm too absorbed in looking over the lake to focus on the cold. The light from the pinprick stars glimmers off of the glassy water, the moon a bright sliver in the black sky. I'm far enough down shore that the laughter of the swimmers is just a faded echo.

I push out farther, the waves lapping up and breaking over my waist, soaking my jeans. I skim my fingertips over the water's surface, trail them lightly back and forth. Everything out here is still and silent. Nothing, it seems, could break the veil of peacefulness.

"Harper? Harper!"

Except that.

Slowly I turn around, the wet sandy mud squishing between

my toes as I do. Jake is up on the dry sand, out of breath, his expression a cross between anger and confusion.

"You've been out here half an hour! I thought you pulled a Jeff Buckley on me. Which—while I would appreciate the extra room in the van—is not something I want to explain to your mother." He stops to catch his breath, his brow furrowed with confusion. "What are you even doing?"

I try to think of how to explain. "The lake—it's… it's *big*."

Jake looks like he's leaning more toward annoyed now. "Uh…so?"

"I mean…" It's difficult to articulate when my tongue feels too thick for my mouth. But I'm desperate to explain, how insignificant I feel in comparison to the lake, to the sky, to the world. "Look at it. I'm *nothing*. It's so much bigger, bigger than me, bigger than my thoughts and my…my…"

Pain, is the word I'm going for, but the line of connection from my brain to my mouth appears to have short-circuited. That's probably for the best. Regardless, Jake seems to get it, because he laughs a little and runs a hand through his hair, making it stick up messily.

"Well, aren't you Mommy's Little Existentialist," he says wryly. The tension releases from his shoulders as he blows out a long breath, like he's been holding it for a long time. "Come on, let's go before you start quoting Sartre. If that happens, I can't be held responsible for my actions."

As I come out of the water, I step on a sharp-edged rock that sends me staggering dangerously to my left. Jake rushes forward and catches an arm around my waist before I lose my balance.

"Easy, tiger," he says, slinging my arm over his shoulder.

I lean into him, and my face momentarily rolls against his

neck. He smells woodsy, like smoke and leather. Probably the jacket, I figure. "Do you believe in God?"

His arm around my waist stiffens. "That's…random."

"No, it's just—what do you have against Sartre? You think the world has *meaning*? That everything happens for a *reason*?" I'm yelling without really intending to. "Because, news flash, Tolan, *it doesn't*."

"Okay, *now* you're just being a nihilist."

I'm not a nihilist. I'm not really anything, I don't think. I don't know what I believe anymore. If God does exist, then He's just an asshole, creating this world full of human suffering and letting all these terrible things happen to good people, and sitting there and doing nothing about it. At June's memorial service, a few people came up to me and said some really stupid things, like how everything happens for a reason, and God never gives us more than we can handle. All I could think was, does that mean if I was a weaker person, this never would've happened? Am I seriously supposed to buy that June's death was part of some stupid divine plan? I don't believe that. I can't. It just doesn't make sense.

We keep walking, and I look at Jake for so long that I almost trip before realizing we've reached the stairs. When we get to the top, I drag my feet, forcing him to slow down, and say, "Seriously, do you? Believe in God, I mean."

A long pause. "You really wanna know?"

"Don't say that. I hate when people say that. Of course I want to know. That's why I asked."

Jake pauses for a bit, considering, and then says, "Sometimes people think they want to know things, but then they hear the answer and realize they'd prefer to be in the dark."

Vagueness is such an annoying trait. I'm adding it to the ever-expanding list of things that annoy me about him.

He shrugs. "Anyway. No. I don't. I don't think the world is meaningless, but if there was ever a God, He's dead now. More dead than hip-hop."

I think of Laney's music tastes, all of the rap she's made me listen to, like the Roots and Mos Def and that Sri Lankan chick who likes to freestyle about third world countries shooting up rich people.

"Hip-hop is not dead!" I protest. "Don't speak of that which you do not know."

"Whatever," Jake says, and I roll my eyes. He looks at me again. "And what about you?"

"You really wanna know?" I mimic his earlier tone, trying not to stumble again. Balance is a really difficult concept to master at the moment. "I don't know. Maybe. Probably not. Lately all signs seem to point to no."

I hold out my hands in front of me in two L shapes, like I'm framing an actual sign. The sign that says God Is Dead.

"I have this rule—" he pauses, fumbling with the knob to the house and pushing the door open, all the while holding me up with his other arm "—of not getting into philosophical debates when one party is sober and the other isn't."

"Well, then you should've gotten drunk. Tequila is good. I mean, it's revolting, but it's good. Sort of. Does that make sense?"

"Absolutely none," he says. "And I don't drink. Not anymore."

Not anymore? Interesting. So far I've learned that Jake has recently given up a lot of things. Pot smoking, political activism and now alcohol. I'm about to ask him why when I notice Laney on the couch—not alone. Very much not alone. She's on top of Seth, the two of them rolling around as they make out eagerly, practically eating each other's faces off in the process.

"Fuck me." Jake kicks the door shut behind him and sighs. "I do not need to be privy to this."

Laney and Seth stop devouring each other long enough to flip us off simultaneously before resuming their face-eating activities. I'm scandalized just watching them go at it, all ravenous mouths and roaming hands.

"I think I'm going to be sick," I say.

"Tell me about it," Jake replies sympathetically.

My stomach turns. "No. I mean, *I think I'm going to be sick.*"

Jake's face pales, and he rushes me into the bathroom with impressive speed. The next thing I know, I'm on my knees, bent over the toilet with him holding my hair back as I empty out the contents of my stomach. Which aren't much to begin with: tequila, tequila and more tequila. Lovely.

I retch into the toilet one last time and, exhausted, slump against the seat. From there I slide bonelessly to the linoleum, my cheek flat against cool, soothing tile. My throat burns. I want to push myself back up, but my hand refuses to move.

Stupid hand. Stupid world.

"Yes, the world *is* stupid," Jake agrees with a soft laugh.

I don't even realize I've said anything out loud. That means despite my current drunken, post-heaving state, I'm still able to formulate syllables into recognizable words—go, Team Me! On the other hand, I'm doing that thing again, thinking something and saying it out loud without realizing it. Where is my filter?

Suddenly the walls move, the cool, comforting floor sliding away from me. Wait. That isn't right. Jake has grabbed me by the back of my shirt and hauled me into a sitting position, the sudden movement causing the whole room to spin in a nauseating blur of beige and white. When my gaze focuses again, I see Jake at the sink, wetting down a washcloth under the faucet.

The world *is* stupid, stupid and unfair. I can't help but think that June would never have ended up with her head stuck in the toilet after a stupid bender. Or if she had, she would've been much more graceful about the whole thing than I am. That's just the way she always was. She was always better.

"Better at what?"

Crap. Did it again. Damn filter!

"Everything," I say as I accept the damp washcloth he hands me.

"I highly doubt that."

I wipe off my mouth and spit a little. "What do you know?"

"Well, you're better at living," he reasons. "You're the one still here, aren't you?"

For a second I think he's trying to be purposefully hurtful, to throw that in my face, but when I look up at him, his expression is neutral. The way he said it, too, wasn't mean. It was just…honest. Like he was merely pointing out an irrefutable fact. Technically he's right, but that knowledge doesn't make me feel any better. I might be living, but what have I done with my life? Nothing spectacular.

"Please tell me you're not a weepy drunk," he says, when I haven't responded.

"No." I fling the washcloth onto the floor. "I don't cry."

Jake looks at me, disbelieving. "Ever?"

"Never."

I stand up slowly, clutching the counter for support. My legs feel all weird and rubbery. I know that the second I step away, I'll probably fall over myself in a spectacular fashion and end up back on the ground in a heap of limbs. I look helplessly to Jake, who rolls his eyes and takes my arm.

"You're like an old lady," he teases as he half carries me into the guest room.

"Yeah, I'm sure you help old ladies cross the street all the time."

"That is how I like to spend my weekends. That, and luring stranded kittens out of trees." He grins. "It's a hobby."

I make Jake look away while I struggle out of my wet jeans, then collapse onto the bed stomach first. I barely have the energy to kick and crawl my way under the covers. Jake steals the extra pillow, easing onto the floor.

"You're sleeping there?" I ask, surprised.

"The couch is...otherwise occupied, if you hadn't noticed," he says.

I watch as he punches the pillow a few times and places it under his head. He tosses and turns, trying to arrange himself into a comfortable position on the hard wooden slats. It's painful just to watch. I know I'll probably regret this later, but...

I sigh and move over on the bed. "Get in."

He picks his head up off the floor. "What?"

"Get in," I repeat, impatient, patting the mattress. "Hurry, before my flash of temporary insanity dissipates."

"How generous of you," he says sarcastically, but he's already halfway to his feet.

The bedsprings creak loudly as Jake settles in, his weight causing the mattress to dip a little. I haven't shared a bed with anyone before, except during sleepovers with Laney, and my mother, when I was, like, five or something and got nightmares all the time. I definitely haven't shared one with a boy.

Did June ever—with Tyler? Common sense would say yes, since they dated for a pretty long time and all, and hormones make teenagers crazy. But still, I can't see it. Would June really have sex? Would she have even told me if she did? She wasn't like Laney, the kind to share details. And I wasn't the kind to press.

I ball up on the other side of the bed, stare at the wall and breathe, slow and even, in an attempt to coax myself into sleep. The leftover tequila churns in my stomach, making my head pound, the room tilted in my vision. I close my eyes and try to push thoughts of June from my mind.

"I didn't know you were such a fan of tequila," Jake says.

So much for sleep.

"I'm not. It's disgusting." I roll onto my back and glance over at him. He's gazing up at the ceiling with his arms tucked behind his head. "I didn't know you could play guitar."

He exhales a self-deprecating laugh. "Not very well."

"Mmm. I didn't hate it."

At this, he turns his head toward me, one corner of his mouth tugged up into a smile. "How would you know? You're totally wasted."

"I'm not wasted." I pause and suppress a smile into the comforter. "Okay, maybe a little." A sudden wave of nausea hits me. I hold my stomach with both hands, take deep breaths and try to ignore it. "Um. And queasy."

"If you throw up on me, I will kill you."

"I can't believe you saw me puke," I groan, pulling the blankets over my head.

It's too embarrassing to think of anyone seeing me like that. I've never gotten so drunk it made me sick. It was nice, I guess, of Jake to hold my hair back, instead of just leaving me there.

"It was a lovely moment," he says drily. "Now there's a band name for you—the Lovely Pukes."

I poke my head back out to shoot him a withering look. "How about the Shut the Fuck Ups?"

"The Toilet Huggers."

"The Imminent Castrations."

"Yes, with our debut album—*Lorena Bobbitt, How Could You.*"

"You know, the husband, John Bobbitt, he formed a band after that whole thing. The Severed Parts," I tell him. "I'm pretty sure he did a lot of porn, too."

Jake just lies there, staring at me. The teasing in his eyes has been replaced with a serious, assessing look.

"What?" I say. God, boys are so weird.

"How do you know that?" he asks. He actually sounds impressed.

"It's called the internet. You might try living in the twenty-first century sometime," I mumble. I yawn and roll back over to face the wall again, and if Jake has a snappy comeback for that one, I don't hear it because I'm already asleep.

six

I wake up to a blast of raucous, thrashing punk attacking my eardrums. My initial reaction is to bolt upright with my eyes wide open, which is also my first mistake, since the sunlight streaming in through the windows only worsens the dull pain behind my eyes. I fall back and shove a pillow over my face to block it out.

Somehow I'm upside down on the bed, on top of all the blankets. When did that happen?

"Rise and shine!" greets Laney in a singsong voice.

I peek out at her only to be welcomed by a blinding flash of white, which causes me to gasp and tumble off the bed, blankets and all, landing on the wooden floor with an ungraceful *oof.* Laney starts laughing so hard she doubles over, my Polaroid camera in one hand. I pitch the pillow at her face.

"I hate you," I say, flailing as I fight to untangle myself from the blanket. "Where did you get that?"

"Found it in your bag. I'm sorry…but…you should have seen…your face…" Between giggle fits, she helps me stand. "Come on. They want to hit the road in an hour. How's your hangover?"

Like death warmed over, actually, but I ignore the question.

"The music. Who. Is playing. The music?" I grate out, blinking as my eyes slowly adjust to the light.

"The wake-up call is courtesy of Gwen," Laney says with false cheer. "Who, by the way, will *not* be accompanying us to Chicago."

This catches my attention. "What? Why not?"

"Because the negative energy of the protest movement is not conducive to her artwork? Because she's an idiot? Who cares!" Laney makes a face. "I don't know what that girl's malfunction is. She and Jake already had it out this morning."

"Really? What were they arguing about?"

"No idea, but it sounded vicious. After they were done, Jake walked into the room and told Seth that Gwen wasn't coming, and then just walked right out. He was totally pissed. I thought for sure he'd freak and punch a wall or something. Weird, right?"

Definitely weird. I climb up on the bed and rub my eyes, then look at her again. There's a glaring hickey right on her neck. A souvenir from her night with Seth, I assume.

"So you and Seth. Did you guys…" I trail off because I'm not good at being casual about these things the way Laney is.

"What? No!" She looks mildly offended. "Seth doesn't even *have* sex. He's saving himself."

"Saving himself? For what?"

"That's what I said! He was all, 'Oh, my body is a temple, blah blah blah,' whatever."

Laney goes to the mirror and applies her makeup, all the while gabbing away about Seth and his bizarre morals (drinking alcohol and smoking pot, apparently, are totally cool in his book, but having sex and eating any animal-derivative food products are totally not), and his kissing technique (very thorough, with lots of tongue usage—but not in a bad way).

I haul my bag onto the bed and paw through the balled-up clothes. So Seth thinks his body is a temple? Maybe Jake adheres to that same belief system. Maybe that's why he doesn't drink. I mean, it isn't a big deal—it's not like I booze it up on a regular basis, contrary to the impression I made by my previous night's behavior—but I'd pegged him as being... different.

I find Jake downstairs, sitting outside on the patio, gazing down the dune and out at the beach. The morning is still cool, a breeze whipping in off the lake. I zip my hoodie up to my chin and sit down next to him.

"You want?" He gestures to the loaf of bread and peanut butter jar positioned between us.

I take a slice of the spelt bread out of the plastic and dip it into the peanut butter. The combination is surprisingly tasty.

"Not bad," I say through my chewing, licking an errant smear of peanut butter from my thumb.

I look out at the lake. It's windier today than it was yesterday, the waves higher and cresting white more often as they roll in. Next to me, Jake stares at his feet and picks at his laces, rubs a thumb across the toe of his shoe.

"I've been thinking," he says, "about California."

I pop another piece of bread in my mouth and wait for him to elaborate.

"My brother has a friend in San Francisco," he continues. "We could stay with her, probably. She's pretty cool. She wouldn't mind."

"Oh," I say. "Okay."

At least that means we're one step closer, right? Now we have an actual destination. Somewhere to pinpoint on a map. Where is San Francisco, anyway? Not in the middle, obviously, because it's on the bay. And they have the trolleys, too, if my memories of the *Full House* opening credits are anything to go by.

"Hi, Daddy. It's me, your favorite daughter." Laney's chipper voice drifts through the door as she steps outside to join us. Her cell phone is pressed to her ear. "I'm just letting you know that me and some friends are going on this little spur-of-the-moment road trip thing—just for a few days. The house is locked and everything, and Martha knows where the spare key is, so she can get in and clean on Tuesday. My phone might be off for a while, but don't freak, I'll call you in a day or two. Have fun with your golf and wine tasting or whatever. Love you. Ciao." She snaps the phone shut and looks at us. "Oh my God. Tell me there is something to drink in this house besides water, wheatgrass juice and soy milk."

"I drank the last of the pop this morning. Sorry. Such are the perils of living in a vegan household," Jake says with a grin. "But we'll have to stop at a gas station before we get out of town anyway."

"I cannot imagine being vegan. I mean, being vegetarian is hard enough. Did you know that gelatin is made out of, like, boiled animal bones? And that they put that shit in Jell-O?" She shudders. "I had to give up Jell-O shots. Greatest tragedy of my *life*."

"And yet somehow you persevere," I say sardonically.

The door slides open again, and this time Seth's head pokes out. "Has anyone seen my gas mask?"

Why the hell does he need a gas mask?

Jake brushes off his jeans and stands. "I think that's my cue to go inside. Be ready to go in a half hour or so, all right?"

"Aye, aye, Captain," Laney says with a mock salute. She takes his seat and fishes a piece of bread from the bag. "Did you need my phone? To call your mom, I mean."

Oh, God, my mother. My stomach jumps. I am so not prepared to face her yet, even over a phone call. Maybe I will be ready when we've put a couple hundred more miles between us. Or a thousand.

I shake my head. "Not yet."

"I can talk to her first. If you want."

"No."

"Harper..." She hesitates, tucking behind her ears strands of her long hair blown loose from the wind. "You know I'm a strong advocate for bucking the system and embracing juvenile delinquency and all that jazz, but soon your mom's going to be boarding the train to Spazzville. Don't you think you should, I don't know, give her a heads-up? She's already dealing with a lot right now—"

"And what about me?" I say angrily. "Does anyone care what I'm dealing with?"

Laney's mouth falls open. "*I* care. Of course I care. Harper, you have to know that."

She looks so desperate for me to see it. I know she's trying— maybe it isn't exactly the support I need, but I don't know *what* I need, or even what I want, from her or from anybody. There's no way to tell her the truth, because the truth is that my heart is broken, and I don't think there's any chance of it being sewn back together. This is permanent. It can't be fixed.

I can't begin to explain it all to her. I can't even explain it to myself.

"I know," I say, more softly. "And I'm going to call. I promise. Just...not this very second. Knowing Aunt Helen, she'd probably pick up and send a bounty hunter after me so I can be dragged back for an exorcism."

Laney looks mollified by my answer. Good. She bites off another chunk of bread. "Your aunt's a fucking nutcase. No offense."

"None taken. Trust me."

★ ★ ★

For the ride down to Chicago, Danny and Anna take Danny's little teal Honda, and Laney, Seth, Jake and I pile into Joplin. Before we leave, Anna gives me a CD.

"Ani DiFranco," she says at my quizzical look. "She'll change your life. I know Jake's a tyrant when it comes to what music he plays in his van, but if he gives you any grief, just ask him how many ABBA albums he owns. That never fails to shut him up."

"Thanks," I say, looking at the picture on the front. It's of a woman with long dreads and an acoustic guitar.

"No problem." Anna shrugs, smile softening. "Hey, by the way. I never told you how sorry I am."

I look up. "What?"

"About your sister," she explains. "I heard what happened."

"Oh," I say, and then, because it seems only appropriate, "Thank you."

"She was a really nice girl."

I open my mouth to regurgitate some polite line, but then I realize what she's said. It's almost enough to knock the wind out of me.

"You—you met her?" I ask. It comes out sort of strangled.

"Well, yeah," she says slowly. "I think that's why Gwen was being rude to you guys last night. She liked June a lot, and I think maybe she thinks it's weird, that Jake is bringing you around, after—"

Anna stops and bites her lip. She's thought better of whatever she was about to say.

"After what?" I prod. I swallow. "Anna—"

"Ask Jake," she says, walking backward. "I mean, I don't really know anything."

Before I can corner her for more, she disappears into Danny's car, leaving me standing there with about a million unanswered questions. On top of the five million unanswered questions I already had.

True to Anna's word, the second Jake starts to object when I replace his Frank Zappa with Ani, all I have to do is ask whether he prefers "Dancing Queen" over "Fernando," and the protest dies on his lips. I suspect that secretly he doesn't oppose the music change, though, considering the way he drums his fingers on the steering wheel along to the song, which is folksy and sharp, just a girl and a guitar. It's hard to get into. The kind of music you have to listen to for a while before you really get it.

We've been on the highway for about half an hour when Laney says, "We should play a game."

Seth, having discovered a deck of playing cards somewhere in the backseat, has spent the last fifteen minutes shuffling them idly. At Laney's suggestion, he stops sorting the cards in his hands and looks up, curiosity piqued. "What did you have in mind?"

"How about Top Three?"

Top Three is a game Laney and I invented when we were thirteen—we'd come up with various topics, ranging from the deeply personal to the philosophical to the downright dirty to everything in between, and the other person has to list their Top Three in that category. Past notable categories include Top Three Worst Childhood Traumas, Top Three Things You Would Say to President George W. Bush If You Faced No Legal Repercussions, and Top Three Places You Would Like to Have a One-Night Stand With Ryan Gosling. Over time, we liked to try to top each other with the craziest, most creative answers we could come up with. Laney claims that Top Three is the best way to reveal a person's soul, inside and out.

After Laney explains the rules (which doesn't take long, since really, the point of the game is that there are no rules;

coming up with the most no-holds-barred categories is half the fun), Seth immediately agrees to play. Even Jake, when prodded, grunts in a way that seems to express consent to being subjected to a round of questioning.

We take turns, and the game kills two hours of driving.

Top Three Alternatives to a Bong (for Seth)

1. A gas mask. ("Dude, it's *hardcore*. Not for the faint of heart. That's all I can say.")
2. Cut-up aluminum can. ("Just make sure it's not from Coca-Cola. Do you know about how they treat factory workers in Colombia? The human rights violations are so screwed up.")
3. Pot brownies. ("Two birds, one stone. The other bird being munchies. Duh.")

Top Three Celebrities You Would Lunch With Given the Opportunity (for Laney)

1. Cary Grant. ("What? You didn't say they have to be *alive*.")
2. Kathy Griffin. ("Imagine the catty gossip you could exchange. We'd rag on Barbara Walters and Ryan Seacrest over Caesar salads.")
3. Brangelina. ("They count as one unit. I want them to adopt me. Or I could be their nanny. They have, like, what, eighteen kids? I'm sure they could always use another nanny.")

Top Three Favorite Albums of All Time (for Jake)

1. *Quadrophenia*, The Who. ("Their peak album. Nothing after ever lived up to it.")

2. *Doolittle*, the Pixies. ("Nirvana, Radiohead—they wouldn't exist without the Pixies. The Pixies are the shit.")
3. *A Love Supreme*, John Coltrane. ("The first jazz album I listened to all the way through. I never got jazz until I heard this. Coltrane is—he's like a *god* when it comes to this stuff.")

Tie for third: *ABBA*, ABBA. ("Fuck you. I know Anna said something. I refuse to be ashamed. They rock, period, end of story.")

*Top Three Things You Want To Be
When You Grow Up (for me)*

1. The person who names nail polish colors. Wouldn't that be cool? I've already thought up some possible names, brainstorming most of them during the snooze fest that is biology class: Strawberry Shakespeare, Mauve It or Lose It, Green With Envy, et cetera.
2. An inner-city school teacher, inspiring those with the odds stacked against them to make something of their lives and break the vicious cycle of poverty—that is, until I remember that even as a kid I hated kids. Plus, school is a nightmare, so why would I want a career that requires me to spend every day there? So that one can get scratched off the list.
3. Happy.

Funny that of all my answers, the last one seems the most unlikely.

"What about that?" Jake asks. When I look at him, confused, he nods to the camera resting in my lap.

"What? You think I should be a photographer?"

"Do you?"

"No. I don't know." I'd be lying if I said I hadn't thought about it. But I don't harbor any delusions of grandeur—I'm no Annie Leibovitz. Just because you enjoy something doesn't mean it'll work out as a career. "It's not a really practical dream to have, is it?"

He stares right at me. It's intense, being under the weight of his full attention. "Dreams have to be practical?" he says.

I turn the camera over in my hands, then pick it up and impulsively snap a picture of Jake. The flash makes him blink, and he swerves a little on the road. Someone in a red BMW leans on their horn as they pass.

He scowls. "Trying to drive here."

"Then keep your eyes on the road."

The picture ejects from the base of the camera. I slide it out, turn it around to look as the photo develops. The cloudy spots dissipate to reveal Jake's face—passive, inquiring. I set it on top of the dashboard.

"Is that what you guys are going to wear?" Seth asks.

I glance down at my outfit: an old green T-shirt and dark jeans. "What's wrong with what I'm wearing?"

"Most of us are going to be wearing black. It's called a black bloc—it helps you blend in so the cops don't identify individuals."

Seth is wearing a plain black wife beater and matching baggy pants. Jake has on a black T-shirt that says Rain Dogs across the front in green, and, as usual, his black jeans. No one notified me of the implied dress code.

"I'll just change, then," Laney says, and immediately strips off her yellow top. She sits there for a moment in nothing but her red bra, then tosses the shirt aside and reaches to grab one of her suitcases. Her tan, impossibly smooth legs, exposed underneath her denim shorts, bend as she leans over the seat. She comes back with a black skinny-strapped tank top in her hands, shimmies it over her head.

"I'm not changing." I blush at the idea of sitting here topless as cars all around us pass by. Laney can be so shameless sometimes.

"Don't be a prude," she teases. "Hey, should I be wearing black underwear, too? Because I have—"

"No," Jake and I cut in hastily at the same time.

"I've got some extra bandannas," Seth offers. "You'll want those. Oh, and you'll want to write this number on your arm, too." He digs into his backpack and hands me a crumpled piece of paper.

"The National Lawyers Guild?" I frown. "Uh, should I plan on getting arrested?"

"Precautionary measure," he says. "Just in case."

Just in case. That's real comforting. Still, I figure it's better to heed the advice of someone who has actually seen the inside of a jail cell, so I etch the numbers on the inside of my right wrist in black marker. Hopefully I won't need to use it.

"You're left-handed," Jake notes, surprised.

I cap the marker and blow on the ink so it'll dry faster. "Yeah, so?"

"So was June." He freezes, glancing at me sideways, then back at the road. "Right?"

My heart hammers against my ribs at the mere mention of her name. How does he remember that detail about my sister? I want to ask, the questions press against my throat, but I swallow them down. I'm not sure whether or not I'm ready for whatever answers he'll give me, even if I can pry them from him.

I ignore him, pop out the Bob Dylan CD he'd put in and shove Anna's disc back in, thumbing up the volume on the stereo and focusing instead on Ani and her righteous anger. Now *there* is music I can relate to.

I've never been really...political. I mean, I have my opinions, and I know enough to laugh at most of the jokes on *The Daily Show*, and I do generally stay up-to-date with current events. I can point to China on a map. I can give you a very broad idea of what is going on in the Israeli-Palestinian conflict, though I can't go too much into detail, because it's all really confusing when you get to the Six-Day War and the intifadas. I've even been known to eschew *People* magazine in favor of Newsweek from time to time. I'm not, like, willfully ignorant, the way a lot of the kids I go to school with are.

But Jake's friends are different. They talk about every topic under the sun, and they have opinions on everything. And I do mean everything. Racism, sexism, classism, disestablishmentarianism and a whole bunch of other *isms* I don't recognize. It's hard to keep up—with the conversation and with how fast they're walking. Plus, I keep getting distracted by my surroundings.

Even though it's relatively close to Grand Lake, I've never been to Chicago. This area of Wicker Park is full of old brownstones and corner cafés. We parked the van near one of the apartment buildings where Seth's friend and fellow activist Devon lives, and are now trekking the few blocks to the train so we can all ride over to the march site. I know we must look bizarre, parading down the sidewalk carrying plastic buckets and a rolled-up cloth banner. But the hipsters and Puerto Ricans we pass don't give us a second look.

As we walk, Seth and Jake and Danny and Anna all talk over each other, but when Devon speaks, everyone listens. He's just that kind of person. Magnetic. He's tall with nicely built shoulders, and he holds himself and speaks in a way that is so full of confidence and poise that you can't help but stare. And when he's listening to someone, he looks them straight in the eye, reacts constantly through his expressions, a frown, a small smile, a nod. You get the feeling he's really absorbing what you're saying, weighing it, taking it seriously. If listening is an art form then Devon is like Matisse or something.

"So this is your first protest?" he asks me as I slide my train ticket through the reader and push past the hip bars to the station platform.

I nod and shift my backpack over my shoulders. I'm sort of embarrassed about the fact, because I'm surrounded by people who know what they're talking about, who have done this before. Well, Laney hasn't, but Laney's not like me. She could fit in anywhere. Except maybe a convent.

At least Devon doesn't sound belittling. Just curious.

"My town is sort of—in a bubble," I explain. It's true. None of this, the politics, the issues, ever seems to reach Grand Lake. People there don't think about these things, or if they do, no one really talks about it. It's like the town is stuck in the fifties' golden era you see in the movies.

Which is totally fucked up, when you think about it.

Devon grins. "It happens. A lot of activists I know didn't get involved until they hit college."

College. I'm going to be a senior next year, and I still haven't decided what I want to do once high school ends. This time last year, June had every school she was applying to lined up, had already toured campuses within driving distance. Laney's GPA puts mine to shame. No way will I be admitted to any of her top choices, even if I bother to apply. It's weird to think about what'll happen—chances are she'll spend four years on the East Coast, while I'm stranded at some state school, if I'm lucky. That means four years apart from my best friend. My only *real* friend these days.

I'm still thinking about this as we board the train. The car sways a little as it kicks into gear, the motion causing me to lean into Jake's side and Devon into mine. Somehow I don't think Laney worries much about the future. Maybe it'll be sad for her not to have me around, but she doesn't need me like I need her. And then she'll have college, and new friends, new boyfriends, new classes, people and things that'll consume her time. I can see it already. I'll end up a footnote in the life she left behind.

I notice the stack of flyers in Devon's lap. They're for the local chapter of Students for Direct Action Now. I take one and read it. It says Drop Knowledge, Not Bombs across the top.

"Clever," I say to Devon.

He looks from the flyer to me. "You are antiwar, right?"

"Well, I'm against people dying in general, so, yes."

"Good answer," Jake says from my other side. I can't tell if he's being sarcastic or not.

"Do you really think, though, that this helps? Running around in the streets waving banners?" I ask. "No offense, I'm just trying to see the point of all this. Does it really change anything?"

Devon frowns. "They have to listen to us. If there are enough people standing up, we can't be ignored. They—"

"No one's going to listen to us," Jake interrupts. "What we do isn't going to stop anything."

I turn to him. His expression is just like his voice: steady, calm. Devon, though, looks thrown.

"Are you saying it doesn't matter?" he says, the question clipped with anger.

"I'm saying this isn't the sixties. The government's not going to see us and be like, 'Oh, oops, our bad.'"

"But what's the alternative? Silence?"

Jake doesn't have an answer for that. Devon smiles smugly, and I'm struck with the urge to smack that smirk off his face.

"You're playing into the government's hand, man," he continues. "They count on people not caring. They brainwash us with the media…" He yammers on, but I tune him out, because I'm now bored with this conversation. It's not that I don't understand being angry, wanting to rail against something bigger than yourself. That part I get, probably too well. I'm just not convinced it isn't a waste of time.

Eventually we emerge from the station to the streets again and walk the distance to the park. I hear the protestors before I see them, a chorus of drums and chants and sirens. When we reach the park entrance, it's easy to spot who is here for the rally—there are about a hundred protestors, gathered on the sidewalk of the cordoned-off street, most of them holding up big signs with slogans like No Blood for Oil and Bring the Troops Home.

"Low turnout," Devon grumbles when he sees the thinned-out crowd.

"Fucking apathy, man," Seth agrees sadly. "It's like a disease."

Devon checks his phone and motions for us to follow him. We wind our way to a group of similarly dressed protestors, decked out in black clothes and bandannas. These must be Devon's friends from Students for Direct Action Now. He fist-bumps a few, taking a megaphone from one of the guys.

"We're going to start walking now," he says. The megaphone seems unnecessary, but it makes him look important, which is probably what he's aiming for.

Laney grabs Seth's arm. "What about us? The scarves?"

"Oh, right!" Seth delves into his backpack and withdraws a black bandanna for each of us. Laney ties hers over her mouth.

I start to do the same when I notice the fabric is damp and smells weird.

"It's wet," Laney tells Seth, eyes crinkling.

"It's soaked in vinegar," he explains. "It'll help protect you from the pepper spray."

"*Pepper spray?*" Laney and I cry out in alarm at the same time, but our identical high-pitched shrieks are drowned out by Devon rousing up the crowd with a chant.

"Whose streets?"

"Our streets!"

"Whose streets?"

"Our streets!"

For the first few blocks, things seem to be going okay. At least, I think so. It's not like I have a political activism track record to compare it to. People chant and bang sticks on plastic buckets and wave their signs around indignantly as we march. I work up a sweat keeping pace with Devon and Seth and the rest of the anarchist group, hoping I don't stick out too much in my decidedly nonblack attire. We push forward until we're at the very front of the march, Devon circling around, talking animatedly with different people and waving his hands like he's giving directives, strategizing. What the strategy is, I have no idea.

The first sign of trouble comes when we pass a cluster of people outside the barriers on the sidewalk. At first I think they're part of the march, but then I see the signs they're holding—Leviticus 20:13 and God Hates Fags.

What I really want to know is how being against the war translates into gayness. But when I look into the frenzied eyes of this one man waving around a Bible and shouting incoherently, I realize it's futile to expect rationality from crazy hate mongers.

"Ignore them," Jake tells Devon and Seth when they move toward the Bible-thumpers.

"Look, man, I know you haven't done this in a while, so maybe you've forgotten. This is what we do," Devon says. He shoots a look at Seth. "You coming?"

Seth's eyes linger hesitantly on Jake for a moment before he nods. "Right behind you, Dev."

As they start to walk away, Jake snatches Seth's shirt collar and drags him to a stop. "Come on, man," he appeals. "Leave it alone. Don't be stupid." There's a frustrated desperation in his voice I haven't heard before. It's the same kind of tone I take when I'm trying to convince Laney not to do something monumentally stupid like sling back four shots in a row of ninety-proof vodka, but knowing all the while she's going to do it regardless.

"Really? You're defending bigots now?" Seth scoffs. "I don't know why you feel sorry for them. They're asking for it."

"Exactly. You're just giving them the attention they want."

"If you didn't want to be part of this, you shouldn't have come."

Seth shrugs him off and follows after Devon, disappearing among the other black-clad protestors.

"What're they going to do?" Laney asks Jake.

His mouth is set in a grim line. "Nothing good."

The demonstration comes to a standstill as more and more marchers, led by Devon, turn to heckle the counterprotestors. Jake, Laney and I weave through the thirty or so people until we're close enough to see the action firsthand. I'm pretty sure Danny and Anna are standing next to us, but it's hard to be sure when they have their faces masked. Everyone is lobbing insults and slurs at the Bible-thumpers. Of course, they hurl them right back.

The man clutching the Bible snarls. It has the effect of making him look like a rabid pit bull. "Take your communist propaganda and go home, you filthy faggots."

"Faggots, huh?" Anna's face is covered in black except for her eyes, but I recognize her voice, shrill and furious. "I'll show you a *faggot*."

She yanks the scarf off her chin and grabs Laney, one arm wound around her neck, and the next thing I know they're kissing. To Laney's credit, she doesn't miss a beat—she enthusiastically opens her mouth to Anna's, mashing their faces together. Everyone goes wild. Everyone except the Biblethumpers, of course. The snarling man's face turns this scary shade of beet red. For a second I almost think he'll have an aneurysm and his head will explode.

You know that story about the Revolutionary War, how no one knows for sure who officially started it, whether it was the American colonists or the British army who shot first that morning in Lexington? Well, this is kind of like that. Because I'm not sure if the first punch is thrown by the Biblethumpers in response to the girl-on-girl macking action, or if it's thrown by the anarchists in response to the snarling man's hocking spit that arcs through the air and lands somewhere in Anna's hair. It happens too fast to tell. There's just a flurry of motion, indignant cries and shouts, the sound of signs being ripped apart, fists flying.

"Come on." Jake latches onto my arm and drags me out of the circle.

I dig in my heels. "But Laney—" I say. I'm not going anywhere without her.

"The cops are going to break it up in a second," he answers. "If she gets arrested—"

Oh, God. I crane my neck to see three nearby policemen descending on the skirmish. The one Laney is caught in the middle of.

I strain forward, but Jake yanks me back by the arm again. "Don't be stupid."

"I'm not just going to leave her!"

"No one's leaving anyone," he says calmly. "I'll go track her down. You, make yourself scarce." He points across the street, to the alley between two buildings. "Wait there and don't move."

"But—"

"Wait. There."

Jake leaves no room for argument. He pulls his black bandanna over his face, heading back toward the growing crowd, and I waver, not sure if I should ignore him and follow anyway. Finally I decide listening to him is the best course, because if the cops grab me, I am so screwed. Beyond screwed. And if Laney gets arrested...

I'm so caught up in worrying about this possibility that I don't even notice the curb until I've tripped over it. My arm and knee scrape roughly against the pavement where I brace my fall. I stay down on the ground for a moment, catching my breath, before I slowly pull myself to my feet and duck between the two buildings. I cradle my skinned arm. It stings really badly, along with the knee I landed on. There's a hole torn through my jean leg. My favorite pair. Fantastic.

I press my back against the brick and close my eyes. God, where are they? I tell myself Laney will be okay. She's always okay. And Jake's handling it. I almost laugh. Yeah, like I trust Jake to do anything. He can't even be up front about June.

Suddenly I realize it has been almost three hours since my sister crossed my mind at all. A new record. It hurts to think about June, but not thinking about her feels like betrayal. After all, this trip is about her. For her. And I deserve to carry all of this. Her ever-present memory. The incessant twinge of guilt in my gut. I deserve every bit of pain I get. I deserve to hurt.

I slam my injured arm back against the brick. On impact the scrape singes with pain. I cry out, feeling like an idiot, but at the same time feeling a little better. It's better than empty numbness. Better than this anger that just sits in my chest, simmering but never boiling over.

The pain brings everything into sharp focus. God, I am so screwed up. I'm no better than those goth girls at school who cut themselves with safety pins and razor blades, the ones with silver scars laced around their wrists like bracelets. Why can't I just feel things like a normal person?

I'm holding the hem of my shirt to my bleeding elbow and panting against the pain when Jake appears with a breathless Laney in tow. Laney grabs me in a tight squeeze, but I'm still reeling too much to reciprocate.

"You're okay?" I ask when I can speak again.

"I'm fine," she tells me. "They're arresting Anna and Devon, though. I have no idea where Seth is." Her eyes widen when she sees my arm. "Oh, shit! What happened?"

"I tripped." I shrug. "It's nothing."

She looks me in the eye for a second longer before she nods. She then turns to Jake. "What do we do now?" she asks him, fingers wrapped around my good wrist, like she's afraid if she lets go I'll just float away into the clouds or something.

He glances over his shoulder and then back to us. "We run."

seven

The moment we find an opening, we don't stop running for two full blocks, where we reach the entrance to some small corner grocery market. And we stop then only because I'm afraid I'm going to pass out. We're all breathing hard.

"We have to go back," Laney says breathlessly. "Seth—"

"Seth can handle Seth," Jake tells her. He gives her a nudge, pushing her over the store's threshold—not hard, but firm. "He's gotten out of a lot scrapes on his own before."

Laney sticks out her lower lip, obviously unconvinced.

"He's probably already gone," he continues. "And do we really need to draw attention from the cops right now? I'm not going to jail for you two."

Would that actually happen? An image of Jake handcuffed in the back of a police cruiser passes through my mind. I haven't spent much time contemplating the consequences for this. Not outside the "grounded for life" thing, anyway.

Laney huffs and marches down the snack food aisle. I follow, watching as she picks up a pack of gum and examines it single-mindedly. She refuses to acknowledge my presence.

"I'm sure he got out fine," I try. "He's done this stuff a million times before. He said so himself."

"I guess," she mutters, still not looking at me.

"I know you're worried, but Jake's right. It'd be useless to go back. He's probably with Danny."

"I just—" She bites her lip. "I wanted to say goodbye."

This stops me. I know a little something about not having the chance to say your goodbyes. But this isn't the same, for obvious reasons.

"We can call him on his cell later, when things have calmed down," I tell her. When she doesn't say anything, I roll my eyes, exasperated. "Seriously, chill out. It's not like he's *dead*."

That last part slips out unintentionally. I want to take it back, but it's too late, and Laney's never looked at me like she's looking at me now. Like she doesn't even know me.

Finally she sighs like she's shaking something off. "Whatever. I'm going to go get a coffee."

She walks off without me, and if I was a better person, I would follow her. But I'm too annoyed to soothe her bruised feelings, too afraid I'll snap at her again if I try. Instead I wander into the back, staring at the array of colored labels in the coolers. I open one of them and stick my roughed-up elbow in. At least it's stopped bleeding by now. The rush of cold air feels good.

"Hey." It's Jake, right at my ear. I jump about a foot in the air.

"Don't do that," I snap. "Jesus."

"Sorry," he says, without sounding sorry at all. "Are you okay?"

"Why wouldn't I be?"

"Hmm, I don't know, maybe because you left half your arm on the pavement of Michigan Avenue?"

"Lovely imagery," I drawl, thoroughly grossed out. I shrug. "I'm fine. Just…kinda sore."

"Let me look."

Before I can object, he takes my arm in both hands and gingerly traces his fingertips over my wrist and elbow. As he touches it, I hiss between my teeth, the pain sharp and sudden. He keeps his hand there longer than necessary. The contrast of his cool fingers—how can they be so cold when it's so warm outside?—on my too-hot skin makes me shiver involuntarily.

"Sorry," he apologizes, quickly drawing his hand back. Is he blushing? "I think you'll be okay. Might want to pick up some bandages, though."

Good idea. I swipe a box of gauze and some antibacterial cream and meet Jake and Laney at the counter. The cashier eyes us suspiciously as we pool our purchases together. He probably realizes we're part of the protesting crowd—he looks prepared to whip out a baseball bat and chase us out of the store at the first sign of trouble. I try for a disarming smile as Jake pays with a twenty-dollar bill; the clerk's dubious expression stays static, but he says nothing, and we slip out of the store unscathed.

All of us are quiet on the train ride back to Wicker Park. I take the window seat, and Laney sits at the other side of the aisle by herself, popping and snapping her gum sullenly. Jake squeezes in next to me, his feet propped up on the seat in front of us. I'm all too aware of his hip pressed up against mine.

"How's the elbow?" he asks.

I shrug, and he rolls his eyes and pulls out the box of bandages. I let him pick up my arm and cover my scrape. When he gently smoothes out the bandage's edges, I feel kind of lightheaded and breathless, and that just makes me feel ridiculous. When I actually think about Jake himself, I'm reminded of the other feelings he inspires: annoyance, anger, exasperation.

Basically any emotion on the spectrum that causes me to roll my eyes so hard they just about fall out of their sockets.

We get off the train at our stop and drag ourselves the three blocks to the brownstone on Albertson, and when we load into Joplin, the sense of relief shared between the three of us is nearly palpable. It isn't until Jake sticks the key into the ignition and starts up the van that he says what we're all thinking: "Time to get the hell outta Dodge."

Laney falls asleep before we even get out of the city, snoring soundly as she curls up against the armrest. I don't blame her; the weight of the day settles over my bones more and more as Joplin eats up the interstate, the dashed lines on the road bleeding together in a blur.

My mind wanders as I look out the window. I think about the last thing I said to June. Before—before. Well. The last thing.

It'd be easy to say that our final exchange was profound, meaningful, or at the very least amiable. No one would be any wiser. The only witness to it was Laney—but that's only because I was on the phone with her, and even she doesn't know that that was the last time I saw June.

I was sitting on my bed. In theory I was doing a reading for World History, but in all actuality, my textbook lay facedown a few feet away, woefully neglected. I'd ditched the adventures of Charlemagne and opted instead to paint my toenails while discussing weekend plans with Laney. Laney, as usual, was advocating an activity that involved public intoxication, nudity and committing multiple felonies.

"So Sara just called me. She said a whole bunch of people are going to get totally trashed at her house and then drive over to the community pool at, like, two in the morning. Apparently Greg's brother was a lifeguard last year, and he told him how to sneak in, so we can all go skinny-dipping. Isn't that awesome?"

"That's not awesome," I said. "That sounds unbelievably lame."

"Come on!" she whined. "We never *do* anything."

"That is such a lie."

Okay, so usually we ended up going to the one-screen dollar theater across town, or to the bowling alley, or to a crappy party serving equally crappy beer. Grand Lake isn't exactly brimming with entertainment possibilities.

I'd just finished painting my toenails black. With the phone cradled between my ear and shoulder, I unscrewed the bottle of red. The idea was to do red stripes down the middle of each toe to match my hands. Just as I started on my left big toe, my door opened, and the sound made me jump a little, the streak of red smearing into a zig-zag blob.

It was June. I don't remember what she was wearing. I don't even remember if her hair was up or down. All I know is that she asked me if I'd taken any of her notebooks. Like I'd have any reason to steal her school notes.

She was being annoyingly relentless about it, like it was so vital to her very existence, and I, already pissed about the nail polish and at being interrupted, snapped, "No, I don't have your stupid notebook, get the fuck *out*," and she said something back—I don't know what. Maybe she yelled, but probably not.

She was already retreating to her room, but I got up and slammed the door anyway. I said something to Laney like, "God, what a bitch," and Laney laughed, and we continued our long-standing debate on whether or not Mr. Collins, the newly divorced physics teacher in his late twenties, was boning Angela Tapely, our fellow junior who was prone to leaning over his desk in low-cut tops and giggling at his stupid jokes about thermodynamics.

So stupid, that I can remember what color I painted my nails, but I can't remember what my sister looked like, what she last said to me, before she killed herself.

I push the thought away and close my eyes to Jake humming along to some Neil Young number under his breath. I know it's Neil Young because he's taken to automatically briefing me on each artist as their songs come on. It's like a twenty-second condensed episode of *Behind the Music* every time he opens his mouth.

I actually do find it interesting, despite myself. But I'm not going to let *him* know that.

The last thing I remember is him schooling me on Grace Slick—"Once she and Abbie Hoffman, the activist, wanted to spike President Nixon's tea with LSD. They came pretty close, too. Oh, and this song's called 'Never Argue with a German if You're Tired or European.' She wrote it about crashing her car near the Golden Gate Bridge in a drag race. She is *badass!*"—right before I drift off.

I dream about riding in June's car with the windows rolled down. No music, no talking, just the two of us enjoying the summer weather and the open road. I can't see her face—every time I turn my head, it's like looking directly into the glare of a blinding light, but somehow I know instinctively that it's her. I tip my chin up to feel the sun warming my face, the wind in my hair. When I venture a glance at the driver's seat again, it's empty, no one at the wheel.

I'm jolted out of sleep when Jake hits a bump in the road. Elton John is wailing about a rocket man, and my head knocks hard against the window, smacked into stars. Great. Now I'm injured in two places. Life can't get any more awesome, can it?

"Careful," Jake warns me. "I don't think you can afford to lose more brain cells."

I glare, still caught in the last threads of the dream, and

rub a hand across my eyes to push it away. I touch the soon-to-be goose-egg spot on my head and ask, "Where are we?"

"Still in Illinois. Not too far from the Missouri state line, though. I pulled off the interstate a few minutes ago." His face stretches with a long yawn. "Getting kind of tired."

"Did you want Laney to drive?" I look over my shoulder; she's still all balled up, mouth slack with sleep. I earned a learner's permit months and months ago, but I haven't gotten around to taking the driver's test yet. What was the point, when I had Laney for rides, and if not her, June? Well. Not June anymore.

Obviously.

"You think I let just *anyone* sit behind this wheel?" Jake says incredulously. "I don't think so. No, I'll be doing all the driving. But I am jonesing for a decent mattress right now."

We stop at a nondescript motel on the side of the road. The vacancy sign glows in yellow neon, the second *A* flickering in and out sporadically. Jake pulls into the drive and cuts the engine. He opens the door, hops out and leans back in for a second. "Stay here," he instructs, and I roll my eyes, because really, what else am I going to do?

A couple minutes later he returns with a plastic key card in hand, and we drive around to the back lot, facing the rows of green doors. Jake elbows Laney awake before giving her the key card. She mumbles something unintelligible and scoots out of the van. When I start to open my door, Jake puts a hand on my arm and says, "Wait," and I do, until Laney's safe inside the room.

"You need to call your mom," he says.

Part of me wants to argue, but I know he's right. And I'd rather get this over with while Laney's not hovering.

After a minute I nod. "Okay."

I get out and head to the pay phone next to the ice machine, Jake following after. I stop and spin around.

"I don't need the moral support, if that's what you're thinking," I snap. The last thing I need is for Jake of all people to get annoyingly protective.

"Stop acting like a five-year-old who missed her nap time. I'm going to call my brother when you're done, *if* you don't mind."

"Don't you have a cell phone?"

"It's one of those prepaid ones. It's only got five minutes left. I'm saving it for an emergency."

Oh. "You can have first dibs, if you want," I offer.

He grins. "No, I think I want to watch you go."

He really would, wouldn't he? Ass.

I glare and snatch the phone off the hook, careful to keep my fingers off of the rock-hard gray wad of gum stuck on the handle. Jake is going to take a perverse pleasure in seeing me get reamed out by whichever member of the familial unit picks up the line.

I pop in my quarters and punch the numbers on the keypad sharply, just to show him I'm not intimidated by his being there. Still, the knot in my stomach slides into my throat as the line on the other end begins to ring. Five rings will get me to the answering machine, and then I can just leave a message, which would be easy. So, so much easier than talking directly to someone.

On the fourth ring, I hold my breath, hoping, but just before the machine can click on, my mother answers, breathless.

"Hello?" A long pause follows, punctuated by her breathing. "Hello? Is anyone—"

"Hi," I whisper, twisting the metal phone cord so tight around my hand that my knuckles whiten.

"Harper!" Mom's voice comes out in a gasp, choked with relief. "What's going on? Where are you? Are you—"

"I'm fine," I cut in. "Laney's with me. We're both safe."

"Where are you calling from? I'll call someone, or come pick you up myself—"

"No." My response is firm, and as I speak the word, I release the coiled cord suddenly. It snaps automatically back into place, swinging from side to side. "I can't tell you. I—I need to be...away. Just for a little while. To figure some things out."

"Figure them out here," Mom says, but it's more of a plea than a command.

Her desperation tugs at me. For a second I think maybe I should listen to her. Maybe I should go home. She's my mother, after all. She's going through so much, and I'm adding to that. But then I think of June, and how she always listened, always followed the rules, and about the California postcard folded up in the zipper pouch of my duffel bag, and I know it's too late. I can't back out now.

"I *can't*, okay? I can't." With a sigh, I turn, bow my head and lower my voice. "Tell Laney's parents that she's fine."

"Your sister..." Mom's voice wavers and breaks, and she pauses for a painfully long time. "The *urn*..."

She starts to cry, low and keening, the same kind of wailing she did at June's memorial. The lump in my throat grows a few sizes bigger, but before I can figure out what to say, the sound of it is suddenly muffled, farther away, background noise.

"Harper. Tell me where you are, right this second." Aunt Helen has commandeered the phone. This is worse than the crying. "I mean it!" she yells when I remain silent.

"Would you stop?" I snap. "I'm only calling so you know we're okay. Just don't, you know...worry."

"Don't *worry*?" Aunt Helen shrieks loud enough to make me flinch. I hold the phone away from my ear. "You disappear without warning, refuse to tell anyone where you've run off to, and that's all you have to say for yourself? To *not worry?*"

"I'm just—"

"Do you not see how *SELFISH* you are being?" She plows on, clearly intent on riding her high horse all the way to the winner's circle. "This is so typical of you, to ignore the needs of this family. To not consider anyone's feelings but your own. If you wanted attention, you should have—"

"This isn't about that!" I shout. My head pounds like it's about to explode. "If you'd just *listen* to me for a second—"

Aunt Helen sighs heavily, a sigh I recognize all too well. Of course. Of course this is what my family would think of me, because it's the same as what they've always thought. This is what I am to them: a failure, a mistake, second best. A constant disappointment. It doesn't matter if June is dead, if June loathed herself and her life enough to off herself in our garage; I'm still the disappointment of the family. Always will be. Nothing's going to change.

Nothing ever changes.

"I don't understand how you can behave this way, Harper, I really don't. You need to hang up that phone right now and come home. You need to—"

I am so tired of people telling me what I *need* that I could puke.

I lean my forehead against the plastic siding of the booth and trace a fingernail across the grimy pane. My throat constricts. "I can't. I'm sorry. I have to go."

Before Aunt Helen can protest further, I slam the phone down on the hook. A few seconds pass as I just stand there and stare at it, imagining her on the other end, entreating to an unresponsive dial tone. The idea of it is disproportionately satisfying. If that thought makes me a horrible person, well. So be it.

I close my eyes and listen to the mosquitoes buzzing around my head, the hum of the nearby rickety ice machine. I know without looking that Jake is right behind me—he hovers close enough for me to smell his aftershave, kind of tangy, and his cigarettes; it's a little weird, mostly because it *isn't* weird. It feels perfectly comfortable to just stand there, breathing in his smells without speaking.

Someone slams a door somewhere above us, jarring him out of our mutual silence.

"How'd it go?" he finally asks.

This time I draw my gaze up to meet his. His hair looks kind of slept-on, sticking out in different directions, his eyes darker in the dim light thrown off by the streetlamp. The same lamp allows me to notice that his black T-shirt clings to him in all the right places.

At first my stomach twists, and I feel vaguely ashamed, or guilty, or something, for noticing that. But then I think—so what. So what if he's hot, sometimes. Like every time I look at him. Besides, annoying he may be, but he's had his shining White Knight Moment, what with the whole saving-me-and-my-best-friend-from-a-brawl-and-probable-jail-time thing. Even if I'm no damsel in distress and he's miles away from Prince Charming, such displays of gallantry, combined with his not-bad-okay-actually-pretty-good looks, make my strange lusty feelings completely justified. Practically obligatory, even.

So really, it isn't as if noticing something like his well-toned biceps or his seriously long eyelashes *means* anything—other than a confirmation of the fact that I'm not blind. Still, I shouldn't be thinking about him, like that. Especially with Anna's cryptic comments lingering in the back of my mind. I take a deep breath and focus instead on my annoyance with Aunt Helen.

"Oh, it went wonderfully," I say sarcastically, glaring at the phone. I tick off Helen's talking points on my fingers as I list them. "Let's see. I'm selfish, I'm a disappointment, I don't care about anyone but myself, and my aunt is convinced I'm systematically destroying my mother's life. You know. The usual."

He smiles with half his mouth. "She sounds like a lovely person."

"Whatever," I mutter, pushing my hair out of my eyes. "It doesn't matter."

And "whatever" truly does sum up my opinion on the whole matter at this point. I am really, really over it. I'm tired, tired of everything, but tired especially of being held solely responsible for everyone else in the world's unhappiness. Trying to keep a handle on my own is hard enough as it is.

So I'm going to do this. I am going to go to California and spread June's ashes in the Pacific like she would have wanted, like she *deserves*, and that is it.

Period. End of story.

eight

When we return to the room, Laney's already passed out on the bed, having not even bothered to pull back the covers. She doesn't stir when we open and close the door or when Jake switches on the television. His conversation with his brother was short and sweet. He didn't let on what they'd talked about as we walked back to the motel room, and I wasn't about to ask. I couldn't glean much from my one-sided perspective—mostly what I heard was, "Hey, not much, okay, yeah, sure, uh-huh, no, not yet, yeah, all right, you too, 'bye."

The room itself is minimally furnished—two single beds, both looking like they've seen better days, a nightstand between them, and the television. There's nothing here that can't be nailed down, except for the Bible in the drawer. I thumb through its thin yellowed pages.

"What was that passage that that one guy with the sign was yelling at the rally?" I ask. "Something starting with an *L*…"

"Leviticus 20:13," he answers without hesitation. "'*If any one lie with a man as with a woman, both have committed an abomination, let them be put to death: their blood be upon them.*'" A small, grim smile tugs at his mouth. "That one's kicked around a lot.

Of course, they never tell you that Leviticus also forbids eating shrimp or cutting your hair. If you run into people who know their stuff, they'll at least refer you to Corinthians 6:9, or something else from the New Testament."

I slam the book shut. For a second I'm worried it'll wake up Laney, but she remains zonked out, sleeping the sleep of the deeply unconscious. "I hate organized religion. I hate that people use it to justify their crappy, bigoted beliefs."

"I know," Jake agrees softly. "But it's not all bad."

"Really?" I say, skeptical.

"Look." Jake sits down beside me, takes the Bible from my hands and flips it open. "Some of the Psalms are nice. And this one—" he skims the pages, hunting for a passage "—is one of my favorites.

'But the souls of the just are in the hand of God, and the torment of death shall not touch them. In the sight of the unwise they seemed to die: and their departure was taken for misery. And their going away from us, for utter destruction: but they are in peace.'

He pauses and looks directly at me as he speaks the last line. *"'And though in the sight of men they suffered torments, their hope is full of immortality.'"*

I'm silent for a minute, absorbing these words. Finally I say, "I thought you didn't believe in God."

His face doesn't change. "I don't."

"Then why do you have the Bible memorized like—like some kind of Mormon?"

"Have you ever even *met* a Mormon, Harper? I was raised Catholic."

"Seriously?" I can't help it, I'm full-on gawking. Jake, Catholic? I wouldn't have guessed, and now I'm totally curious. "Like with confession, and…everything?" I ask.

He nods. "Confession, rosaries, Hail Mary, the pope…the whole shebang, pretty much."

"That's weird. I mean, it isn't weird, but it's weird trying to picture it. Trying to picture you." I'm stumbling over my words, trying not to sound like the world's biggest moron. "In a church."

"Well, let's just say I wasn't exactly the ideal church-going child," Jake says wryly. "Still, could've been worse. I could've pissed off a nun—trust me, you do not want to do that." He drops the Bible and sighs. "You know, I'm an atheist, but I get it. I get why people have faith in a higher power. Some people need it. They need to believe they're not alone."

I have a sudden flashback to a reading from my first-semester religions class. "Opiates for the masses?"

"Maybe," he says after some thought. "But you can't judge everyone by what you believe."

"You don't think that way about music," I point out, remembering his earlier argument with Laney.

"That's different."

"How is it different?" I demand. "You know, just because you think bubblegum pop on the radio represents all that is wrong with society, that doesn't mean there's not someone out there who needs that shitty pop song. Maybe that shitty pop song makes them feel good, about themselves and the world. And as long as that shitty pop song doesn't infringe upon your rights to rock out to, I don't know, Subway Sect, or Siouxsie and the Banshees, or whichever old-ass band it is you worship, then who cares?"

He shifts on the bed and looks over at me. "Okay, you may have a point," he concedes, a little reluctantly. His lips curl like he's trying not to smile. "Does this mean you actually listen when I talk about music?"

"Did June?" I counter, feeling bold. I'm sick of this tiptoeing around the subject. I want to know what he knows. I want to know everything about her I missed out on.

"We had a deal," he explains. "I listened to her yap about math and books and whatever, and she'd listen to my music."

"Do you know if she liked any of it?"

The halfway smile on his face fades. "Only the sad songs," he says.

For a second I can't catch my breath. Jake must take my silence as the end of the conversation, because he picks up the remote and flicks through the channels. He stops on *Skye Desmond: Wild at Heart*. Skye is one of those wildlife gurus with a show on one of the nature channels. The premise involves him being dropped in various geographical backdrops with a camera crew, surviving the rough wilderness via dramatic tactics such as drinking his own urine and disrupting bee colonies in order to forage their honey.

It's actually one of my favorite shows, too—though, granted, it has less to do with the nature stuff and more to do with the fact that Skye has cheekbones you could sharpen knives on, a yummy Australian accent and washboard abs. It certainly doesn't hurt that he almost always finds an excuse to take off his shirt at least once per episode.

As I settle back in to watch Skye trek across the snowy Alaskan tundra, I think about everything Jake said. He's right; some people *do* need that faith in a higher power, like Aunt Helen, who depends on her religion for every answer to every question, no matter how trivial, and Laney, who believes every life has a predestined path. Part of me wants to have that— but wanting is not the same as needing. And then I think of June, and wonder what she would have to say about all of this.

She would've understood. She would've known what to say. I wish I'd talked to her about what she believed before she died. If only we could have had one conversation like that, just one, instead of the countless petty fights and tiffs. Now I'll never know what she thought—about that, or anything.

There is so much I'll never know.

"Tell me what *Nolite te bastardes carborundorum* means," I say.

Jake doesn't look away from the television. Skye Desmond is stripping off his parka and sweater layers—something about conserving body heat. "You already know what it means."

"I'm not talking about the translation. I'm talking about what it means—meant—for you and June."

"It's none of your business."

"Of course it's my business!" I explode. "She was my sister, I have a right to know!"

"Trust me," he insists, "it really isn't a big deal."

But I don't believe him for a second. "Then why do you keep clamming up?" I ask. "Why was it on the CD you made her? Did you know that CD was playing in her car when she—" I can't say it. Why can't I just say it? *When she killed herself.* The words refuse to come out.

"Wait, what?" Jake's eyes widen. He looks away from me, and then back, rubbing a hand over his mouth. "Look. It's just something I read in a book for my lit class, and she thought I could relate to it. She told me to say it every time I wanted to blow off studying. It was just a joke, okay? A stupid inside joke."

"What about—"

"No. The Jake Tolan Inquisition portion of this evening's entertainment has come to a close. Go to sleep."

He hits the mute button, throws the remote onto the nightstand and yanks the lamp chain off. I fall back against the pillows next to comatose Laney and glance at the screen. Skye

Desmond is flashing a dazzling-white smile at the camera, waving a knife around in his hand as he talks, answering every question I could ever have about how to slice up and prepare a raw salmon.

The first thing Jake does the next morning is buy a map from the closest gas station. The second thing he does is drive to a diner for breakfast, since we're all starving, and Laney's always catatonic until her first cup of coffee. We stop at the first place we come across, a greasy spoon that pulls out all the stops as far as clichés go: a lunch counter at the front, red vinyl booths, Formica tables, black-and-white checkered floors, waitresses wearing pale pink uniforms.

We order—coffee, Belgian waffles and French toast with strawberries for Laney, hash browns, pinto beans and bacon for Jake, and a blueberry short stack with a side of poached eggs for me. While we wait, Jake spreads the map out on the table, holding down the corners with salt and pepper shakers.

"We're not going through Indiana again, are we?" Laney asks. She dumps a sugar packet into her second cup of coffee, her eyes hidden behind those huge pink sunglasses. "Indiana is boring and full of Amish people."

"You won't have to worry about the Amish," Jake says. "At least, not the ones in Indiana. We're going through Missouri first."

She raises the cup to her mouth and frowns. "What's in Missouri?"

"St. Louis," I tell her. "They have the arch thing. And Jefferson City is the capital."

"I'm glad one of us paid attention in sixth grade," she grumbles, turning her gaze to Jake. "So what comes after Missouri?"

He squints at the map. "Well, it depends. If we go north, Nebraska."

"Ew. Pass. What's south?"

"Oklahoma."

"Those are our only options? Lame!"

"I think we should go south," I say. "Call it a gut instinct."

Our thirtysomething waitress—Dottie, if her name tag is anything to go by—comes to the table, balancing two trays. She fills out her pink uniform in every way, looking round and soft and puffy. Dark roots show through peroxide-blond hair—the kind of dye job a single mother does with a home kit, bent over the bathtub, scrubbing it in while her kids take a nap.

Dottie sets down my blueberry pancakes and eggs and Laney's waffles and French toast. "I'll be right back with yours, sugar," she tells Jake.

Jake pulls his spoon out of his coffee mug, licks it and says, "Thanks." And then he winks, tipping back on his chair and watching her legs as she saunters to the kitchen.

I reach out with my feet and slam his chair back down. "You're a pig."

"What, I'm not allowed to say thanks?"

"Not like that, you aren't." I spear a piece of pancake and stuff it in my mouth. "So we've got Missouri, Oklahoma, then... Texas, is it?"

"Yup," he says. "But only a little part of it. See?" He draws a line across the map with his finger. "After that, New Mexico, then Arizona. I'd say we should make a side trip to Nevada and hit up Las Vegas, but what's the point in going to Vegas if you can't gamble? So that's out. We can cut straight through Arizona to California, drive up the coast to San Fran."

Dottie returns with Jake's food, flashing him a smile that dimples her round apple cheeks and crinkles the corners of her tired eyes. "Here you go. You need anything else, you just holler."

Jake looks up at her as he bites into a piece of bacon. "Do you happen to know how far St. Louis is from here?"

"I got some cousins down in Kirkwood, right around those parts," she says. She taps her finger on her chin, considering. "I'd say it's about a two-hour drive, 'pending on traffic."

"And the famous arch thingamabob—can you, like, go on top of it?" asks Laney hopefully.

I can't believe she wants to play tourist. We already wasted hours of travel time going to the protest. Then again...maybe dragging this out isn't such a bad idea. Last night's phone call just reminded me of how much I do not want to go home yet.

"The arch? Sure can! One year I took my baby girl Pearl on the tram. Course, she just 'bout screamed her head off all the way to the top." Dottie laughs and tilts her head at us curiously. "Where you kids from, anyway?"

Laney tells her we're from Michigan, and that we're on our way to California. I kick her shin under the table as subtly as I can—why does she feel the need to give our exact destination?—but she just sticks her tongue out at me like a two-year-old. Jake doesn't seem to mind that she's said anything, though, so maybe I'm just paranoid.

"California?" Dottie's eyebrows shoot skyward. "I've never been. I bet you'll see movie stars!"

Laney's face lights up. "You think?"

"I imagine the place is crawling with 'em. Now, you do me a favor. You run into George Clooney, you let him know Dottie sends her love all the way from the best damn breakfast diner in the state of Illinois. Tell him he needs to swing by and try one of our peach crumb pies—they're legendary. World's best. And you can quote me on that!"

"Hey, Dottie, could I take your picture?" I grab my camera out of my backpack and hold it up. "I'm trying to document our trip."

She smiles nervously, hands twisting her ponytail. "Me? I don't know, I'm such a mess—"

"Come on," Jake needles. "You can write your message to George Clooney on the back. If we see him, we can pass it on. Once he gets a look at you, he'll be booking the first flight to Illinois."

"Aren't you sweet?" she says with a laugh. "Deluded, but sweet. All right, take your picture if you must."

I peer one eye through the viewfinder. When the picture has been taken and materialized, it shows Dottie, her cheeks flushed, one hand cocked on her hip and the other balancing a tray. She writes, *Dear George, You should get your cute butt down to New Sun Diner in the fine state of Illinois, ASAP. Call me!!! Love always, Dottie,* on the back. She dots all of her *i*'s with little hearts.

As we finish our breakfasts—admittedly, the food *is* really delicious—we decide that the best course of action is to drive to St. Louis and spend the day there. Riding in the car for so long makes Laney restless, plus she's really into the idea of visiting the arch, and Jake mentions wanting to stop by some jazz clubs or something. I'm not interested in any of it, but they can drag me along, if they want. Otherwise I'll end up just sitting around and thinking about how sad I am. Might as well do that and the touristy stuff at the same time. Yeah, I'm multitalented that way.

Dottie clears our plates when we've scraped them clean and brings out three slices of peach crumb pie in Styrofoam containers. "On the house. You can save a piece for George," she says airily, and dismisses our modest objections with a wave of her hand. Jake lays some crumpled bills on the table, including what looks to be at least a sixty-percent tip, give or take.

Jake Tolan: Secret Overboard Tipper, at least when it comes

to overworked, yet resilient, bubbly waitresses with bad dye jobs. Who would've thought?

The afternoon is blazing by the time we hit St. Louis, and once we find it, Laney drags me along for the ride to the top of the arch thingamabob—or, as the plaque underneath it proclaims, the Gateway Arch. There are white pod-type cars for the trip up, and in a few minutes we're at the top viewing area, where the small windows treat us to a breathtaking view of the city sprawled out below, tall buildings jutting into the picture-perfect blue sky. It makes me wish I'd brought my better camera instead of my Polaroid.

When we come down, Jake is waiting for us, juggling two chili dogs, three Cokes and some fries. He hands one chili dog and a Coke to me, and the fries and a Coke to Laney.

"How was the ride?" he asks.

I shrug. "Okay."

"It was awesome!" Laney plops down on the grass and shoves a handful of fries into her mouth. "You have, like, no sense of adventure."

"I do too!"

"Oh, come off it. You'd never do anything fun if I didn't drag you into it, kicking and screaming."

"Maybe I'm just not in the mood for having fun right now," I retort sharply.

A wave of instant regret hits me at the hurt look on Laney's face.

"It was a joke, Harper," she says. Her voice is calm but firm. "Look, I know that this is a…bad time for you. The worst, even. I get it. I get it, and I'm trying to be patient, because I know you don't mean it when you turn me into your punching bag. But cut me some damn slack already, would you? I'm on your side here."

She's right. Of course she's right. I know if I don't stop being so awful and pushing her away like this, one day she'll reach her breaking point, and she won't be there at all. And what would I do then? She's my best friend. My only real friend. I need her.

"I'm sorry," I say quietly. I sit cross-legged on the grass beside her, and after a minute, I bump my shoulder against hers. "Anyway, your idea of fun is driving to Canada to get your tongue pierced."

I steal one of her fries and smile a little, and Laney smiles back, which makes me feel better.

"What's your point? It'd be wicked. I'd do it just to see my mother's face." She pauses to mop her mouth off with a napkin. "Hey, Jake, thanks for the fries."

"Yeah, well, I figured you might be hungry," he says. "By the way, I found a pay phone and got hold of Seth. He got back to White Haven with Danny and Anna. Devon's the only one in the group who got arrested. He's still in jail."

"He can't afford bail?" I ask.

"Oh, he can afford it. His parents are loaded. But Seth tells me he's really stoked about starting a hunger strike."

God, what an idiot. Laney rolls her eyes and says, "He says that now. Just you watch, boy's gonna get shanked." She stands up and pulls out her cell phone. "I'm gonna go call Seth."

Jake and I watch her walk away, and then he looks at me with his eyebrows raised. "So, what do you want to do next?" he asks. "Museums? Garden tour? The zoo?"

"No zoos. They make Laney depressed. During a third-grade field trip, she tried to convince me to help her liberate the penguins and set them free in the North Pole."

"There aren't any penguins in the North Pole. They're native to the southern hemisphere."

"I know, but she thought they were Santa's pets."

He laughs and shakes his head. "She's funny."

An unsettling feeling creeps into my stomach. I'm used to boys who chase after Laney and her long blond hair and even longer legs, but for some reason, the idea of Jake doing the chasing annoys me. I don't know if it's because part of me is stupidly attracted to him, or if it's because I'm trying to be protective of Laney. If I'm honest with myself, it's probably a little of both.

"You're not trying to get into her pants, are you?" I ask, eyes narrowed.

Jake's mouth falls open with surprise. Then he closes it again and says, a little tightly, "I said she was funny, not that I wanted to bang her. But good job on jumping to conclusions."

"I know how guys look at her, okay? Especially guys like you."

Apparently that was the wrong thing to say. Jake scrunches the hot dog wrapper up in one fist, the paper crinkling sharply. The way he's staring at me makes me want to break eye contact, or take back what I said, but I don't do either.

"*Guys like me*'?" he throws back at me cuttingly. "You don't know anything about me, Scott. Even if I did like Laney that way—which I don't—I wouldn't do anything. Not when Seth's made it clear he's interested."

I scoff. "Because guys never abandon all codes of friendship in pursuit of a piece of ass."

"No, some of us don't," he snaps. He rises to his feet abruptly and throws his trash in a nearby garbage bin, then pulls out a pack of cigarettes from his back pocket.

I actually almost believe him, is the thing. Or maybe I just *want* to believe him. It'd be nice to think there are some guys out there who are better than that, but I know I'm right. I know how boys are. How men are. My father, Tyler, that asshole Kyle—they're all the same. They all have a bottom line. Jake, too, has an agenda; I just don't know yet what it is.

"Hey," I say, standing up. He turns, and I gesture to his cigarette. "I want one."

"Why should I share when you're being such a bitch?" he sneers.

So, I guess we're back to that. One step forward, two steps back.

I walk over to him and say, "Don't be an asshole."

"*I'm* an asshole?" he echoes incredulously. "Are you freaking kidding me right now?"

"Just give me one."

He does, and he lights it for me, leaning in close as he does. God, those eyes. They really pull you in. And I can't help it; I kind of enjoy pushing his buttons. Maybe because he's so willing to push mine right back. In some twisted way, it makes him even sexier. Fucking teenage hormones. I wonder if this is what it's like for Laney, with all those boys she messes around with. It would explain a lot.

"You know that'll kill you," Jake deadpans, nodding toward my cigarette.

"Maybe that's the plan," I shoot back, which is stupid, because it's not like— I don't want to *die*, really.

I just— I want— I don't even know. I want to scream. I want to want to cry. I want to feel like a person again. I want June here, so she could lecture me on what an idiot I am for picking up such a nasty habit. I want to be back in Grand Lake, sitting on my roof with her next to me, smoking one of my mom's stolen cigarettes, knowing that my sister is there without even having to look. The same way it felt in my dream.

I close my eyes and breathe in the mingled smoke of our cigarettes because it's the closest I'm going to get. Because I want so many things, and I'm not going to have any of them,

ever again. Because there's no way to fill in the empty spaces
June left behind.

When I open my eyes again, Jake is staring at me. He shakes
his head. "You're a real piece of work, you know that?" he says.

I exhale a stream of smoke and sigh, staring up at the blue
sky overhead. "Trust me. I know."

nine

The pizza in St. Louis tastes different. Not bad different, just... different.

"It's called Provel cheese," Laney says. Laney watches way too many cooking shows.

We've just finished up an early dinner at some pizza place after spending the day doing, well, pretty much nothing. Jake napped on a bench in the park for a while, his hat pulled over his eyes, leaving Laney and I to entertain ourselves with playing cards and newspaper crosswords. Finally we got bored enough to wake him by tipping the bench until he rolled off and onto the grass. We were highly amused by the startled girlish yelp he made when he hit the ground. Jake, not so much.

Now we're in some place called the Blue Lounge, because Jake claims it would be nothing short of tragic to pass through St. Louis without soaking in some jazz.

I don't know if I'd go so far as to use the word *tragic*, but I am enjoying the band. And I'm not the only one—there are a few older couples on the wooden floor, holding each other close and swaying to the music. Everyone looks like they belong in one of those old Rat Pack movies; it makes me glad

Laney insisted we change before coming here. She looks stunning in her short red dress, not that that's a surprise—she looks stunning in anything. And I don't look too out of place wearing one of Laney's skirts with a belt and a strappy tank top. Jake, of course, fits in seamlessly with his black fedora.

I know Laney sensed something had transpired between me and Jake to mess with my mood when she came back from her phone call with Seth. On the way to the jazz club, she kept looking at me weird, asking if I was okay, asking if I'd had enough to eat, asking if she could do anything.

After the tenth time she asked if I was sure I was okay, I said, exasperated, "Laney. I'm fine. Relax."

"Of course she's not *fine*," Jake said to Laney. "Her sister is fucking dead. But that doesn't make her an invalid. Get off her back."

That shut Laney up. She fell silent, and I punched Jake in the shoulder and told him to shove it, even though I was grateful he'd put an end to the line of questioning.

I know Laney is worried, so I'm trying to pull it together for her sake. It's hard not to think of everything in the context of what it would be like if June was here, to not want to curl up in a ball and remain in the fetal position until we reach California, but I'm trying.

This is what I tell Jake, after we've staked out a table in the club and Laney's disappeared into the bathroom. I don't mean to bring June up; it just sort of spills out of me. Somehow it's easier to talk to Jake about her than it is Laney. Maybe because I know there's nothing I could say that would hurt him. And he's clearly not afraid of hurting me.

"Think of it this way," he says. "You're experiencing everything she'll never get to. It's, like…a tribute, or something. Not living your life won't help anyone."

It is comforting, I guess, to think of it that way. I take my camera and snap a shot of the dance floor, then turn and take one of Jake's profile, his face thoughtful as he listens to the band play. He gives me a look when the flash goes off but doesn't comment.

When Laney returns to our table, Jake pushes back his chair and says, "Now, which one of you ladies is going to take the first dance?"

"Not me." Laney wrinkles her nose. "I'm still feeling a little gross. Too much grease on those fries earlier, I guess."

"I suppose that leaves you then," he says to me.

"No way." I shake my head, tugging at my skirt. I haven't worn one of these things willingly since...well, pretty much never. "Not happening."

"Why not?"

"I don't dance."

"She really doesn't," Laney says around the lime from her water glass. "Trust me, I've tried to get her to, many, many times. Like I said earlier—she's got no sense of adventure."

"That's not true," I say defensively, but my cheeks heat up, and I realize that, okay, maybe she has me on this one.

"Prove it."

Jake holds out his hand and waggles his eyebrows. I know both he and Laney expect me to wrap my ankles around my chair legs and refuse to budge. That is, in fact, my first instinct, but then I think: Jake is right. I need to experience things. Push beyond my comfort zone. Even if I make a fool out of myself in the process.

With a defiant look shot Laney's way, I accept Jake's hand and let him draw me onto the wooden dance floor. He wants to play it that way? Fine. Then it's on.

At first I move to wind my arms awkwardly around his neck, the way I did ages ago at the sixth-grade dance when nerdy Arnold Beaman asked me, and I said yes, partly because I felt sorry for him, and partly because Laney was too distracted flirting with her harem of prepubescent boy toys to bail me out in time. But Jake stops me, guides one of my hands to his shoulder and takes the other in his, entwining our fingers. His other hand rests lightly on my hip. The contact makes me feel flushed all over.

"This isn't freshman year homecoming," he reminds me. "Don't worry. I'm not going to cop a feel."

"You better not." I pause, feeling awkward and cumbersome as he starts to shuffle across the floor with me stumbling along ungracefully. "Wait, wait— I don't— I don't know even how to dance like this!"

"It's easy. Just follow me."

I stare down at our feet, trying to move in time with him, but it's like no matter what I'm a half step behind. I'm about to inform Jake of my reneging on this dancing thing, when all of a sudden his Converse comes down on my toes. I jump and cry out in surprise. And now everyone, including the band, is staring at me. Oh, and what is that I spy out of the corner of my eye? Laney, stifling a giggle into her hand. Some best friend she is.

"You're overthinking this," Jake says.

I glare. "Maybe if you'd stop stepping all over my feet like a—"

"Does it always have to be the push and pull with you?"

"Yes. When it comes to you, yes, it does."

"Look. Stop. Breathe." His hand on my waist slides to the small of my back, pushing me in closer to him. It's all I can do not to shiver. "Don't look at the floor. Don't think about it. Just move with me."

Jake steps back, and I hesitate for just a moment before sliding with him. His grip on our interlaced fingers tightens as he begins to lead me around. On the fourth step, he twirls me in a fluid movement, pulls me back to him expertly. My breath catches a little in my chest at the look in his hooded eyes.

"You seem surprised," he says, amused.

"You're not half-bad at this." My hand relaxes on his shoulder. "I'm almost impressed."

He takes a sudden swinging step to the right, guiding us closer to the band. I glance over at the sax player in time to see him cock his head and wink, smiling around his mouthpiece. When I look back to Jake, his mouth curves in a playful grin.

"Careful, Harper. Someone might think you're actually enjoying yourself."

I can't suppress a smile. "Huh."

"'Huh'?" He quirks an eyebrow. "What was the 'huh' for?"

"This just doesn't seem like your type of music."

"That's because you've caught me in the middle of a nostalgic British Invasion phase. The first—not the second. You know, the Stones, Cream, Pink Floyd. But I don't restrict myself to certain genres. Labels are substantially irrelevant."

"Wow," I say. "You are truly obsessed."

"Yeah, I kinda am," he agrees, grinning. "Without music, life would be a mistake."

"Did you coin that one yourself?"

"Nietzsche did, actually. But it's a common mix-up."

"And you believe that?"

"Isn't it obvious?"

He spins me once more, draws me in close and dips me dramatically. When he rights me on my feet again, I'm grinning back, matching him step for step.

"I'm starting to realize that nothing about you is as obvious as I thought," I say. "The penchant for ABBA. The no-drinking policy. The generous tipping habits."

"What can I tell you?" He shrugs. "I'm a complicated guy."

I know he's joking, but the truth is, he *is* a complicated guy, more complicated than I ever would have guessed. I wonder if June realized the same thing during all of their study sessions. Maybe she saw what I'm just starting to see—that there is a lot more to Jake than meets the eye. She must've seen *something*, since they were friends and all. Or at the very least, friendly.

The quartet's jam comes to an end, the last sax note sounding out in a long, high trill. It's met with scattered applause from the peanut gallery, including Laney's. She puts two fingers in her mouth and blows an earsplitting whistle. Jake tips his hat at me, then leans forward, his mouth brushing my ear.

"Has she been drinking?" he asks jokingly.

"Nah," I say. "I think she was just born like that."

I'm feeling…kind of good, actually. This is the most I've smiled since June died. I don't know whether I should feel guilty about that or not, so I decide not to. As we walk back to the table, I bump my shoulder into Jake's.

"So, you still think I have no sense of adventure?" I ask him.

He smiles. "You know, Scott, you're starting to change my mind."

Oklahoma is almost as boring as Indiana. The good news is that after wasting the entire day in St. Louis, Jake seems anxious to hit the road and put some serious mileage behind him, so I don't have to endure too much of it. He drives all through the night, and when he thinks I'm asleep, he slips in some ABBA.

Laney stays asleep—I guess her stomach is still bugging her—and I drift in and out until around four in the morning, when I open my eyes to Jake singing "Take a Chance on Me" under his breath, his fingers drumming on the steering wheel. I watch him for a while, amused, then look out the window. We're on some side road, off the highway. It's still pretty dark outside.

When he notices I'm awake, Jake stops singing and turns down the stereo. "I need to gas up," he says.

"Okay." My voice comes out all thick and scratchy from sleep. I clear my throat, sitting up straighter. "Are we still in Oklahoma?"

"Yeah. Got a pretty long time before we hit Texas."

Texas. Holy shit. I rub my forehead and calculate how many states we have left to pass through. Half of Oklahoma, Texas, New Mexico, Arizona and then we're there. California. It feels so close and so far away at the same time.

Jake swings into a gas station, climbs out and fills up Joplin's tank. A minute later he yanks the pump nozzle out and heads inside to pay. I glance over my shoulder at Laney sleeping behind me. She looks younger when she's asleep, snuggled deep into her sweatshirt, legs drawn toward her chest, her whole body curled in like she's making herself as small as possible. It's like nothing has touched her and nothing ever will.

I unbuckle my seat belt and climb over the seats, all the way into the open back, careful to avoid Laney's sleeping form. The lights from the gas station's parking lot illuminate everything with a dim yellow glow, and I squint under them until I see it. The trunk with June's ashes. Its battered top feels smooth under my hands, old leather and brass. I unsnap the latches as quietly as I can manage and lift the heavy lid.

The urn is swaddled in Jake's blanket. I pull it out and into my lap, brushing my fingers across the cool marble. All this time I've been avoiding the urn, afraid of— I don't know. Afraid, I guess, that looking at it will make this real. Will drive home the fact that June is gone. She's gone and that's permanent. I can't pretend otherwise when I'm looking at her remains.

"Hey." I turn when I hear Laney's sleep-heavy voice. She

climbs over the backseat and slides down next to me. "Every-thing okay?" she asks.

I nod without taking my eyes off the urn. "Yeah. I just..." Miss her.

"Me, too," Laney says softly, resting her cheek against my shoulder.

"I called her a bitch."

She looks up at me. "What?"

"The night before... I yelled at her." My throat is like sandpaper when I swallow. "She barged into my room, and I was— I was *mad*. And I said all these things—"

"Everyone says stupid shit," Laney cuts in. "It doesn't mean anything. It doesn't. June knew you didn't mean it. I know you two didn't always get along, but she loved you. And she knew you loved her. I know she did."

Before I can respond to that, the back doors pop open and Jake sticks his head inside.

"Sorry to interrupt the powwow," he says. He raises his eyebrows curiously at the urn.

I quickly place it back in the trunk and close the top. "What do you want?"

He tosses something into my lap. I look down; it's a pack of cigarettes. Camel Lights.

"Now you can stop stealing mine," he tells me.

Laney gives me a look, but she knows better than to say anything. The same way I never say anything about her drink-ing. We let each other have these things, even though we shouldn't. We have our reasons.

The sky gradually lightens as we drive on, deep midnight-blue giving way to flaring orange and dusky pink. Outside the landscape is flat, and everything looks dead: the barren trees, the brown grass. It'd be easy to be lulled back into sleep by the monotony—Laney doesn't seem to have any trouble drifting off again—but I'm too keyed up at the moment for that. My head buzzes with thoughts that twist around each other like vines.

Maybe Laney's right. Maybe June did love me. But I'm far less certain that she knew I loved her. Did she realize how much I needed her around? It's not like I ever told her. I was too wrapped up in my world to notice what was going on in hers. Even if she did know, it wasn't enough to count. It wasn't enough to make her stay. So really, what did it matter, in the end?

The bottom line is, it's my fault. I didn't love her enough. I didn't do enough. *I* wasn't enough. There's no excuse. There is nothing that will ever make that okay.

I press the heels of my hands into my eyes while Jake replaces ABBA with something else—it doesn't even sound like music. It's weird and warped and grating. Chaotic noise. I make it about three and a half tracks in before I can't stand it any longer. I take my hands off my eyes and press the eject button, yanking the disc out with my fingers.

"What the hell is this?" I demand.

"Uh, it's Captain Beefheart," Jake explains, nonplussed.

"It's crap."

"It's avant-garde."

"No. It's *crap*."

"Okay," he relents, "it's not the most listenable album ever. You have to experience it a few times in its entirety before it grows on you."

I seriously doubt that. I almost throw the damn thing out onto the side of the highway, except Jake snatches the disc out of my hand before I can roll the window halfway down.

"All right, all right! I'll play something else." He glances away from the road and at the stack of CDs on top of the dashboard. "How about… Pink Floyd?"

"Blah. No."

"Bob Dylan?"

"We've listened to him a ton already."

"Okay," he says slowly, and I can tell he's working to not let his impatience creep into his tone, "so what music *do* you like?"

"I dunno." I shrug. "Usually I listen to whatever Laney listens to."

"I didn't ask what music you *listen* to. I asked what music you *like*."

I stop and think about it for a minute. "Well… I like some of the more indie stuff. You know—Arcade Fire, Regina Spektor, Magnetic Fields, Tegan and Sara, Ted Leo and the Pharmacists. Rilo Kiley's first album was awesome. Laney listens to this Sri Lankan female rapper, I forget her name, but I enjoy her." I pause. "And the Beatles. I can't lie. I love the Beatles."

"*Now* we're getting somewhere," he says with the hint of a smile. He squints at me appraisingly. "Let me guess. You're a Paul girl?"

"Please! I happen to think Ringo is severely underrated," I say. "But let me guess—you're a Lennon fan?"

He's totally that type. Probably thinks he's bigger than Jesus, too.

I know I've pegged him right when he shrugs and says, "Guilty as charged."

So predictable.

He roots through the stack of CDs and slides one out, pops it into the stereo. I realize what it is when I hear the first song—the *Let It Be* album. "The last Beatles record ever," I say.

"Well, to be released," Jake amends. "Technically it was recorded before *Abbey Road*."

Whatever.

We drive for another ten minutes or so before the title track comes on. Paul sings the words with a quiet, strong conviction, accompanied by striking, solemn piano notes. As the song goes on, I think about June. Surprise, surprise. All of a sudden anger bubbles up in my chest so hot and furious I can barely breathe.

I want what Paul had. I want the faith that there will be some kind of an answer, something more than these endless questions taking up so much space in my head, this feeling that nothing matters and nothing has a point. It isn't fair. It isn't fair that I have no answers. It isn't fair that June isn't here to give them. Most of all it isn't fair that she did this to me, that she left me to deal with this mess on my own. That's how I feel: completely and utterly alone. Even with Laney here. Even with my mother. I'm still alone.

Hot tears prick behind my eyes like tiny searing needles. The feel of them there surprises me as much as it does Jake.

He glances over at me, confused. "Hey. What's—"

"Shut up," I retort reflexively.

I turn to the window and watch the ground slip by through my unfocused vision, trying to keep myself under control. I can't get June out of my head. The worst part is not knowing if I want her out of there or not. But I don't have a choice when I'm listening to this song, to these lyrics all about guidance and comfort, so sad and hopeful at the same time.

A minute later the headlights wash over a sign indicating an upcoming rest stop. I try to blink the wetness out of my eyes, but it doesn't work.

"I need to pee," I say, my voice wavering.

Without a word, Jake pulls off at the next exit and drives down the sloping road. The tears form thick in my throat until I can't hold it in anymore.

I grab the door handle. "Stop the car."

"Harper—"

"Stop the goddamn car!"

I unfasten my belt and tumble out the door as he skids to a stop. The lot is mostly empty; thankfully no one is there to witness my mad bolt toward the bathrooms. But I don't even get that far before I stumble and drop to my knees on the grass.

A song. A stupid song is making me cry like a baby, when I couldn't even muster up a single tear for my own sister's funeral. What does that say about me? The sobs that have been building in my chest burst out, ragged and painful. I rock on my heels, crying and crying, ripping out chunks of grass by the fistfuls. I hate this. I hate feeling too much and not enough at the same time. I go on ripping at the grass and crying and hating myself some more.

I'm not sure how long I've been doing that before I sense Jake behind me. I don't turn around.

"Paul is wrong, you know," I say as I wipe my grass-stained palms on my knees. I'm still crying so hard I'm barely coherent. "There's not going to be an answer."

There will never be answers. Just more and more questions. And maybe I'd be okay with that if I didn't have to hear someone sing those lies so beautifully that it makes me want more than anything to believe that I'm wrong. That one day this all might make sense. That my life is shattered now, but one day I'll be able to glue the pieces back together and make it whole again.

Jake hovers a step closer. "Hey—" he starts.

"Don't," I say. I put my head in my hands and try to get a grip, get myself under control. Stop acting like an idiot. I hate that it's Jake who always sees me when I'm acting like an idiot.

"Don't…what?"

"Don't say something nice. It'll make me feel so pathetic I'll want to die."

Jake kneels down and sets one of his hands lightly on the middle of my back. It's like his touch cracks open my insides, and I start crying freely again, even harder than before.

"Good news," he hisses in a stage whisper. "I was just going to tell you how puffy and red your eyes are. You look like you tested out Seth's gas mask."

I laugh a little through my tears, brushing them away with the back of my hand, and the sound surprises me as much as the crying. I can't remember the last time I laughed.

I blow out a shaky breath. "Jerk."

Everything's starting to feel a little more normal now; my breathing coming a little easier, my voice a little steadier. The hysterical feeling fades and leaves me with the all-too-sharp awareness of my stupid meltdown.

"This is so ridiculous," I say, embarrassed. I want to dig a hole in the ground right here and crawl inside it. "Crying over a *song*—"

"It's not dumb," he tells me. He hasn't moved his hand from the center of my back. I kind of like it, though, its weight and warmth. Holding me together. "It makes sense."

What is he talking about? It totally does not make sense. It is the opposite of sense making.

I roll my eyes. "Whatever."

"I mean it," he stresses. He pauses, the silence between us lengthening until I finally meet his serious gaze. "You want to know why I love music?"

"Enlighten me." I sniffle. My face must be such a mess right now.

"Eric Clapton had a four-year-old son who fell forty-nine stories through an open window of their apartment and died," he says.

I stare at him in return, waiting to see how this could possibly be relevant to his point.

"Clapton wrote this song about it, after, and it just—It rips your heart out," he continues. "It is the best kind of devastating there is. He took his pain and he turned it into something beautiful. Into something that people connect to. And that's what good music does. It speaks to you. It changes you." Jake leans in toward me a little closer, voice softening. "What I'm trying to say is, it's just nice, I guess, knowing that someone else can put into words what I feel. That there are people who have been through things worse than I have, and they came out on the other side okay. Not only that, but they made some kind of twisted, fucked-up sense of the completely senseless. They made it mean something. These songs tell me I'm not alone. If you look at it that way, music...music can see you through anything."

I close my eyes as his hand rubs a small circle on my back. It's the first time in so long that I've been touched by someone—anyone—without my every instinct screaming at me to run away. The first time when I feel like someone is reaching out without expecting anything from me in return.

"Everything is so screwed up." My voice trembles, tears flowing again. "I'm doing this all wrong."

Jake looks unsure of how to respond. "You seriously need to give yourself a break here, kid," he says after a minute. "There's no right way to do this." He stands, moving his hand from my back to the top of my head. "Look, it's not ever going to stop hurting. That's the reality. But after a while, it'll get... easier. You'll get used to living with it."

I don't want to get used to living with it. I want things to go back to the way they used to be.

Jake gives me a hand up, and I notice the way he doesn't let go right away when I'm on my feet. But then, I don't really want to let go, either. I like having something to hold on to.

We walk back to the lot in silence. Joplin is parked next to a blue minivan, where a mother shepherds three sleepy-looking boys out of the back and toward the bathrooms. The shortest of them carries a raggedy blanket that drags across the ground as he follows his brothers.

Jake opens the back doors of the van, and the two of us sit on the ledge, feet dangling. We eat two slices of Dottie's peach crumb pie and then chain-smoke cigarettes, watching the sun begin its slow climb over the horizon.

"I need a nap," he sighs. "I'm going to clear out the back and lie down."

"I'll help."

We manage to toss the bags and Laney's suitcases into the front without waking her. The only thing we don't move is the trunk holding June's urn—Jake just gently pushes it against the wall. He spreads a blanket over the floor, pulls out two pillows.

"I can take the backseat," he says. He glances at Laney, still asleep. "Uh, if we can get her to move."

"That's a pretty big if. I don't think we'll be able to render her from unconsciousness for hours."

"Well, what do you want to do then?"

"We can sleep together." I immediately blush. "I mean— you know what I mean. I could use a nap, and there's enough room."

Jake stares at me, stammers out, "Um, yeah, sure," and tosses over one of the pillows.

I set it under my head, curling up on my side and sliding off my shoes. Jake shuts the van's back doors and lies down next to me. He's really close, so close I can feel him breathing on the nape of my neck. I could put more space between us, but instead I scoot backward, leaning into him, my back pressed into the pleasant warmth of his front. Jake holds his breath for a moment, but he doesn't say anything. And he doesn't move away.

"Have you played me that Clapton song?" I whisper. I don't want to wake up Laney. I don't want her to find us like this. Even though we're not really doing anything. Still, it feels like we're doing…something. I don't know what, exactly, but this—the way I'm curled into him, the way his face is in my hair—it isn't nothing.

Jake stirs behind me. "No, I don't think so."

"How does it go?"

He moves so his mouth is right under my ear, brushing the skin there, and one of his hands slides up, resting on my rib cage. My whole body tingles as he starts to sing softly into my ear. I'm not facing him, my eyes are closed, but I can imagine the look on his face. I listen to the words, and I have that feeling again, the same one I had right before I started sobbing in the grass. A tidal wave of emotion rises inside of me.

It's like I'm on the cusp of something desperate and dangerous, but I don't know what it is. And then it doesn't matter because I'm asleep.

ten

It seems like only minutes pass before Laney shakes me awake by my shoulder. I sigh and roll onto my back, blinking up at her. She folds her arms on top of the backseat and grins down at me. She's practically glowing, even sans makeup.

"Nice nap?" she asks innocently, shooting a pointed glance at Jake's rumpled pillow.

The memory of Jake singing, his arm wrapped halfway around me, comes flooding back, and my cheeks heat up against my will. I don't know how much Laney saw. If anything.

I struggle into a sitting position. "What time is it?"

"Almost ten," she informs me. "Jake's taking a leak. Wanna go freshen up?"

We traipse to the bathrooms to wash our faces and brush our teeth. Mine feel fuzzy and gross; I really, really want a shower. Maybe we can check into a motel at the end of the day. I wonder how far we'll be by nightfall.

I'm splashing water on my face at the sink when Laney emerges from the stall, comes up behind me and says, "You know, Jake's pretty cute."

"S-seriously?" I sputter. I'm dripping water all over the counter.

"What? I'm just saying!" She approaches the mirror and whips out her dental floss, but totally looks at me the whole time. "Don't worry, it's not like I'm interested or anything."

What is that supposed to mean?

I meet her eyes in the mirror. "Why would I be worried?"

"I've decided to adopt Seth's philosophy." She continues like she didn't hear me as she twists the floss around her hand and runs it through her bottom teeth. "I'm embracing a life of celibacy. Everything above the waist is fair game, but that's it."

"Wow. You're practically a nun now."

"I know, right? Maybe I'd become a real one if the outfits weren't so terrible."

She snaps off the mess of floss string and takes out her lip gloss, rubbing it into her lower lip with her index finger. I want to tell her that she's prettier without all of the makeup. It kills me a little, the fact that I'll never be effortlessly beautiful the way Laney is.

"Sex turns boys into idiots," she says sagely, like she's imparting some profound wisdom. "Since they're already idiots to begin with, it just makes them worse."

"Do you think Seth is an idiot?" I ask.

She presses her lips together, weighing the question. "Bottom line, Seth is a boy," she says after a minute. "Ergo, idiot."

Is Jake just a boy? He's only eighteen, but he seems older sometimes. Like he's not hung up on the same things as most kids his age. And yeah, he can be insufferable, but he's insufferable in different ways than other boys I know. So where does that leave him?

I'm still mulling it over when we go back to the parking lot to find Jake leaning up against the driver's side door, munching on some pretzels from the vending machine.

"Took you long enough," he says gruffly.

"It takes hard work to look this good," Laney retorts, flipping her hair and flouncing around to the back door. "Learn it, live it, love it."

Jake looks at me briefly, but it's not any different than usual. It's almost like he never saw me cry, or like we didn't fall asleep together in the back of his van.

Okay, so I guess we're pretending none of that happened. I can roll with that.

We get lost for the first time not long after we've crossed the Oklahoma border and into Texas. Jake stops to pick us up some fast food, and we get all turned around trying to get back on the highway. Somehow we end up heading back east.

"You were supposed to turn left! *Left!*" I yell over Mick Jagger. Jake's been blasting the Stones for the past hour. I like them, a lot, actually, but come on. Enough is enough.

"Jesus, Scott, maybe you should've let me know when that fact was relevant. Like, five exits ago."

"You two are driving me insane." Laney squeezes up front between us, cell phone in hand. "Get off here," she instructs, pointing at the next exit.

Jake's mouth falls open. "But—"

"Just do it."

He does. Laney calls out directions from her BlackBerry to navigate until we're back on the highway, going west again, the right way.

When we pass a billboard advertising some Texan steak house, I look over my shoulder at her and say, "I bet your father would be horrified that we're going through Texas without stopping for steak."

"Probably." She's lying across the backseat, scrolling on her

BlackBerry, her long legs stretched out across the seat. "What about your dad? Think he's freaking out?"

"No," I say. I stare out the window; the next billboard is for a Hooters restaurant. Ew. "I think he'd rather pretend my mom and I don't exist." That much has become crystal clear since June died.

Jake cuts his eyes toward me for a moment before focusing on the road again. "What about the urn?" he asks. "Isn't he going to be pissed about not getting the ashes?"

"Maybe." I shrug. I don't particularly care about his reaction.

I'm probably being unfair. June was his daughter, after all. But for the first time, I think I truly understand the intensity of my mother's anger at him. It hurts to be treated this way, like a mistake, like something someone is trying to erase. Melinda is his clean slate. Mom and I, we're his baggage, the kind you abandon on the side of the road because it's inconvenient.

"It's his own fault," says Laney. "He's just like my dad, dumping the first wife for a newer model. It's sick."

Jake catches her eyes in the rearview mirror. "Your mother is the newer model in this scenario, I assume?"

"I have no illusions about my parents' marriage," she replies. "My mom didn't really want a kid—stretch marks, oh, the horror—but I was, you know, an investment. Financial security. Tummy tucks cured the rest." There's a bitter edge to her voice underneath the flippancy. She shrugs. "At least they stay off my ass most of the time. As long as it doesn't interfere with their lives, they don't care what I do."

"My mom—" Jake starts, and then stops just as suddenly. I turn my head to look at him, but he keeps staring out at the stretch of highway. The line of his throat works as he swallows. "She never cared, either. Sometimes I feel like things would've been really different. If she had."

We drive along in contemplative silence for a few minutes.

"Parents suck," Laney eventually comments from the back.

"True that," Jake concurs.

He drums his fingers on the steering wheel as Keith Richards bursts into a guitar solo, and it strikes me then that this is the first thing the three of us have agreed on since we started our trip. For once, we're all on the same page.

The harmony between us lasts most of the day, until a few miles outside of Santa Fe, when Jake stops to use a pay phone so he can check in with his brother.

"A cell phone without a monthly plan that you can't even text from? No iPod?" Laney scoffs when he returns a few minutes later. "Are you technophobic or something?"

"It's time to embrace the twenty-first century, Tolan," I tease.

"You know what they say. If it ain't broke…" Once he's pulled onto the highway again, he turns around to look at Laney. "Besides, you're sixteen. What does a sixteen-year-old need with a BlackBerry anyway?"

"I'm seventeen," she corrects, like that changes everything. "Harper's the baby here."

"Being ten months younger than you does not make me an infant!" I protest. "We're in the same grade! It's not my fault I got a head start and you went into kindergarten late."

"Whatever." She turns to Jake. "Remember, this Black-Berry just saved your ass. Have a little respect."

"Sorry, but I don't have respect for—"

I raise my Polaroid camera and take a picture of the two of them bickering. They both stop to glare at me. Well, at least they're not arguing anymore.

"Give me a little warning next time!" Laney runs her hands over her tousled hair in distress. "I have total bedhead, and my makeup melted off my face hours ago, and my left foot is asleep, and—" She stops abruptly mid-sentence, looking past me. "Hey, what is that?"

I face the front just as we fly by a hand-painted sign that reads Fridgehenge: Next Exit.

Laney strains forward against her seat belt. "What do you think it means?" she wonders.

"It's code for Stupid Tourist Trap," Jake deadpans.

She grabs his shoulders and shakes them from behind. "Come on, we should check it out! We've been driving all day. I am so bored I could die. I want to breathe in New Mexico's fresh summer air. I need to *breathe*, Jake!"

He rolls his eyes and looks at me. "And what do you think?"

"I think it's probably dumb," I say, which elicits a sound of protest from the backseat. "*However*, I'm required to automatically side with her in this situation in fear of violating extremely sacred best-friend codes. Let's stop."

Laney beams. "Now, that's the spirit!"

Jake reluctantly turns off at the next exit, following a series of hand-painted signs until they lead to a bumpy dirt road. It stretches out for about half a mile before ending abruptly. Joplin's headlights click on, swarms of bugs catching in their light, and illuminate another sign that reads Fridgehenge. An arrow points straight ahead toward a worn path in a brown field. We all look at each other as the engine idles, wondering what to do next.

I shrug. "I guess we park and walk."

When we unload from the van, I dig out a can of bug spray from my backpack and spray each of us down thoroughly, until we're all coughing from the fumes. Not the most pleasant aroma, but it does allow us to hike up the hill without constantly fending off the feasting mosquito herds or having to fear dropping dead of malaria or West Nile or whatever.

At the top is a circular wire fence surrounding what looks to be a landfill.

"Well, isn't this exciting," says Jake. He swats at a fly near his face.

"It's a dump," I say to Laney, trying to catch my breath.

"There's got be something more to it—" She peers around on her tiptoes, then points. "Look, that must be it! Fridge-henge."

Jake and I swivel our heads to find whatever she's gesturing to. And then I see it: in the middle of the landfill, someone has stacked old refrigerators on top of each other in an artful—and surprisingly accurate—replication of Stonehenge.

"Can we get any closer?" I ask, but Laney's one step ahead of me, already headed toward a break in the fence. She ducks through and motions for us to follow.

Up close, the spectacle is even more strange—and somehow, also weirdly magnificent. The refrigerators, yellowed with age and many of them tagged with graffiti, all look sort of beautiful and majestic, what with the vividly colorful purple-and-red sky lighting them from behind. I snap a good deal of Polaroids in the fading twilight, trying different angles, doing my best to show the scope of the arrangement someone has built here.

Laney tips her head to the side thoughtfully. "What does it mean?"

"I think it's supposed to be a statement about America's reliance on and addiction to rampant, wasteful consumerism," Jake says.

"Interesting." She then turns to scan the horizon with one hand on her hip. "Hey, do you think there's a Starbucks around here? I would punch a monkey for a macchiato."

"*I* would punch a monkey for a shower," I groan, yanking at my sweat-ringed shirt collar to let some air in. I take the developed photos from between my teeth and stick them in a zippered pouch of my backpack.

"Me too," Laney agrees. "And mmm, a nice, comfy bed."

"You can have your shower, but don't hold your breath on the comfy bed part." Jake smirks. "Girls, we're going camping."

There has to be some irony in the fact that we use Laney's BlackBerry to find directions to the nearest rustic campsite. When I point this out to them, however, neither is amused. Guess you can't win 'em all.

I can tell Laney is trying really hard not to complain; she must know that if she did, I'd call her out on her "sense of adventure" crap she wouldn't shut up about earlier. It isn't until Jake pays for the site that it seems Laney can hold it in no longer.

"Where do you expect me to pee?" she demands indignantly.

"They have bathroom facilities," he says. He slaps the sticker on his windshield. "And if that's too far, you can walk around and find a spot where no one's looking. Just be on the lookout for rattlesnakes." I can't tell whether or not he's kidding.

Laney's eyes go comically wide. "There are *rattlesnakes*?"

After that, she vows to barricade herself inside the van until we've crossed state lines. As soon as we park, she digs up some blankets, clears out the space in the back, and burrows under them, clicking away on her BlackBerry. I bet she's googling to see what kind of snakes are native to New Mexico.

When Jake steps outside, I follow without thinking. No way am I ready for sleep yet. I worry that if I do sleep, I'll dream of June, even though I haven't yet, except for that one time. And that wasn't the nightmare I keep bracing myself for—some terrible reenactment of the morning I found her.

In the garage. I've successfully repressed that memory so far, but I can still feel it, bubbling right under the surface, ready to jump out at me when I'm least expecting it. A poisonous snake hidden in the high grass.

Jake jumps onto Joplin's hood, extends a hand and hoists me up beside him. We stretch out side by side, arms laced behind our heads, gazing up at the stars. It's amazing—they seem bigger out here, brighter, and there are more of them.

"Do you know any constellations?" I ask.

"Not really," he says. "There is this one, called the Southern Cross. But you can only see it in the Southern Hemisphere. Actually, there's a song about it—"

"Of course there's a song. There's *always* a song."

He ignores me and continues "—by Crosby, Stills and Nash. I prefer most of their stuff when Neil Young was in the group, but it's a great song."

Jake starts singing it under his breath, voicing the verses he knows and humming the rest. It's a pretty song. He has a pretty voice. Though I'm pretty certain if I called him "pretty," he'd get royally pissed off, regardless of the context.

When he trails off at the end of the song, I say, "Are you in a band? You should be."

"Me?" He sounds surprised. "No, I just play Eli's instruments sometimes. He's in one, though. Mostly they just jam in the drummer's basement, but…yeah. Making music, that's his thing. Not mine."

I get that. It's sort of like how it was with June and me—how I knew from the start I would never live up to her, so it was easier to not even try.

"Have you written any songs?" I ask.

"No. I'm not a writer." He shrugs one shoulder. "I don't have anything to say."

I sit up and raise my eyebrows at him. "You? Not have anything to say? Hmm, somehow I'm not buying that."

Jake shrugs again, and I lie back down, staring up at the star-filled sky. I wonder what the Southern Cross looks like. All I know is the Big Dipper. June taught me how to find that one, when we were little kids.

"It's so quiet out here," I say, just to say something. Anything at all. The silence is getting to me.

"What, are you bored? Want to play a game?" Jake shoots me a mock-serious look. "Something *other* than Top Three."

"There's always Truth or Dare."

"Truth or Dare? Do you think I'm a twelve-year-old girl?" he says. He nudges his foot against mine.

I nudge mine back, our legs hooking together, crossed at the ankles. "Sometimes I do, in fact."

After a beat, he says, "All right, I'll play," much to my surprise. He turns his head and adds, "But only if I can go first."

"If you must." I sigh and throw an arm over my eyes. "Okay. Truth."

"What are you thinking, right now?"

That's his question, of all things? I move my arm a little and open one eye to look at him. His face is completely serious, waiting me out. My arm slides down so that my hand rests at the base of my throat, and when my thumb brushes up against the thin skin there, I can feel the *tick-tick-tick* of my heartbeat.

"I'm thinking that…" I breathe in, just for a moment. "My sister really would've loved to have seen that. Fridgehenge, I mean."

He digs out a cigarette from his pocket and lights it, looking at me the whole time. "Really?"

"Yeah. June liked that kind of stuff—I guess you'd call it ironic, right? Making art out of other people's trash." I smile. "She had this shirt with a can of tomato soup on it that she'd wear all of the time. She said it was by some artist, and she tried to explain to me why it was art. I never got it. It was just a can of soup."

Jake inhales on his cigarette, the tip flaring bright orange against the descending darkness. "People see art in a lot of things."

"I guess." I hug my hoodie tighter around my middle. Who knew the desert could get so cold? "Now it's my turn. Truth or dare?"

"Dare," he says automatically. How unsurprising.

I hate coming up with dares. Laney always picks them, and there's only so many times I can dare her to run around her front yard naked at two in the morning when no one's looking before it gets old.

And I am not asking Jake to get naked. Even if the thought is a little tempting.

"Oh, I've got it!" I sit up on my elbow and grin down at him. "I...dare you...to write a song."

"Right now?" he says, making a face.

"Uh, obviously not. But at some point. When we get home." *Home.* The word churns in my stomach. It won't be long before I'll have to face that reality. Mom and Aunt Helen and June's untouched bedroom and everything else I don't want to think about right now. I'd rather be here. "Promise me you'll at least try," I say.

Jake looks away. "I don't know. Maybe."

I shouldn't be disappointed by his response, but I am anyway. Stupid of me to think I could talk him into it. That my thinking he could do it would make a difference. What does my opinion matter to him? What do I matter? I'm just some girl whose sister he knew.

"Fine." I drop down onto my back again and look up at the immense night sky. It's better than looking at Jake and his closed-off face. "I get to ask a truth then. Tell me. What happened to your parents?"

He takes a deep breath like he's steeling himself. "My dad left when I was four, and he's been in prison since I was nine. Armed robbery with a side of possession, if you're curious."

"Oh," I say. I'm sort of stunned; partly because I didn't expect a real answer, and partly because I've never known anyone who's even been arrested. Aside from Seth and Devon, of course. "That…sucks."

"It's for the best, really. He was…" Jake hesitates. "Not a good person."

"And your mother?"

"After a while…she got tired of being a mom. So she stopped."

And that's all he'll say about it.

"So what about your parents?" he asks.

"I didn't pick truth."

"Okay, then I *dare* you to tell me about your parents."

That's totally cheating, but instead of calling him out on it, I say, "Did June ever tell you anything about them?"

"A little. I know they're divorced," he tells me. "Let me guess. Your dad had the cliché affair with the secretary? Mixing business with pleasure?" He waggles his eyebrows.

"Not quite. He does have a girlfriend—her name is Melinda and she is a caterer. But supposedly it wasn't an affair. All parties claim it happened after the divorce."

"Your family's lack of scandal is shocking. And a little disappointing."

"I know, it's a boring story. I guess they just stopped loving each other. How mundane." I sigh, shifting on the metal hood. "My dad is pretty much happy to pretend what little is left of his former life doesn't exist. My mother made up her mind that all men are evil and conniving and out to destroy you."

"I wondered where you got that philosophy from," Jake says. He's probably only half joking.

I swat him on the shoulder. "Whatever. It's my turn."

"Truth. Take your best shot."

Oh, I will. I've been waiting to ask this since Chicago, since Anna so casually mentioned knowing my sister. This is as good a time to ask as any. "June," I say. "Were you—were you like her secret boyfriend, or something?"

Jake stiffens beside me. "Why would you think I was her boyfriend?"

"I don't know, let's see." I roll my eyes. "Maybe because you clam up whenever I ask how you knew her. Maybe because I know she met Anna and your friends, on at least one occasion."

"Anna told you that, huh?" he says, but he doesn't sound mad. He takes a hard drag on his cigarette and goes quiet for a minute. "I was never... She only met them a few times. We hung out sometimes. She wanted to—get out of the house, I guess. I know things were...intense. With your parents. With college. It was hard on her. And she'd just dumped that loser jock boyfriend of hers."

"You mean Tyler."

"Tyler, is that his name? Yeah." He frowns. "Anyway. One of Seth's friends was playing a show in Detroit, so we drove up there together."

This is news to me. "A show? Like, a punk band show?" I sit up again, surprised. "June went to see a punk band?"

"Well, they were a shit excuse for a punk band, but yeah. Don't worry, I'm pretty sure she hated it. Said she 'didn't get the scene.'" He laughs. "It's so weird. Sometimes I can't believe you two are related. You're nothing like her."

That's just what I need. Another damn comparison. Another person stating the obvious.

"Thanks," I say. Yeah, I'm bitter.

"It's not an insult," he clarifies. I don't know what he means by that, but then he explains. "I know I didn't know June as well as…some people, but she always seemed… I don't know. Uncomfortable in her own skin. Maybe that's why she wanted to spend time around me. Do things she didn't usually. Maybe she had an identity crisis or something."

"Yeah. Maybe." It would make some sense—June hated the life she'd constructed, so she tried something new, hoping it would fit better. But it didn't. So she gave up. I slide out the pack of cigarettes from my hoodie pocket, and say, "So, you're saying that I'm what? Comfortable?"

"I'm saying," he says, leaning over to light my cigarette on cue, always on hand to corrupt the youth of America, "that you're not fragile like she was. God, she was like a china doll."

Easy to crack. Unlike me.

"And I'm just made of metal. I don't feel anything." I take a sullen drag off my cigarette. "You never answered my original question. Okay, so you were friends with June, but you and her. You never—"

"Never," he answers sharply. He says it in a way that makes it clear this round of Truth or Dare is officially over.

He slowly rolls off the hood, and a second later I hear him open the driver's door and climb in. The slam of the door shutting makes me wince. I feel kind of bad, and kind of pissed at the same time, because why should he be angry? He has no right. None.

I swing my legs over and slide off the hood, walk around to the driver's side. Jake's window is rolled down, and he's draped over the steering wheel, chin tucked on top of his hands, staring straight ahead.

"I have one more," I say. I curl my hands over the window frame's edge. "Truth."

He doesn't blink. "Game's over, Scott. Not your turn, anyway."

"One more," I insist, louder, and grip the rubbery strip around the car window frame. I wait until he eventually turns his head to look right at me. "I want to know. Did you have any idea—with June, that she would—or *why* she would—" My voice shakes. I'm looking right at him, but it's all one big blur.

"No," he says quietly. He sighs and rubs his face with both hands. "I think… Some people are just sad, all of the time. Too sad to deal with—everything. Life, I guess. I don't know. There doesn't always have to be a reason." His face softens. "I wish I knew."

"Yeah, well. I guess if June wanted us to know, she would've said something, or at least left a note," I reply bitterly.

I start to step away when Jake catches my wrist and draws me back, flush against the side of the van.

"Hey." His other hand reaches out, pushing a stray lock of hair off of my face and behind my ear. "You're not, you know."

"Not what?" My voice is barely a whisper. My heart races wildly, like I've just finished a ten-mile marathon. Jake shifts forward so that his face is only inches from mine. If he moved forward just a fraction, our mouths would be touching.

"Made of metal," he says.

Kissing him would be a stupid move. Monumentally stupid, epic levels of stupid—the kind of stupid that gets written down in the history books. And I'm not going to, but in that moment, I think if he closed the gap between us, I'd probably kiss him back. I can blame it on a number of things: the dry, cold New Mexico night air getting to my head, homesickness (okay, not that), temporary insanity. If he kissed *me*, then I'd just be reacting, which would be beyond my control—

isn't that like one of Newton's laws or something? And then maybe I could live with myself. If I had physics on my side.

But Jake doesn't make a move to kiss me. He just looks at me for a really long time, his fingers sliding down my wrist and grabbing my hand.

My chest tightens, and suddenly I feel like crying, for no reason at all. "Like you would even know," I spit at him, then yank out of his loose grip. I turn on my heel and stalk away, shivering. All of a sudden the night seems so much colder.

eleven

"Daddy, I know. I didn't think you'd be so upset. No! We're not in any trouble. I just thought we could use a little...vacation."

The sound of Laney's voice stirs me out of sleep. I sit up on my elbows and look over to see her perched next to me, legs crossed yoga-style, talking into her cell phone. She winds one of her loose curls around her finger absentmindedly. When she notices I'm awake, she glances over briefly, but doesn't quite smile.

"Yes, I'm telling the truth," she says into the phone. "No, we don't need any money. Okay, I will. I promise! Tell them everything is cool. Daddy, it's just an expression. All right, I know. Of course. Love you, too. 'Bye." She clicks off the phone and holds it out to me. "You need to call your mom."

I wrap the blanket around my shoulders. What I really want to do is hide under it and pretend I didn't hear any of that conversation. It only serves as a reminder of what is waiting for me back home. "Why?"

"Because if you don't, our parents are going to sic the cops on us."

There's a motivation if I ever needed one.

"They're bluffing," I say, but I don't really believe myself.

Neither does Laney. "Harper, I'm serious here," she says. "My dad is not happy about this."

"Did he freak out?"

"He's not exactly jumping for joy at the moment. Especially since your family is flipping out. He was all, 'I know you and Harper are close, and you need this healing time, but you've worried everyone and have a responsibility to come home and cope with this properly, blah freaking blah.' The only reason he's sympathetic is because he read too much Jack Kerouac in his twenties."

I worry at my bottom lip. "Do you really think they're going to call the cops?"

"Apparently your aunt Helen keeps threatening to call them herself, but he's managed to prevent her from doing it so far," she says. "But he says he can't keep stalling if you won't call to let them know you're okay. I hate to say it, but he's right. You owe them a phone call."

My stomach tightens in knots. "I'm going to," I tell her. "When we get to California."

"No," Laney says adamantly. "You're calling now." She starts to dial, and before I can steal the phone from her hands, it's ringing. I glare and press it to my ear.

On the third ring, someone answers. "Hello?" It's my mom, her voice surprisingly breezy, like I've caught her just coming in or about to leave. I breathe a sigh of relief. I can't handle another conversation with Aunt Helen.

"Hey, Mom."

"Harper?" Her tone changes. At least she doesn't sound angry—but then, how much of someone's mood can you infer from two syllables? "Is that you?"

"Who else would it be? Unless you have some illegitimate

children you'd like to tell me about," I say, trying to keep it light.

"It's good to hear your voice." Okay, pleasantries. I haven't really prepared myself for that. I expected something more along the lines of vicious screaming, maybe some drunken sobbing and *how-could-you-do-this-to-me-you-ruin-everything* ranting. "Are you okay?" she presses. "Is anything wrong?"

"Nothing's wrong. I'm fine. We're both fine." I can't quite keep the note of surprise out of my voice. I clear my throat and glance at Laney, who gives me a supportive smile. "Um. How are—things? With you?"

She pauses for a really long time before saying, "I don't know how I'm supposed to answer that, Harper."

Point taken. I pick at the hole in my jeans at the knee, pulling up white strings of thread. "So…have you gone back to work yet?"

"What? Have I—? Harper, I just lost one daughter, and the other has run away. What do you think?" She sounds incredulous.

"Yeah, stupid question, I guess." This is even harder than I thought it'd be. "I'm sorry," I say, and mean it. "This isn't about hurting you. I know you don't believe me, but I mean that."

"Does this mean you're coming home?"

I can't yet. "I will soon," I promise. "I swear. I just— I have to do this first."

"Do *what*?"

"It's for June," I whisper. "Trust me on this. Please, just trust me."

Her breath hitches. I expect crying, but instead she says, "Okay. Okay, I trust you, Harper," the sound of her voice like shattered glass.

By the time we hang up, I'm pretty sure I've convinced her

to keep Aunt Helen reined in for a little while longer. I hand the phone back to Laney with a long sigh.

"She must be really freaked out," Laney remarks. She sounds almost...jealous.

"You're lucky your parents let you do what you want," I tell her.

She shrugs and tucks her phone into her jeans pocket without answering. When she looks back up at me, she's smiling.

"Totally," she agrees. She climbs out of the van before I can say anything else.

I never would've thought in any universe, existing or alternate, Laney Sterling would ever be jealous of me. She always acts like she loves her freedom. Her parents basically give her free rein, as long as she keeps her grades up, and turn a blind eye to everything else. I don't think she's ever been grounded in her life. Really, even after this whole mess, her father seems more mildly annoyed than actually angry.

Laney makes me feel like a shitty daughter, and an even shittier friend, and the worst part is that if I asked her if I was either, she'd tell me to shut up and stop being an idiot. Even if secretly she thought it was true.

And I'm pretty sure it might be true.

Apparently Jake has decided we aren't talking, because he barely says a word to me when we pack up our things and drive out, just hits the highway and turns the music up loud. No *Behind the Music*-esque history lessons for me today. I do see the front of the CD case before he tosses it on the floor—Fleetwood Mac. They have some corny lyrics, but the melodies are enjoyable enough.

Being on the receiving end of Jake's silent treatment isn't so bad; at least New Mexico is a nice change of pace. We drive by long stretches of desert, sparse bushes, and I can make out some rocky areas in the distance. I don't mind leaning my forehead against the window, letting the vibrations chatter my teeth and thrum through me as the scenery flies by.

Laney pulls out her bag of nail polish colors and begins to work on her nails. I look down at my feet, remembering the last time I painted them. The color has somewhat flaked off, but I can still pinpoint that zigzag red smear on my big toe, from when June interrupted me and—

I force myself to not think about it. The next time we stop, I'll pick up some polish remover and take care of it once and for all.

"Hey, Laney, can I have some?" I ask over my shoulder.

"What color?"

"Black."

She snorts. "I'm shocked." But she searches in the bag and withdraws the small bottle, drops it into my outstretched palm.

I brace my hand against the dashboard, unscrew the bottle top and very carefully swipe the brush over my thumbnail. The process is tedious; Joplin's rattling over every little bump in the road doesn't help matters.

"You're stinking up my car," Jake complains as I start on the middle finger of my left hand.

I roll my eyes. "I'm almost done." I finish the last two fingers, topping off the pinkie with a flourish. "So, you've decided we're good enough to speak to again?" I raise my eyebrows at him.

"Keep up the attitude and I might change my mind."

"Your silence would be a gift, Jake." Laney shakes out her hand and examines her freshly painted nails. "You know, if it was up to me, we would extend this road trip to last all summer. When I get home, my mother is going to ground me just as an excuse to make me study for the SATs twenty-four seven."

"Is she still pushing for U of M?" I ask. The University of Michigan is her mother's alma mater.

"Of course. I'd so rather go to NYU, or USC. Somewhere where things are *happening*," she says. "My dad thinks I should go to Dartmouth. Like I could even get *in* to Dartmouth if I wanted to! My GPA is not that stellar. I don't know if it'll even get me into any of my top choices."

"That must be hard," Jake says flatly. "Let me guess, Daddy is the one who will be footing the bill for this dream school of yours?"

"What's your point?"

"Do you even listen to yourself?" he asks, voice rising with a mix of disgust and incredulity. "You might not get into your number-one college. Poor you! Let me pass you a tissue so you can cry over it some more while the rest of us deal with *real* problems."

"What crawled up your ass and died, Jake?" Laney bristles. "You don't know me. You don't know what my life is like."

"I know *exactly* what you're like," he retorts. "You're one of those types—'Oh, let me constantly whine about my privileged, perfect existence and whore it up around town because Daddy doesn't love me enough.'"

Laney recoils like she's been slapped. I twist around to stare at him, shocked. "What the hell did you just say?"

Jake clenches his jaw. "I don't know why I bother with spoiled brats. The both of you."

"Apologize," I demand in a low voice. "Apologize, right now, or I am getting out of this car and walking to California if I have to. Do you hear me?" He slides his eyes over at me wordlessly, so I know he's listening. "Do you hear me?" I yell it so loud that he flinches, hands jerking on the steering wheel.

Suddenly there's a loud popping sound, and Laney screams. I brace my hands hard against the dashboard as the van swerves to one side, the seat belt cutting into my collarbone hard enough to break skin. Jake curses loudly, slams on the brakes and pulls over onto the shoulder of the road.

For a few seconds we all sit there, no one breathing a word, and then Jake says, "Is everyone okay?" He sounds out of breath.

"What—what was that?" Laney asks shakily.

"I think we've got a flat." He looks over at me, but I just stare straight ahead. "Harper? Are you okay?"

I don't answer. I undo my belt with trembling hands and climb out of the van, slam the door and then kick it as hard as I can. My big toe throbs and it's so fucking hot and dry out here but I don't care. I can't be here right now. I turn toward the desert and start walking. I hear the back door open, and Laney's voice as she calls my name, but I don't stop, not until I've reached a massive gray rock a couple yards away. It's weird to see a random, big-ass rock in the middle of nowhere. I put my hands on the granite, scramble for a foothold and clamber on top of it.

There's nothing in front of me but miles and miles of flat desert, yellow and gold and orange, stretching out until the sky meets the horizon, the deepest, clearest blue I've ever seen. I stand there and look out at it, the blazing sun stinging my eyes until my vision goes liquid fuzzy, and I wonder how far it goes before it hits anything. How far you'd have to walk before finding civilization.

God, I hate everything. I hate Jake and I hate his stupid van and I hate that people can be so horrible to Laney and she just *takes* it, because—because why? Because she likes the attention? Because she thinks she deserves it? I've always thought of her as this totally fearless person, but then she just lets herself get walked all over like she's a freaking doormat.

And I hate that I expected better from Jake. I should've known. He's no different from anyone else.

A scream bubbles up in my chest, rips out of my throat from somewhere in the depths of my gut and reverberates into nothing. Even after I've stopped I can hear the echoes ringing in my ears. And then I'm just standing there, breathing raggedly, everything in me empty and aching.

"Harper, stop it!" Laney's behind me, screaming too, on the verge of frantic tears. "Stop it! Stop!"

I turn around slowly so I'm standing sentinel over her and Jake. Laney looks panicked, but he is perfectly calm, unmoving.

"It's okay," Laney says. "It's okay. It's okay."

"Stop saying that! It is not okay!" I yell. "It is so *not* okay! It isn't okay for a guy to treat you like you're a piece of crap—" I point to Jake "—and it isn't okay for you to be a raging asshole for no reason, and we have to stop pretending things are okay. *Nothing* is okay."

I can see the road from here. A pickup truck rolls by, slows as it approaches the van but doesn't stop. None of us speak until it's out of sight.

"I'm sorry," Jake says. He turns to Laney. "I didn't mean it."

She lifts a shoulder and drops it. "Yeah, you did," she says, very pointedly avoiding eye contact. "Whatever. It's fine. I mean. It's not fine, but I forgive you or whatever." She looks to me. "Will you get down now?"

"All right." I sit and shimmy off the rock, land on the dusty ground. "Let's go fix the damn tire."

"Shit." Jake stares into the back of the van with one hand slapped over his face. "Shit. Shit. Shit."

"You're an idiot," I tell him. "A spare but no jack? You are such. An. Idiot."

"Eli must've borrowed it and not put it back," he says. He's still moving around bags and blankets, searching for the jack even though we've torn the van apart five times already. "Shit. *Shit.*"

I look at Laney, sitting on the side of the road, squinting down at her cell phone. She's been texting Seth for the last fifteen minutes. "What does Seth say?" I ask.

"Seth says, and I quote, 'Jake is an idiot,'" she says. Seth is a good study of human character.

Jake curses a few more times and stalks off around the van, jumping up and sitting on the hood. I follow and watch as he paws his pockets madly, until he eventually fumbles out a cigarette. I walk around so I'm standing in front of him.

"What should we do?" I ask.

He doesn't look at me as he shakes his lighter and tries to flick up a flame. "Do I look like I have an answer to that?" I really could just punch him in the mouth, I swear.

"What is wrong with you?" I snatch the lighter out of his hands and throw it on the ground. "Why are you being such a dick?"

He stares at me with the unlit cigarette hanging on his lower lip and says, "We're not friends, Harper. Don't act like we are."

I'm wrong—Jake isn't the idiot, I am. Because somehow these words sting, even though I know they're true. We aren't friends. After California, this'll all be over, and I'll go back to never thinking about Jacob Tolan and his stupid unkempt hair and his sucky attitude, and my life will be better for it.

Probably.

Maybe.

I can't quite look him in the eye when I say, "Fine. I'll have Laney call for a towing service."

"Wait, don't. Not yet. Give me a minute to think."

"We have to do *something*. We're stuck in the middle of nowhere, in case you hadn't noticed."

"If someone comes out, sees the two of you and starts asking questions—"

"You're being paranoid."

"That's easy for you to say! It's not your ass on the line here, Scott."

"You chose to come," I remind him. "Nobody put a gun to your head. If it's really that bad, why are you even here?"

Jake looks uneasy again, but before I can question him further, his eyes shift to some point over my shoulder. I turn to see a beat-up station wagon painted with black-and-white stripes rumbling up the road in our direction. It passes, then skids to an abrupt halt and zooms back in Reverse, tires squealing. The dust hasn't yet settled when the engine cuts and the driver's door opens.

A boy with dyed pink hair sticks out his head. "What up, motherfuckers? Got some car trouble?"

"Um…" Jake hops off the van hood and brushes off his jeans. "Yeah, actually. Flat tire. I've got a spare but I'm missing my jack."

"Oh, we can fix that," the boy says easily, and Jake and I share a glance. We?

The back doors of the station wagon fly open, and out tumble five more kids: four boys and one girl. The boys are dressed in ratty T-shirts and baggy pants with silver chains, their hair dyed every color of the rainbow (and then some), with all kinds of piercings from noses to eyebrows to lips to ears. The sole girl has tightly coiled red curls and bright eyes and is wearing a pair of knee-high leather boots and a barely there miniskirt. It's the most surreal thing I've ever seen—a bunch of punk kids in a zebra-striped station wagon in the middle of the desert.

"Am I hallucinating?" I mutter to Jake under my breath as the kids walk toward us. "Is this some mirage brought on by severe dehydration?"

Jake tilts his head to one side as the pink-haired boy pops his trunk. "I'm...really not sure."

The boy comes back with a car jack and wrench in hand, and he and Jake walk over to the busted rear tire. The rest of the kids crowd around Laney and me and rattle off their names—I don't remember any of them because it's too hot to focus, so I decide to call them by what they look like. There's Redhead Girl, and Goonies T-Shirt Boy, and Boy With So Many Piercings You Can Hardly See His Face, and so on and so on.

Goonies Boy joins the pink-haired boy and Jake, and I follow, standing back to watch them work.

"I hope you know what you're doing, dude," Pink-haired Boy says to Jake. "My dad makes me keep the tools, but I am *so* not mechanically inclined."

Jake seems like he's done this before; with the other boy's help, he loosens the nuts with the wrench, jacks up the car and sets to replacing the tire. In a few minutes the spare is snugly in place.

Pink-haired Boy looks at Jake and says, "Holy shit!"

"It wasn't that hard," Jake says modestly as he wipes off his hands on his jeans.

"No, not the tire. Your shirt. Holy shit, that is one sick design!"

I look at Jake. His black shirt has the words Robot Suicide Squad splashed across the front in white, and below that a stencil of a square robot holding a gun to its head.

"Classy," I tell him. "Is that a band?"

"Yeah. They're heavy grunge, slash numetal, slash hardcore,

depending on the album." He glances down at his shirt and back up at Pink-haired Boy. "So you must be a fan, I take it?"

"Hell yes!" Pink-haired Boy exclaims. "So, you guys are on your way to their show, right?"

"Show? What show?"

"Dude. They're playing in Flagstaff. We're all road tripping just for the occasion, man. Seriously, you should come. It's going to be *legendary*."

Jake hesitates. "I don't know—"

"We should," I cut in. "I mean, if you want to, we should. We're not exactly on a tight schedule here."

I don't know why I'm being so nice; Jake's acting like a jerk, but maybe he needs a break from the driving and the monotony. Yes, he chose to come, but he can't be having the time of his life carting Laney and me around, and we've driven this far, so what's a few more hours? We could all use the opportunity to blow off some steam before we implode.

"Well..." Jake purses his mouth as he considers. "I guess—"

"So that seals the deal," Pink-haired Boy crows, pumping one fist in the air. "Next stop, Flagstaff, baby!"

Three and a half hours later and I'm in the middle of a mosh pit.

Being in a mosh pit is what I imagine being packed in a tin of sardines must be like. I'm squeezed in at the very front of the stage, crammed in with the other people crowded there, and as soon as the music starts, it's basically a free-for-all—dancing, jumping, elbowing, pushing, knocking people down... nothing is sacred. Doing things that would normally get you an aggravated assault charge in real life is not only acceptable, but encouraged.

I've never moshed before. I never had the opportunity— the best you can get in Grand Lake is a lame group of white boys playing crap guitar in their parents' basements on Saturday nights, thinking they're hot shit, with a few underclassmen jumping around like a bunch of morons and pretending to be drunker than they actually are.

The venue in Flagstaff is totally different. Sure, it's in a basement, but in the refurbished basement of a nightclub. Also, there are ten times more people present than any local "show" I've attended in the past. Even with the crowd, Jake, Laney and I manage to sneak to the front with the help of Pink-haired Boy and his posse.

"R.S.S. are kickass!" Redhead Girl shouts in my ear to be heard over the din. I still don't know her name, which makes it a little weird since she's practically on top of me. "You're going to love them, for fucking serious!"

I decide to take her word for it. I look around and realize that aside from Redhead Girl and Laney, there are no other girls in the pit.

"Hey, where are all the girls?" I yell to Redhead Girl.

She scrunches her face at me and yells, "What? You're going to hurl?"

It doesn't really matter that she can't hear because in five minutes I get my answer: the opening band, who call themselves the Big Fear, roars into their first song, and everyone begins to thrash around, all at once. Some burly guy twice my size slams hard into my shoulder, and then another one does on the other side, and it's only a matter of seconds before I'm smashed out of the pit and into the outer edges of what seems to be a safety zone, which has a far higher ratio of girls.

I'm still gathering my bearings and my equilibrium when Jake brushes past a few people and comes up to me. I'm afraid he's going to look concerned. I don't want to be the kind of girl who needs to be checked on and looked after—and as soon as I think it, I realize it's because I don't want to be like my mom.

Thankfully, Jake looks more amused than anything else. He leans in close to my ear, his hand on my waist to pull me in closer, and says, "You're not going to let some assholes chase you off, are you?"

I glance down at where his hand is and try not to blush. When I look back up, his face is only centimeters away from mine. God, why does he have to be so pretty in such close proximity, even when he's all sweaty? Why do I have to get these fluttery feelings when I look at his face and feel his hand on my hip, even though he's been an utter dick all day?

It was so much easier when all I felt toward him was annoyance.

"Please," I scoff. "I'm just strategizing on the best way to get back in."

"Keep your elbows up and you'll be fine."

He's right. I keep my elbows up and don't hesitate to shove back, and I'm able to hold my own. By the time Robot Suicide Squad takes the stage, plugging in their leads, my shirt is drenched in sweat. The room is almost too hot to breathe in. I don't care. There's something exhilarating about being in the pit—knowing that everyone has fought to be here, that we're all here for the same reason.

We slam-dance all the way through Robot Suicide Squad's set. People frantically shove, and I receive a few whacks from those behind, but I avoid getting the crap kicked out of me. The band is equally hardcore as the crowd—the bassist throws himself against the wall, against the floor, and the lead singer beats himself over the head with his mike until he gashes open his forehead. The wound bleeds in a sluggish trail down his face. Every time I glance over at Jake, he's staring at me with this huge grin, and when I yell "What?" over the music, he just shakes his head and turns his attention back to the band.

As soon as the last riff of the last song fades into screeching guitar feedback, the band members all drop their instruments and abandon the stage. The drummer pauses long enough to hurl his drumsticks into the audience, one after the other. Apparently he isn't concerned with being responsible for any concussions.

Of course, with the moshers already beating the crap out of each other, they probably don't care much, either.

I'm hanging outside the bathroom, waiting for Jake, when Laney runs up and pulls me into a sideways hug and says, "That was *amazing*!"

I don't really like being hugged and she's pretty sweaty, but then, she's Laney and so I let her. I lost her halfway into the opening band's set, so it's a relief to see she's all in one piece.

The guy behind her says, "I'll show you something amazing, babe." His words come out all slurred. He's huge and bald and has this crazy spiderweb tattoo on his neck, and there's this weird piercing in his nose with a silver chain connecting to his ear.

"Don't bother. I'm sure I've seen it before," she tells him drily.

"Oh, I don't think you have." He moves in closer, and I almost gag on the overwhelming stench of liquor. Ew. Someone's been spending quality time with Jack Daniel's. "So tell me—your tits. They real?"

"About as real as my interest in you," she says, turning away.

He laughs too loud, reaches forward and grabs her ass. She gasps and whirls around to face him, and I pull her back so she's hidden behind me. What the hell? Who does that?

Oh, right. Stupid assholes drunk out of their minds.

I glare at him. "Leave her alone."

"No one's talking to you, you dried-up cunt."

"Is there a problem?" Jake's suddenly here, stepping between us. Even though he's taller than me, the other guy still has a few inches on him. Not to mention, like, seventy pounds.

The guy squares his shoulders and says, "I think you need to keep your bitches on a leash."

"Maybe you need to go die in a fire," I snap.

The guy's face twists with anger. He rushes forward, but then Jake pushes me out of the way, and for all his trouble gets welcomed with the guy's fist flying into his face. It makes a sound, but not as loud as the sound of him tumbling to the floor. The people around us gasp and laugh in shocked surprise.

Oh, it is *so* on.

I lash one hand out and snatch the guy's silver chain. He cries out in pain as I rip it out of his nose.

"Stupid bitch," he spits, and that's when I mentally punch him in the face.

Except it isn't just mentally—it's for real, my closed fist is actually moving. It hits him square in the nose with a sickening crunch.

"Oh my God," Laney breathes from behind me.

"Oh my God," Jake says from the floor.

My eyes widen. "Oh my God."

There's a moment that's barely even a moment—it can't be more than a second or two—where everyone around us falls dead silent, collectively holding their breath as the guy staggers back with his hands covering his nose, which is gushing blood like a fountain. But then the moment of stunned silence is over, and someone pushes him to the ground, and all of a sudden people are shoving and fists are flying everywhere.

I'm elbowing some guy in the face when strong arms wrap around my stomach from behind and heft me up high. I kick and struggle and scream at the top of my lungs as the person drags me out from the crowd, and it's not until I'm unceremoniously dumped in the back alley that I roll over and see that it's a security officer who grabbed me.

"And stay the fuck out," he says, right before slamming the door in my face.

I sit up slowly to assess the damage. The elbow I scraped at the protest flares with pain, and I'll definitely be bruised in a lot of interesting places by tomorrow morning, but I think for the most part I'm okay.

Someone laughs and says, "Having a rough night?"

I twist around, wincing a little at the movement, to see that the disembodied voice belongs to someone standing farther down in the alley. All I can make out is a silhouette and the orange embers glowing from the tip of his clove cigarette, but then he steps into the pool of light emanating from the lamplight above. He's all jet-black hair and winter pale skin, and he has the widest smile I've ever seen. It splits his face and shows all of his shiny and even teeth.

"I've had worse." I stand up a little shakily and inspect my elbow. Not bleeding. So that's something.

"You're not from around here, are you?" the guy asks.

"What makes you think that?"

"You don't look like you fit in this scene."

I'm not sure if that's supposed to be an insult. "If that's how all the guys in this 'scene' act, then that's probably a good thing."

He waves smoke away from his face and grimaces. "Those stupid horny fucks? Ignore them. Half the guys who come to these shows are just idiots wanting to indiscriminately beat the crap out of each other. Or worse, neo-Nazi assholes co-opting the scene as their own. They don't even listen to the lyrics. Otherwise they'd know we're anti-Nazi. Antisexism, antiracism, anticorporate tools, antiestablishment—"

"Anti-everything?"

"Practically," he laughs.

He leans against the grimy brick, and the light slashes across his face in a way that illuminates the large white bandage plastered over his right temple.

"You're that guy," I realize. "The singer. From Robot Suicide Squad."

"Quentin Williams, at your service." He pushes himself off the wall and does this little bow thing that makes me grin, before sticking out his hand.

I shake it; his palm is hot and dry. "Harper Scott."

"As in *To Kill A Mockingbird*-writing, friend of Truman Capote, reclusive author Harper?" he asks.

"The one and only." I'm surprised. It isn't often people recognize my namesake.

"So if you're not local, where are you from?"

"Michigan, born and bred. It's a lot cooler there. Weather-wise, I mean."

"You traveled all the way here for our show?"

"Not exactly. This was sort of an unplanned detour. We're on our way to California." His face falls a little. "But you guys were great," I assure him. "Really."

"Overinflated ego. It's an occupational hazard," he says, recovering with a self-effacing grin. "So, who is this 'we'?"

"Harper!"

Footsteps pound on the pavement, and I turn to see Laney and Jake running down the alley. They stop a few feet short of us, out of breath.

"Are you guys okay?" I ask.

Laney's bent with her hands on her knees as she pants. "Us? You're the one who punched a dude in the face!"

"Nice," Quentin says appreciatively.

"I've got a few scrapes, but I'll live," I tell her. "So, this is—"

"Quentin Williams. I know." Jake looks to me, then to Quentin, and then to my hand, which Quentin is still holding. I drop it quickly. "You were great tonight, man," he adds.

"And my wounded pride makes a resounding comeback," Quentin says with a smirk shot my way. "You know, the band's chilling in the bus right now. You guys wanna come check it out?"

twelve

It turns out a tour bus looks a lot like a Moroccan opium den: clouds of pot smoke and strange decor. Who knew punks were into tasseled throw pillows?

"This place is awesome," Laney says, shouldering past me and farther into the bus. "You guys must have a blast touring."

Quentin tosses his head to the side, flipping his shaggy hair out of his eyes. "Touring's cool. Flagstaff is too hot for me, though. At least the turnout was good," he says. "Let me introduce you to the band. The guy with the neck tat is our drummer, Dom, and next to him is our bassist, Shane—"

"Wait," Laney says, "you mean *them?*"

I peer over her shoulder to see what she's gawking at. The drop-dead gorgeous drummer with high cheekbones is on one of the couch benches, making out with the bassist.

The very male bassist.

"Oh," I say, out loud.

Laney stifles a laugh into her hand, leans into my ear and hisses, "That is *so* hot."

It really is. I stare, transfixed.

"So," Quentin says, "what'd you think of the set?"

"It was amazing," Jake says. "I mean, the bass line alone in 'Revolution Is an Excuse to Party' kills me every time. And the crazy chord progression after the second verse—that took forever for me to learn." His cheeks go red, much to my amusement. He's such a fanboy.

"Hey, Dom!" Quentin calls to the drummer. "You should hear this. Someone is actually complimenting your boy's skills. Maybe you oughta document this occasion with a picture or something, you know, since it happens so rarely."

"Fucker." Shane, the bassist, extracts himself from Dom, the drummer, and punches Quentin in the shoulder. Then he nods at Jake. "I heard that, man. Thanks. So you play, too?"

"Not really. I mean, I mess around a little, that's all. The bass isn't even mine. It's my brother's."

"He's really good," I insist, overly defensive. Jake *does* have talent. Why's he trying to brush it off like it's nothing?

Shane glances at me and then back at Jake. "You write any original stuff?"

"No," he says quickly with a shake of his head. "Definitely not."

"Too bad."

I remember then that I have my camera on me. I grabbed it from the van before we went to the bus.

"Hey," I say, pulling off my pack and reaching for it, "would you mind if I—?" I hold up the Polaroid tentatively.

Dom pauses from rolling a blunt between his fingers to frown. "Wait a minute. Are these going to wind up on the internet?"

"Uh…" I pause. "No?"

"Fair enough."

I snap away as everyone else sits down, getting comfortable. At first Quentin, Shane and Dom make faces at the camera, alternately growling and sneering and leering lewdly, but after a few minutes they drop the poses. That's when I get the best shots—Jake, in intense conversation with Shane about chord progressions; Laney laughing at some elaborate story Quentin is telling about getting pulled over by the cops in San Antonio; Dom, beating out a rhythm on his thighs and nuzzling at Shane's shoulder.

I feel part of it all and completely separate at the same time.

I turn to Quentin, who is closest to me, and tell him I'm going to go get some air.

"I'll come with you," he says.

He follows me down the bus steps and out into the dark and empty parking lot. The feeling in the night air is weird, like it's at a standstill. No breeze.

"So what's in California?" he asks, bumping his shoulder into mine.

I look down at the camera in my hands and shrug. "I don't know."

"Aw, don't hold out on me. You've gotta have a reason for going."

I don't really want to explain it to him in detail, so I keep my eyes down as I fiddle with the camera strap. "Some people think that a place can save them," I say. "Like if they could just be somewhere else, their lives would be totally different. They could finally be the people they always wanted to be. But to me, a place is just a place. If you really want things to change, you can make them change no matter where you are." I look up at him. "Does that make sense?"

Quentin stares at me, his face schooled in a pensive expression, and for a second I think maybe he understands. Maybe someone does.

But then he cracks a bemused smile and says, "Wow. That shit is too deep for me."

Well, it was a long shot. My thoughts don't make sense even to me most of the time.

Suddenly Quentin lunges forward and steals the camera from my hands. He lifts it up, pointing the lens at me, and I instinctively cover my face with my arms.

"Come on," he cajoles. "No fair. You take everyone else's picture, but no one can take yours? That's how it is?"

"That's *exactly* how it is. I hate having my picture taken."

I peek at him cautiously through my fingers as he lowers the camera. I rush forward to dive for it, but he quickly raises it over his head again. Since he's at least half a foot taller than me, no matter how high I try to jump, I don't come close. Finally I stop, huffing, and cross my arms over my chest.

"Give it back," I demand.

"I will," he says, "if you let me take your picture."

"Fine." I toss my hands up in defeat. "Go ahead."

He holds the camera to his face and peers through the viewfinder as I glower. A second later he pulls it away, head shaking. "Nah, it's no good unless you're smiling."

"I don't smile unless I have a reason."

"All right. Then I'll give you one."

Quentin ambushes me, his hands grabbing at my rib cage, tickling my sides. I jerk backward and stumble so hard my back rams up against the side of the bus.

"Stop," I gasp, trying to bat his hands away. "Seriously, Quentin, don't—"

He does stop. He slides his hands down from my ribs to circle my waist. I try to remember, through wheezes, how to breathe normally as he leans down, his breath hot against my face. I know that he'll kiss me if I don't stop him. Part of me doesn't want to stop him, because Quentin doesn't know who I am, doesn't know about June—he just sees a girl with a camera who rambles nonsensically. Maybe that's the same reason he wants to kiss me; before tonight I'd never even heard of the legendary Quentin Williams, I don't own any Robot Suicide Squad albums, I just see a guy with black hair and pale skin and a killer smile.

Too bad that at this range, all I can focus on is how he reeks of pot and stale beer and sweat.

"Dammit. Shitty piece of—"

I glance to my left to see Jake, cigarette dangling between his lips. He shakes out his malfunctioning lighter and curses a few times. And then he looks up, and I'm looking at him, and Quentin has his hands around my waist, and—

Jake stops dead in his tracks. He stares at us for a few seconds, frozen, before whirling around and rushing off, all without a word.

"Get off me," I choke out through gritted teeth. I shove Quentin back a few steps and snatch my camera from his hands.

He fixes me with a bewildered look and says, "It was just a joke. I didn't mean to—"

"Well, it wasn't funny," I snap hotly.

My legs won't stop shaking. God, Jake's face—

"Is that guy your boyfriend or something?" Quentin asks, more curious than anything.

"No! God, he's not—" I stop and take a breath. *"No."*

He raises one eyebrow at me like he thinks I'm full of shit.

"I'm not anyone's anything," I insist. "Believe me."

I tug down my shirt from where Quentin's hands rucked it up, angry, embarrassed. At least my camera didn't break in our scuffle. There's a picture sticking out of the bottom—I yank it out to see a reflection of myself, hands blocking my face from view. I rip the photo down the middle and drop the remnants.

He watches both halves flutter to the ground. "You're pissed," he observes.

"You think?" I sigh, running my hands through my hair. I hate that I'm so flustered. "I just didn't expect to get jumped on. It freaked me out."

"Some girls like the element of surprise."

"I'm not *some girl*," I shoot back.

A half smile curves Quentin's lips as he looks at me. "You're really, really not, are you?"

I expect Jake to act all weird and annoying when we get back. But he doesn't. He acts totally normal, even when Quentin and I board the bus together, my face still flushed. Not long after that, Quentin announces they have to hit the road.

I'm halfway out the bus when he puts a hand on my shoulder and says, "Hey."

I glance once at Jake, his arms crossed, eyes on the ground like the cigarette butts littered there are fascinating, before I turn to face Quentin.

He flashes me that sparkling smile. "You should Facebook me or something," he says.

Facebook. How very punk rock.

I don't know what else to do but nod. Quentin waves and heads back into the bus, and Jake, Laney and I walk to Joplin, parked on the other side of the lot.

Jake continues to act like nothing is wrong as we pore over the atlas and navigate toward the main westbound route. I feel guilty, and even more than that, irritated with myself for feeling guilty when I have no reason to.

Before getting onto the highway, Jake pulls into the parking lot of a drugstore. "We should stock up on supplies," he explains.

Laney has been quiet since we left the bus. After picking

myself up a wrapped turkey sandwich, some Skittles and a water bottle, I find her in front of the pop coolers, considering the different brands.

"What's up?" I ask.

She doesn't answer for a moment, then snaps out of whatever daze she's in and looks at me. "Oh. Just the eternal debate. Trying to decide between cherry and diet."

"Ah, yes." I nod gravely. "A question for the ages."

"Exactly," she says. She glances over her shoulder toward the door. "Why don't you pay and wait in the van? I might be a minute."

I shrug. "Okay."

As soon as I've checked out and pushed through the door, I nearly barrel smack-dab into Jake. He has a coffee in one hand, a lit cigarette in his mouth (big shock there) and two white plastic bags hanging off the other arm.

I falter for a second before deciding the best approach is to adopt his: act totally normal. "Hey," I say carefully. "What did you buy?"

"Stuff," he replies. He doesn't elaborate.

"Thanks for the clarification." I roll my eyes.

He doesn't even look at me. Apparently staring at the pavement is more interesting than engaging in conversation with me.

Suddenly I blurt out, "Quentin and I—we didn't do anything."

Ahhhhhhh! Why, why, *why* does my mouth never listen to my brain? So much for playing it cool. So much for maintaining my dignity.

Jake taps the ash off his cigarette and regards me impassively. "Okay."

"And even if we did, which we didn't, it's none of your business."

"Okay."

"I just wanted you to know."

"Okay."

"If you say okay one more time, I'm going to punch you in the solar plexus."

His eyebrows jump. "The solar plexus, huh?"

"Yes," I say. "I'm not exactly sure where that is, but I will find out. And then I will punch you there. Hard."

"Look," he says. He inhales sharply. "You're right. It's not my business. You are free to do whatever you want with whomever you want. It really doesn't matter to me."

I wonder if he believes me. I wonder why I care so much that he does. Jesus, it's *Jake.*

I study him for a long beat and say, "Good."

Except it isn't, because somehow what he's said only makes me feel worse.

"So, how far is California from here?" Laney joins us outside, a piece of licorice stuck in her mouth. She tears a big bite out of the strand and chomps on it loudly.

"I talked to the guy inside, and he said it's about five hours to L.A.," Jake says. "I'm thinking we drive past and hit up a motel in Huntington Beach near the shore, since we're going to take the highway up the coast anyway. We can spend tomorrow chilling out before driving to San Fran."

"Finally!" She pumps one fist in the air. "All of this driving is making me crazy."

I have to admit I'm getting stir-crazy, too. Not so much that I'm ready to go home yet, but I am starting to long for the comfort of a warm bed instead of a stiff car seat. It feels like we've been on the road forever.

"Are you going to be able to stay awake for the drive?" I ask Jake.

He holds up the coffee cup, jiggles it with a grin. "Isn't that why they invented caffeine?"

★ ★ ★

The moshing experience combined with getting pounced on by a certain overeager Robot Suicide Squad band member has taken its toll on me; I try to stay awake for Jake's benefit, but about an hour into the drive I nod off to the strains of some Nirvana jam. The closer we get to California, the more willing Jake is to play recent music. This means R.E.M., Soundgarden, the Pixies, even Courtney Love's old band—a lot of grunge and punk and alternative. Jake says that's because the only good music made during the nineties fits into those genres.

When he said that, Laney made an indignant noise from the back. "You're ignoring rap," she complained. "If you think you're too indie or alternative or whatever to appreciate Tupac and KRS-One and Tribe Called Quest, then you can eat shit, because you're missing out on something amazing."

I lean my head against the window and close my eyes. I'm so not in the mood for more arguments. Sleep comes easy, dreamless and deep, until Jake rouses me a while later. The first thing I see is his hand on my thigh, shaking me awake. When he notices my open eyes, he quickly draws his hand back.

"Hey," he says softly as I push myself up. "We're in California."

My heart speeds up. I push myself straight in the seat and catch the spreading smile on Jake's face as he senses my growing excitement. Outside in the night, things look the same, mostly. The same endless stretch of highway. Still, knowing that we've made it, finally, makes me want to sit up and drink in everything.

"California?" Laney's leaning forward from the back, rubbing the sleep from her eyes. "We're here?"

Jake looks sheepish. "Sorry. I probably shouldn't have woken you up. I know it's not the most exciting thing ever."

"No," I say quickly, "I'm glad you did." And I am. I want to remember this.

"Oh, I know what would make this perfect!" Laney exclaims. She unbuckles her belt and clambers over the seat, rummages around in the back and returns a minute later with June's urn in her arms. "She should be here for this," she tells me.

I know the urn isn't June. I know that, but I still feel myself choking up a little.

We did it. We're actually here.

The three of us sit and appreciate the significance of the moment for a while. And then Laney says, "I still can't believe you punched a guy in the face."

She giggles, and after a second Jake laughs, and I can't help but laugh, too. It is sort of hilarious in retrospect. Bizarre, and surreal, but hilarious.

"What's even funnier is that Jake here was so quick to defend our honor," I tease, grabbing his chin with my hand.

"Our *hero*," Laney sings as she presses her cheek to his.

I pick up my camera from between our seats and, without warning, take his picture. He makes a face as the flash goes off.

"I hate it when you do that," he says.

"I know, but we need a portrait to commemorate your heroism." I wave the emitted photo back and forth lightly before placing it in the glove compartment with the rest. I listen to the music coming out of the speakers, the low, melancholy singer warbling about the California stars. "Who is this?"

"Wilco," he answers. "Have I told you about them?"

"Not that I remember."

"Ah, now see, that must be remedied. Would you ladies care for some background information?"

Laney snorts. "Like we could stop you if we tried!"

"True."

He grins, and I return his with one of my own, settle into my seat and close my eyes. In front of us the road to California stretches out, and above us the California stars shine, and next to me Jake begins his latest lecture.

thirteen

When we stop at the seaside motel in Huntington Beach, Laney and I get our own room. Jake says it's because he's going to lose it if he doesn't get some alone time—and then Laney is all, *ohhh, alone time, I know what that means, hope you have some extra socks,* and Jake goes to the room adjacent to ours and shuts the door firmly, makes a big show of turning the lock.

I'm happy to have an entire bed to myself, even if the mattress is old and stiff and smells weird. It's more space than I've had in a while, and I want to take up all of it. I reach my arms out so they're braced against the headboard, stretch my legs until my toes curl, and fall asleep to the ancient fan groaning in the corner.

I wake to the sound of muffled sobbing. When my eyes open, my first thought is that it's my mom. Except it can't be her, because she's two thousand miles away from here. I sit up and notice there's a light on in the bathroom. And then I notice Laney's bed is empty.

"Laney?" I pull the sheets off my legs, pad over to the bathroom door and rap my knuckles on the wood. "Laney, what's going on? Are you okay?"

I try the knob, but it doesn't budge. Locked. Shit. I knock a few more times, rattle the knob in vain. She doesn't answer, but I can still hear her crying. I'm getting really, really worried. Panicked. I need her to say something, to tell me she's okay. All I can think of is June and the garage. My chest tightens. I'm having a panic attack. Oh, God.

Jake. Jake will know what to do.

I run out of our motel room in nothing but my long T-shirt and bare feet and pound on his door as hard as I can with both fists. I don't stop pounding until Jake opens it and squints at me.

"What's up?" he asks around a yawn. I hear faint strains of music behind him from the portable CD player he must have set up somewhere.

"Something's wrong with Laney." My heart is racing about a million beats per second, but I'm already feeling a little calmer, having him here in front of me.

He follows me into our room and to the bathroom door. He's smart enough not to waste time trying to coax her out—if she won't come out for me, she won't come out for anyone.

He turns to me. "I can probably jimmy this open."

"You know how to pick locks?" I ask. Before he can answer I say, "Wait, never mind. Of *course* you know how to pick locks."

"Do you have a bobby pin?"

"Yes, right here in my pocket along with this stick of gum, a shoelace and a number two pencil. Will that be enough for you, MacGyver?"

"What about a credit card?"

"What do *you* think? I'm sixteen!" I try to think. "Wait. Hang on." I rifle through my bag for my wallet. "My library card. Will that work?"

Jake slides the card through the crack between the door

and frame. He leans his weight against the hard wood, bending and angling the piece of plastic, jiggling the knob until a soft click sounds. As soon as the door gives, I push past him and into the bathroom.

Laney sits on the floor with her back to the tub, legs drawn to her chest. She turns her tearstained face away from me, body twisting as one hand grabs blindly at the shower curtain. I drop to my knees in front of her, try to make her look at me. The points of her shoulders shake under my hands.

"Laney, stop. Stop for a second. What is going on? What's wrong?"

She closes her eyes as fat tears squeeze out, one after the other, and then holds up one hand. I glance down to see her trembling fingers curled around something that looks like a thermometer.

"What—?" I don't understand. I twist around, searching for Jake. He stands next to the sink, a small cardboard box in his hands.

And then I realize. Not a thermometer.

A pregnancy test.

"Laney…" I turn back to her, swallowing hard, and say, "Are you… Laney, are you pregnant?"

She opens her eyes and nods.

My heart turns to stone in my chest. It does not compute— Laney, my best friend, pregnant. Pregnant by that scumbag Kyle, who apparently got her drunk and took advantage of her while she was three sheets to the wind. For a few seconds I'm too shocked to move, absorbing this information. But when Laney's face crumples again, I put my arms around her, pull her close.

"What am I going to do?" Her body-racking sobs wane into a steady stream of silent tears. "I can't have a baby. What would I— How would I—" She stops, too overwhelmed to consider the possibility.

"It's okay," I soothe. "We'll figure something out."

She shakes her head. "I can't have a baby," she cries. "I can't. I *can't*."

I hold her tight against me. She says I *can't* again and again into my shoulder, until her voice fades and she just breathes raggedly, in and out. It's not like it's rare for Laney to cry—she cries a lot, compared to me—but I haven't seen her fall apart like this. Ever. But she's never had a reason before.

"Laney, if you want to…" I hesitate. "If you want to…end it—"

"You mean, have an abortion."

"Yes," I say. "If you want to have an abortion, we'll figure it out. And—and if you don't, we can figure that out, too. Whatever you want to do, we'll do it."

She goes quiet for a long while. "I—I don't know."

"Okay." I gently smooth the hair off her forehead, and keep stroking it. Laney likes to be touched, and I'm not a touchy-feely person, but I'd do anything for her. Anything to make it better. "It's okay," I say again. "You don't have to make up your mind right now."

She cringes. "Even if I decided to—you know." Her voice gets all wobbly, mouth bending like she's on the verge of tears. "How would I pay for it? It's not like I can hit up my dad and ask to put it on his Visa. Are you kidding? He'll disown me if he finds out! And my mom— Oh, God."

"Don't worry about the cost. I can get you the money."

I'd almost forgotten Jake was in the room. He steps forward, face serious and drawn.

Laney glares. "Oh, that's rich. Why would you do that? I'm just a slut, right? I bet you think I should've kept my legs closed and none of this would've happened."

I could kill Jake for what he said earlier. Laney has problems, I know that better than anyone, but it wasn't his place to say something like that. It's not anyone's place. And now she's going to think this is her fault, and it so is not. There's no excuse for what that Kyle guy did.

On second thought, it's him that I want to kill for hurting my best friend.

Jake looks chagrined. Good. He should.

"I don't have any excuse for what I said before," he says. He's looking Laney right in the eye. "It was wrong. I know that. Look, I'm not telling you to do one thing or the other. But whatever you decide, don't let it be because you don't think you have a choice."

I thought after all of the driving and all of the drama that I would lapse into a coma the second my head hit the pillow. Things don't quite work out that way. While Laney crashes hard, I rise with the sun. As soon as I open my eyes I'm completely awake, staring at the ceiling. It's a dingy white and there's a mysterious rust-brown stain, possibly a handprint. I close my eyes and count backward from one hundred. When that doesn't work, I count again. No luck.

So I decide to run.

June was always the athletic one. She spent three years on the track team—it wasn't her best sport, but it was the one she loved most. She used to tell me that running cleared her head.

Well, my head could use some clearing. Everything is so complicated. The mess with Laney. How I feel about Jake. How I feel about my sister. I want someone to make things black-and-white. Someone to tell me, *These are the people worth caring about, who won't hurt you or let you down. These are the people who will put you through the wringer and abandon you in the worst ways. When it really counts.*

The beach is close—down some stairs, around a corner

and boom. There it is. The ocean. I've never seen the Pacific before, and now it is spread out all in front of me, an endless wall of blue. Less blue than I'd imagined. I'd envisioned that picturesque jewel-turquoise from June's postcard. Waves cap white and roar into the beach, one stacking on top of the next. I hike over the sand to the shoreline, stopping just short of where the tide ripples in, and jump back when it splashes over my toes. Only a few people are out here, some early-morning surfers braving the cool temperatures and paddling out into the water, stomach-down on their boards.

I turn and run as fast as I can. Seagulls caw and fly off in different directions when I cut straight through their cluster. I run, my shoes sinking into the spongy sand with each step, run until my lungs burn and my legs ache. I don't pace myself, I just run and run and June is right, she is so right, I'm not thinking, not about anything, it's just me and my heartbeat in my ears and the sound of the ocean and the sky above it.

I run until I feel like I'm going to pass out, which doesn't take very long, since I have next to zero stamina. I know you're supposed to walk it off, to keep your muscles from cramping and locking up, but my legs wobble and buckle beneath me, so I collapse in a heap on the sand and look out over the waves. For a few seconds I think I feel a crying jag coming on, but it dies somewhere in my throat, and then I think I might throw up, but I don't.

June is gone. For the first time, the enormity of that hits me. Every muscle aches, my heart most of all. I am throbbing with how much I miss her. It hurts worse than anything. I don't know how I'm supposed to be expected to live day to day carrying this kind of pain. I don't know how I'm supposed to go out there, spread her ashes and let her go.

I want to stop running away from everything.

I want to find something to run toward.

★ ★ ★

It's a long time before I head back to the motel. The wind whips my ponytail off the back of my sweaty neck, the air heavy with the scent of salt and morning. Laney is up by the time I return to the room, sitting on the bed and drinking from a foam cup as an infomercial plays on the television.

"I really want a BeDazzler," she says.

I glance at the studded pair of jeans on the screen. "I'll remember that for your birthday."

"I'm holding you to that," she replies. She looks me up and down. "So where were you?"

"Took a walk," I answer evasively on my way to the bathroom. I shut the door and sit on the closed toilet lid for a while with my head in my hands, trying not to feel so shaky, then come back with a towel and eye the coffeepot on the dresser. "I'm surprised you're up," I say. "And you made coffee? Very ambitious."

She shrugs. "You know what they say. Desperate times, and all that."

We watch infomercials for a while, since every other channel comes in static snow. Laney keeps making cracks in a voice too loud and overly enthusiastic; she wants to pretend everything is normal. I don't have the heart to do anything but play along. We'll have to talk about the hard stuff eventually, but for now, it can wait.

Around eleven, I pour a cup of coffee, grab a handful of sugar packets and knock on Jake's door. No answer. I assume he's still asleep. With all of that driving, I hardly blame him. But as I start to walk away, the door creaks open, so I turn back. And nearly drop the coffee.

"God, Jake!" I shield my eyes with one hand. "Put on some pants, would you?"

"Cut it with the histrionics, Scott. It's not like I'm naked." He pauses and adds, "You should be so lucky."

Jesus, isn't it a little early in the morning for suggestive comments?

It's only after he's taken the coffee cup out of my hand that I dare to venture another look. Jake lounges against the doorway with an amused expression. His cheeks are smooth—he must've shaved—and there's a white towel wrapped dangerously low on his narrow hips, revealing the defined V of his pelvic bone.

It's *definitely* too early to be seeing all of that.

I try, and fail, not to stare. "You are so gross," I tell him. Not very convincingly.

"Yeah, and you love every second of it," he says, shaking out his shower-wet hair and spraying me with tiny droplets. I jump back with a surprised squeak. "Besides, you're one to talk. At least I'm not parading around in a sports bra like you."

"I would pay good money to see that, though."

I turn my back until I hear the rustle of denim as he steps into his jeans, the sound of him doing up his zipper, and when I look again, he's in the middle of fastening his belt.

"What's on the agenda today?" I ask.

"There isn't one. That's kind of the point."

He rakes a comb through his hair until it lies flat against his head. It's funny seeing it like that, rather than all disheveled and messy. For the first time I notice his ears—they're nice, close to his head and not too big or too small.

Only *I* would notice a guy's ears when he's half-naked. There's something seriously wrong with me.

"I thought you'd still be sleeping," I say, not looking at his ears. Or his chest. The floor. That's a good, safe place to keep my eyes. "All of that driving—how are you even able to function?"

"A divine combination of caffeine and sheer force of will," he explains. He takes the coffee cup off the nightstand and sips from it. "Where'd you get this? It tastes like shit."

"Laney made it."

"Ah," he says, and drinks some more. "Why don't you guys go hang out at the beach? I'll go pick up some breakfast. Donuts. Donuts sound good?"

I borrow one of Laney's swimsuits, and we stretch out on our towels near the shore, her working on her tan while I read Kurt Vonnegut. When Jake returns, he tosses a greasy white paper bag onto the ground and plops down beside me with little fanfare.

In full daylight the water is a brighter blue, and more surfers have joined the early-morning crowd, riding in the tumbling waves. With the sun out like this, it looks more like June's postcard. Laney sleeps on her stomach, soaking up the rays—which seems unnecessary. Summer has hardly started and already she has a perfect tan, dark and even. I always wanted skin like that. Mine only burns a fierce red and peels before fading to its natural white state.

Jake has a deep tan, too. Not as dark as Laney's, but his skin is a nice ruddy brown. It makes his eyes look even greener.

For lunch we walk down the street to a farmers' market on the pier. Laney buys a homemade decorative birdcage, its metal bars painted a vibrant teal. Jake picks up a loaf of homemade bread, all kinds of fruit and, curiously enough, a bouquet of fresh carnations. Back at the beach Laney and I try to braid the flowers into each other's hair. Mine is too slippery and thin, but a stem weaves into her long curls perfectly, swaying slightly with every turn of her head.

It's a good day. Relaxing. Just what we needed. We spend the afternoon combing the beach for shells and lying out on our towels until the heat is unbearable, then plunging into the surf to cool down. You can't make it too far out before a massive wave rumbles in and sends you toppling. Jake hoists Laney onto his shoulders and lets me try to push her off—he has the height advantage, but I have moxie, and eventually I'm able to tackle him into the water.

"That was not due to your moxie," he says later that night. The sun set a while ago, and we'd all trudged back to the motel; Laney decided to curl up under the covers and watch television while Jake and I sit in the outside hallway, playing cards. "That was due to the monstrous wave that knocked me off of my feet."

"Then that just means the gods are on my side. The god of the sea. Which one would that be? Triton?"

"No, you're thinking of *The Little Mermaid*. You meant to say Poseidon. Unless we're talking Roman mythology, then it would be Neptunus."

"You know, for someone who needed a tutor, you seem to know a lot."

"Mmm." He pauses to light his cigarette, then lays down his last card—the king of clubs. "Well, for someone with such *moxie*, you're pretty bad at Crazy Eights."

I roll my eyes and pool the cards together. "All right, your deal. I'm going to go check on Laney."

I let myself into the room. On the television a bright-eyed woman flails and gestures excitedly with her hands toward a vegetable juicer. I look over at Laney; the glow from the television makes her skin look eerily blue. She's on her back with her eyes closed, and she looks so still.

Too still.

Just like that I'm back in the garage, looking through the backseat window at June, sprawled there, motionless, pill bottle in her limp hand. And I'm throwing open the door, shaking her as hard as I can, saying her name over and over, *oh God please wake up June June June oh God please don't leave me you have to wake up wakeupwakeupwakeup,* but she's cold already, she's so cold, and then someone else is there, saying my name, but I'm not listening because I have to wake up June, June, *wake up*—

"Harper. Harper. *Harper!*"

I blink and the image is gone. My hands are on Laney's shoulders, shaking her, and she's staring at me with eyes like saucers, confused and scared. And breathing. She's breathing. Relief cuts through me so sharply that it knocks me back a step—which is when I realize Jake is there, too, his hand steadying between my shoulder blades.

"I'm sorry," I choke out. "I'm sorry. I thought—"

Dead. I thought she was dead, but I can't say that out loud. I turn on my heel and stumble into the bathroom, retch into the toilet a few times until my stomach cramps and spasms because there's nothing more in it to expel. Laney crouches behind me, her hand stroking my hair.

Eventually I shrug her off and stand. "I'm fine," I promise, after I've rinsed out my mouth and splashed my face with some cold water. "Go back to bed. I just need some air. I'm *fine*. Really."

It's a lie and she knows it, and she knows I know she knows it, but she won't call me out on it.

No one ever calls me out on it.

Once I've convinced Laney to go back to bed, I step into the outside hallway. Jake stands at the railing, his back to me, and turns quickly when I close the door, like he wasn't expecting me, like he hasn't been waiting. It's obvious this is exactly what he was waiting for, though. His eyes give him away.

I lean back against the wall and slide slowly to the ground. I don't think I'm going to throw up again, but there's still this twisted nervous feeling in the pit of my stomach. Like when you forget you had an essay worth half your grade due until the teacher starts collecting the papers.

Jake sits across from me and asks, "Is everything all right?" I know that by *everything* he means me, specifically.

"Yeah," I say. "I'm still alive." And then I laugh, but it sounds weird, hollow, and that must not be the appropriate reaction because he's looking at me like he's concerned, and I kind of hate it, so I say, "I already told you not to do that."

"Not do what?"

"You keep being…nice. And then you do a total dick move, and then you redeem yourself by doing something stupid like letting yourself get punched in the face."

There's a shadow of a bruise under his right eye. I want to reach across and touch it. I would, if I think he'd let me.

"It's not the first time I've been laid out," he says quietly, and I know he's not talking about stupid high school fisti-cuffs, but something more. His dad, probably. I wonder what it's like, to live with that, to fear your parents. My dad isn't around, and even when he was he was like a ghost, never re-ally there. Still, I know he would never raise a hand to me. I've never had to be afraid of him causing me any physical harm. Emotional, on the other hand…

Parents are supposed to protect you, but they seem to be really, really lousy at it.

I look down, push my hair behind my ears and change the subject. "Uh, so I meant to thank you. For earlier, when you offered to—to pay, for Laney's—"

Jake cuts me off with a shake of his head and says, "Don't mention it."

He eases two clementines out of the bag, my pocket knife in one hand. I gave it to him earlier to cut the white net-ting. He uses it to peel the clementines, his hands working in smooth, practiced motions.

"I'm surprised you have that much money, just lying around," I say, and he shoots me a sharp look. I realize he probably thinks I'm insulting him for being—well, for being unlike Laney, comfortably upper middle-class, or even unlike my family, less comfortably middle-class, but generally able to stay afloat. "Not that I think you're— I'm not trying to…" I blush guiltily. "It's a good chunk of change, for anyone."

"I know what you mean," he says. He doesn't sound offended, at least. "Plus, you're right. I don't have the money lying around. But I can get it."

"What do you mean?"

"Well, I spent most of my savings on this little expedition, but between what I'll have left over and what I can get off of selling the Hendrix record Seth gave me, it'd be enough to cover it." He holds out a slice of clementine. "Here, try this."

"What?" I don't take the fruit. "Jake, you can't do that."

"Fine then. More for me," he says, popping the slice in his mouth and smiling around it.

"I'm talking about the record."

He sighs. "I know."

"You can't sell it. It's too valuable. It means something to you." If not on a monetary level, a personal one.

I can't believe Jake is willing to sacrifice that autographed record—he'll never admit it, but I know how much it means to him. I saw the way he looked when Seth handed it over, how impressed he'd been. That total awe written across his face. Music is everything to Jake.

"I'm not nearly as sentimental as you paint me to be, Scott."

I stare at him. "Yes, you are. I know it's important to you."

"Not as important as some things." He pushes a clementine into my hands. "Come on, eat this. I'll deal."

Not as important as some things. Like what? Like Laney? Like me? Like June? I'm still trying to understand what she meant to him. I believe him when he says they weren't, you know, *involved*, but there had to be something there to make him care so much. To compel him to drive us all the way across the country on her behalf.

"Do you think it's my fault?" I blurt out. Jake frowns at me, so I clear my throat and say, "For not knowing anything was wrong. With June." I look down at my hands. "I know you probably blame me for it."

"I don't blame you."

I scoff. "Come on. Admit it. When I saw you at the wake, you *hated* me. You didn't even know me and you hated me."

"That's not— I didn't— I mean..." He rolls a clementine back and forth against the ground. I watch the movement so I don't have to look at his face. "I... I guess maybe I did hate you, a little, when I first heard what happened," he admits.

He lets go of the clementine, and I look at him, even though it hurts to hear this. At least he hasn't lied to me. He only knows how to hurt me with the truth.

"But that was stupid," he adds. "I just wanted to think it was someone's—anyone's—fault. I thought someone closer to her, someone in her family, should've seen something was wrong. I was so pissed at myself for not realizing." He takes a breath, drawing his gaze up from the clementine to meet mine. "And...and all that was before I knew you."

Does Jake really know me? It is weird, that I've only known him for so little time, but I feel like I've told him more about myself than anyone I know, maybe even more than Laney. I guess it was easier, since we didn't have any history, for me to be honest. Because even if he judged me, it wasn't like it mattered. Except that doesn't feel true anymore. It feels like it does matter, what he thinks. I want him to know everything and still not hate me for it.

"I'm the one who found her," I say. I don't know why I say

it. Maybe because it's harder to not say it—like trying to contain a thunderstorm in a mason jar. Maybe because I feel like I owe it to him, for driving us all the way out here, for being here and not expecting anything in return. Maybe because I want to touch his bruises and his scars and let him touch mine, the ones that aren't on my skin.

He freezes in the middle of dealing the cards, sets them down slowly and just looks at me. Waiting.

"Laney picks me up in the mornings, because June always went to school early to study or tutor or do whatever it is she did, and I went through the garage to wait." I can remember that part perfectly: stuffing books haphazardly in my bag, grabbing a half-finished essay on Nathaniel Hawthorne off the table and an apple from the fridge, annoyed because I'm running late and if I'm tardy for first period again I'm going to get another detention. "All of the lights were off, which was weird, and June's car was there and the engine was on. So I turned on the lights and opened the garage door, and I went to ask her for a ride since Laney wasn't there yet. It smelled like there was a lot of exhaust, but I didn't really— I mean, I didn't think about it. I went around to the driver's side, but it was empty, and then I looked in the backseat."

I thought she was sleeping at first. Her eyes were closed, and she was curled up on the seat, one arm hanging down to the floor. It wasn't until I opened the door to wake her up that I realized something was wrong. It was her skin—it was so pale. Not just pale, but sallow. Eggshell-white. Like there was no life in it.

Jake is silent, so I take a deep breath and go on. "I thought she was taking a nap," I say, and almost laugh a little to myself at the strangeness of it. "I went to wake her up, and I saw her face, and—and I knew, you know? I knew. She didn't look like herself. I knew she was gone."

Some people say that if you experience a traumatic event, your mind blacks out and represses it as a coping mechanism, so it's just this empty void. Like selective amnesia. I guess it's like your brain's survival tool because if you remembered, you'd be too traumatized to function.

Well, I remember everything. I remember exactly what she looked like in that car. I remember my mom's face when the paramedics told her the news. I remember how I screamed and screamed and didn't stop. I remember it all.

I wish so much that I didn't.

"I am *so* mad at her," I tell him. It's hard to admit that. I'm ashamed for being as angry as I am. I mean, she was in so much pain, she had to be, to do what she did, and logically I know it's not fair of me to hate her for it. But no one said emotions are fair. Part of me still thinks she was a selfish bitch, for bailing on me and our mom and everyone else, for leaving me with nothing but the pieces of so many shattered lives and a guilt that will never, ever go away. "She didn't even say goodbye, or leave a note, or anything, and I hate her for that. I should've seen it coming. I should've *done* something."

The night air is clear and cool and silent, save for the bugs humming around the buttery-yellow lamps overhead, a car's wheels sounding against pavement as it guns out of the parking lot. And beyond that, faint echoes of the ocean tide.

"You can't hold yourself responsible for what she did," Jake says, so softly I barely hear him. "There's nothing you could have done. Nothing."

I shake my head. "You don't know that."

"Come on, Harper. You're smarter than that. It was her choice. Hers, not yours."

I feel like he's lying, except he's never lied before, he never sugarcoats anything, so why would he start now? And if he's right, it doesn't really change anything. It may not be my fault, but she's still gone, she still chose to leave. I'll still always wonder why I wasn't enough.

My eyes water, my breath catching in dry not-quite sobs. Jake moves toward me, but I wave him off.

"I'm fine," I insist, swallowing hard, trying to shove the emotion down again.

He says, "You're not fine. And that's okay. No one is expecting you to be okay right now."

"It doesn't matter, okay?" I whisper. "How I am—it's not important. It doesn't matter."

One of his hands falls across the inside of my knee. I turn my head to see his face, hovering inches from mine. His expression is so open and understanding and sympathetic that my throat closes up just looking at it.

He leans close and says, "It matters to me," right against my mouth, and then kisses me like he means it.

I've thought about what it'd be like to kiss Jake over the past few days, way more than I'd care to admit. But I don't even have time to register the firm press of his lips against mine, without breath, before he pulls back. His face freezes, eyes wide with *oh shit* written across them. Maybe I'd be offended if I wasn't so sure that my own expression matches his perfectly.

"I shouldn't have done that," he blurts out. "I'm an idiot."

"Yeah," I agree, "you really are."

I grab the collar of his shirt and tug him back to me. He makes a muffled sound of surprise in the back of his throat, hesitating for a heartbeat before his mouth opens against mine. Suddenly we're kissing for real—clumsy at first as we feel each other out, but then I shift forward into his lap, fall against his chest and tip my head down, and it's like two puzzle pieces snapping into place.

He tastes exactly the way I thought he would, of cigarettes and citrus and salt. The ocean. And he kisses like I thought he would, too, hard and hot and urgent, and way better than anyone I've made out with before. Not that there's a long list or anything, just a few sloppy hookups at parties I can count on one hand with guys who used too much tongue and didn't know what to do with their hands.

Jake knows *exactly* what to do with his hands. One cups my jaw while the other wraps around my back to pull me in flush against him. I grab at his neck, and one of his legs accidentally knocks into the bag of clementines. A few roll out across the floor.

He falters for a second like he's contemplating reaching for them. I shake my head, mumble against his lips, "Leave it," because I don't want him to stop, and then he's pressing back, hands moving down to fit around my hip bones. He uses them to push me to my feet.

We stumble through the door to his room, never breaking contact, and he shoves me up against the wall, kisses me as hard as he can. I think I'll float up out of my body, being kissed like that, but he anchors me down with his hands pinning my wrists to the wall, his hips pressed against mine.

I push back, break my arms from his grip so I can wrap them around him, pull him even closer. God, I love his mouth, love his hands. I'd climb inside his skin if I could. We kiss like we're drowning, gasping and desperate.

"Wait." Jake breaks away first, leaving both of us out of breath. For a second I think he will pull back completely, say something like, *We can't do this, it's not right, I'm sorry*, but instead he grins and says, "How about some music?"

He moves to the CD player on the dresser. I stand behind him, pulling his jacket off his shoulders as he flips through his collection case. I don't want to stop touching him. I can't get enough now that I've started.

"One-track mind much?" I say into the back of his neck.

"Hey, the sound track is vital. It sets the mood."

This feels more like us. It's easy to slip into this comfortable back-and-forth banter with him, helps to ease the anxious ache in my stomach. But I'm still nervous, because I know what this is leading up to. What I want to do with him.

"I'm sure." My sarcasm has to be predictable at this point, but it's my most reliable defense mechanism for a reason. "So what do you have in mind?" I ask. "ABBA's *Greatest Hits*?"

Jake laughs. "Tempting, but I'm thinking something more along the lines of—" He pauses. "Hold on. I found the perfect choice."

I try and peer around him to see his pick, but he jams it into the player and presses Play before I can sneak a look. The first track cues up and answers my question anyway. The beginning riff of "Touch Me" by the Doors blasts out, startling me into laughter. Jake turns and serenades me, his arms wrapped around my waist, swaying us back and forth in time to the music. I sing along until the sight of his exaggerated facial expressions breaks my voice off into laughter again, and then I'm laughing into his mouth.

As we kiss, my hands creep underneath his shirt and up his taut stomach. The muscles there tense, his grip on my waist tightening. When I slip a hand beneath the waistband of his jeans, Jake jerks back and stares at me with his mouth parted.

"Do you have—" I start, and then stop. Okay, new rule. If I'm not mature enough to talk about sex, I'm not going to be having it. My heart is beating so hard it could burst out of my chest and go flying across the room at any moment, but I suck it up, grit my teeth and tip my chin upward to look him square in the eyes. "Do you have protection?"

He blinks in confusion, and then I see it click in his head, and then he just looks kind of bowled over. Like all he expected was for us to make out against walls and go our separate ways. Normally that would be more than enough for me, but tonight… I don't want to be alone.

I want to be with him.

"Y-yeah," he stammers, throwing a glance over his shoulder at the wallet on the nightstand, "I mean—I do, but—is that really what—"

I cut him off. "Yes. I want to."

"Harper," he says, struggling for words. "We don't—we don't have to. I don't think—"

It's kind of sweet, and at the same time kind of condescending, that he'd try to protect me from myself.

I roll my eyes. "Of course we don't have to," I say impatiently. I yank his shirt up over his head, discard it on the floor and take a moment to appreciate the sight of him shirtless. "No one *makes* me do anything. I don't let them. Haven't you realized that yet?"

He laughs. "Yeah, I guess you're right."

I reach out and put my hands on his bare chest, steer him to the bed, where I push him down on the mattress and straddle him awkwardly. Some fumbling ensues, and then my shirt is off, and I am kissing Jake again, our knees knocking, legs caught in a clumsy tangle. His hands hover before eventually settling over my ribs. They move up my back, over my bra, thumbs rubbing across my shoulder blades, and then around to my front, lower, lower—

I pull away and say, "I've never done this before." The blood rushes to my face. If he laughs, or pushes me off in disgust, I don't know what I'll do. Punch him in the head before crawling into a corner to die of embarrassment, probably. My heart flutters in my chest like a spastic hummingbird.

An expression I can't place passes over his eyes. "Maybe we shouldn't," he says.

The knot in my stomach reappears with a roaring vengeance, twisting painfully. I try to keep the hurt out of my voice when I ask, "So is it because you've suddenly become a noble defender of womanly virtue, or because you just don't want to?"

He must've detected it, though, because he shakes his head fervently. "Are you crazy? Of course I *want* to. Believe me. I just… I want you to be sure."

"I am," I promise. "I'm a big girl now. I know what I want. I want you to—"

He cuts me off with a kiss before I can finish and rolls me onto my back. Behind us Jim Morrison has moved on to singing about running to L.A. Yes, sometimes the melodies are repetitive, but I can't deny that his voice is like liquid sex. And the song—the song is fitting, when I stop to think about it, which I don't for very long because the way Jake kisses me and the places his hands roam are incredibly distracting.

He lifts his mouth from mine as he unbuttons my jeans with tentative deliberation, looking to me for permission. "You okay?"

I nod shakily. It's so hot I can hardly breathe, and still I shiver like crazy all over, like someone's tossed me into a tub of ice.

Jake draws back to look me in the eye. "You're sure?"

I don't want him to stop, I want him to keep going, I don't want to have to think about it. It's like running: if you don't stop, you don't have time to think. It would be so much easier if he'd just do it, get it over with, instead of all this talking.

I want this. I want this. So why do I feel like crying?

"Yes," I say. His skin is so hot, like there's a furnace under it, and my arms and legs feel like Jell-O. I put my hands in his hair, pull him down into another kiss, breathe into his mouth. "Yes."

I want this, and Jake— I don't have to ask him twice. He

presses his mouth to the curve of my jaw, my throat, my collarbone, kisses a line down my stomach. I arch off the bed
and into his touch, stare up at the stained ceiling that swims
in my vision, and all around me hear the music, rising, rising.

fourteen

Sex is not something June and I talked about. Ever. I don't know if she ever did it with Tyler or not—I would've bet good money she was waiting for prom night, so he could book a hotel room and make love to her on a bed strewn with rose petals, surrounded by candles or some sappy shit straight out of *The Notebook*. But then they broke up and June didn't even go to her senior prom because she was too upset about the whole mess.

I can't imagine her having a first time like mine—then again, if you'd told me a month ago my sister was going to kill herself, I would've laughed in your face, so what do I know?

When I wake up the next morning, there are five blissful seconds where I don't remember anything at all. Not about what happened with Jake, or about June, or even where I am. But then I stretch and roll over onto my side, and the thin starched sheet slides over my sticky bare skin, and that's the moment I open my eyes, lift my head off my pillow and realize I'm naked. And in Jake's room.

And, oh yeah, did I mention *naked*?

Last night filters its way back into my consciousness in bits and pieces, fitting together like a jigsaw puzzle—Laney in the bed, me throwing up in the toilet, the clementines, the king of clubs, the crying, the kissing, my back pressed against the motel room wall, Jim Morrison's heavy, raspy baritone echoing in my ears.

I rub my eyes and let my head fall back on the pillow. Jake's side of the bed is empty; the CD player lies mute. I wonder where he went. Maybe he wanted to distance himself, make it clear this was a one-time deal. We didn't talk about it, after; we just lay there, sweaty limbs tangled together under the sheets, my head cushioned on his bare shoulder while we listened to the record on repeat until we fell asleep.

I have no idea how he feels about all of this. Maybe he regrets it so much he can't stand to see my face. Probably couldn't wait to get away from me as fast as possible.

Asshole.

I fight back a wave of anger and embarrassment and dress as quickly as I can, snatching the closest articles of clothing off the floor—which happen to be Jake's boxers and a baggy T-shirt with the acronym CBGB across the front. Whatever that means. It doesn't matter, I just need to be covered enough to get into my room, where I can do a quick change, hopefully before Laney wakes up and gets a clue.

And then I open the door, and there's Jake, leaning against the outside railing and smoking a cigarette. He's wearing that silly hat of his again, and he looks over his shoulder when I come out, a small smile curving his lips. My stupid heart betrays me by doing this weird flippy thing in my chest that feels like fifty million butterflies ricocheting off each other.

"Hey," he greets me.

I step up next to him. "Hey."

I keep a little distance between us, bending over the railing and staring down at the parking lot below. I try to compose what I want to say in my head, but the problem is, I still haven't sorted out how I feel about things myself.

I like Jake, I do, but it's complicated, like everything else. Last night was probably a bad idea. At the same time, I don't feel bad about it, or like I have anything to apologize for.

Jake nudges his elbow against mine. "How'd you sleep?" he asks, and at the same time I blurt out, "This doesn't mean I want to have your babies."

We stare at each other for about ten seconds in awkward silence.

"Okay," he says slowly, smiling with his mouth closed, like he's holding back a laugh.

"I mean, I don't want you to think..." Is there a non-lame way to phrase this? Doubtful. "I'm not going to get all clingy and weird," I explain, "and want to, like, carve our initials into birch trees inside a little heart and start planning our wedding or whatever."

"In that case, I guess I need to call the Radisson and cancel the booking for the reception," he replies. His smile softens. "It's okay, Harper. I get it. I don't expect anything."

That's what I want, isn't it? No expectations. No pressure. So why do I feel so disappointed?

Jake says, "We can talk about it more later, if you want," and drops a quick kiss on my forehead. "Go pack. We should get on the road as soon as we can. It's going to be a long day."

I don't know what constitutes as "later" in Jake's mind— we don't discuss it after we've checked out of the motel, or on the drive to the nearest Denny's for breakfast, and as soon as we get there, he ducks into the bathroom, leaving Laney and me alone in a side booth. If I really wanted to I could follow him and force him to have this conversation, except, what is there to say? And if I figured out what I did want to say, is it something I'd want to confront him about in such close proximity to a urinal?

I don't think Laney suspects anything. She was still sleeping when I crept into our room, and she's acted normal all morning. Maybe a little quieter than usual. It'd be selfish of me to worry her with my crisis when hers is so much more critical than mine. She's gotta be a level red on the personal-crisis color scale.

Between the three of us, we have enough fodder for a year's worth of Lifetime made-for-television movies, easy.

Laney pulls a newspaper out of her giant handbag and smiles at the waiter as he sets a big-ass pot of coffee and three glasses of water on our table.

"So what's new in the world?" I ask, pouring myself some coffee. I don't really like plain coffee, except for the smell. But today I feel older than ever. I can act like an adult. I can drink plain coffee if I want.

Laney quirks an eyebrow from behind her newspaper. "Let's see…war, famine, disease. One of the Olsen twins is in rehab again. The usual, it would seem." She flicks past a page, feigning surprise. "Oh, wait, listen to this: *'Harper Scott has sizzling one-night stand with Jacob Tolan.'*"

My hand jerks, and coffee spills all over the tabletop. Jesus.

I gape at her stupidly. "You—you know?" Seriously, does she have a sixth sense for these things or something?

"Pick your jaw up off the floor. It's not exactly a state secret, what with you coming into our room wearing his underwear this morning," she says, pointing to me with her spoon. "Yeah, that's right, I was awake, you thought I wasn't, but I totally was. I can't believe he wears Looney Tunes boxers." She rolls her eyes. "So tell me. How was it? Good? Bad?"

"Um." I grab handfuls of napkins from the dispenser and mop up the spilled coffee, stalling for time, hoping she might change the subject on her own. But she doesn't; she just keeps her eyes on me. "It was… I don't know." I shrug. "It just was."

She leans in over the table, grinning wickedly. "Was it, like, super-romantic Kate-and-Leo-in-the-back-of-the-car-in-*Titanic* sex, or take-me-now sex, like when Clark Gable drags a protesting Vivien Leigh up the stairs in *Gone With the Wind*, but it's obvious she's secretly totally into it?"

Of course that's what Laney would want to know.

I crumple the napkins in my fist and sigh. "I am so not talking about this."

"Come on! A girl needs *details*. I've always shared details with you, when you've asked."

"I never ask for details. You share them willingly. In fact, if anything, you force them on me when I'd rather not hear. I'm not a fan of the overshare."

"Okay," she says, and sits back. She eyes me carefully. "Just tell me—are you okay?"

I toss the soppy napkins aside and say, "I hate when you ask that."

"I know you do. Are you okay?"

"Yes." I look up and meet her direct gaze. "I mean. I've been better. But last night…" I can feel myself blushing red. "Laney…your first time. Was it…good?"

"No," she replies bluntly. She spins the spoon around in her fingers. "Memorable? Yes. Good? No. Not in any sense of the word."

I don't get it. If she didn't enjoy it, what made her want more of it? Dustin Matthews was her first, but not her last. I'm certain of that much. I think there are some things about Laney I will never understand.

Now it's her turn to change the subject. "So," she says, "what about Jake?"

"What?"

"Are you in love with him?"

Love? No. Definitely, absolutely, positively not. What happened last night was just two people missing the same person, combined with some serious raging hormone action. A weak moment. I don't regret it, but it isn't like we're in *love*.

You cannot be in love with someone you've really only known for barely a week, and on top of that, someone who drives you crazy most of the time. No matter how good-looking and charming and interesting and understanding he may be. Not even if he's the one person who makes you feel like yourself.

Right?

It's a straight shot to San Francisco off of the Pacific Coast Highway. The drive will take most of the day, but we all feel reenergized from the sabbatical in Huntington Beach. Being in California in itself is a shot in the arm, too; all of us chat more over the music, point out different sights along the way.

Things are going swimmingly, in fact, until Jake cuts across three lanes, gets off the I-5 north and onto the 46.

I look from the map to Jake and back again. "You're going the wrong way. We're supposed to stay on I-5 until—"

"I know. This is the last detour."

"Detour? Haven't we had enough of those already?"

"Trust me. It'll be worth it."

It takes everything I have not to pester him the whole way about what, exactly, we are doing on this detour. It's hard to stay annoyed when Jake turns on the music, though. Seriously, who can be in a bad mood during a Beach Boys song? It is impossible. Even Laney isn't immune to the infectious beats; she hums along in the back as she flips through a fashion magazine. I prop my bare feet out of the open window and swing them to the tune, the salty ocean-shore air rushing in through the van.

I feel pretty content, all things considered. I figure if anything I should be receiving a medal of some kind for holding my shit together this well. My sister is dead, my best friend is pregnant and I've just lost my virginity to a guy I hate. Sort of.

Well, *hate* is a strong word, one I usually reserve for expressing my feelings toward, say, P.E. class and FOX News. I don't *hate* Jake. Sometimes I am annoyed by, frustrated by and irritated by him. And confused. I am pretty much always confused by him, by what he says and how he acts. Sleeping with him has only made things that much more complicated.

But I also enjoy him, erratic behavioral patterns and all. I like that he isn't too cool to openly geek out over ABBA, and that he is so passionate about music, that he gives as good as he gets and doesn't back down from a good argument. He makes me feel safe, without being overbearing, and at the same time totally stripped bare, forcing me to confront the things I want to keep locked up inside.

But maybe that's better. You can only cover a bullet hole with a Band-Aid for so long. Maybe I need to bleed out.

Maybe I need to stop with the lame metaphors.

The detour turns out to be a town called Cholame.

"Cholame?" Laney gasps and sits up, eyes bugging out of her head. "Shut up. Seriously? This is Cholame?"

I don't see what the big deal is—this place makes Grand Lake look like a metropolis in comparison. But then Jake explains that this is where James Dean died after crashing his Porsche.

I squint out the window. "On this road? Right here?"

"Not exactly," he says. "They realigned the intersection back in the seventies, and the crash site's on private property. You can see it from the road, though."

Laney's reaction suddenly makes sense. Dead movie star, prime of life—how many times has she made me watch *Rebel Without a Cause* and *East of Eden*? James Dean is one of her favorites. The only thing that could top this would be flying to whatever island Grace Kelly is buried on.

Jake pulls Joplin into the parking lot of a small café, where someone has constructed a memorial. The monument is built out of steel planks wrapped around a tree, surrounded by a Japanese rock garden and plaques inscribed with quotes by people like Elia Kazan and Lord Byron and James Dean himself. No one is around except for us. I snap a few Polaroids, then step back with Jake while Laney reads each and every inscription.

"How'd you know where to find this place?" I ask.

"I stopped here once, with my brother. It's pretty easy to find. All you do is shoot straight from—"

"Wait, when were you in California?"

He looks at me funny. "I was born here. Well, not *here*—Echo Park."

"I didn't know that." Dumb response—of course I didn't know that. How could I? Jake hasn't volunteered the information up until this point, and I'm not a mind reader. I glance at Laney and ask Jake, "So why'd you choose this for our last detour?"

"I figured she could use some cheering up," he says. "Life's hard enough, you know, without..." He trails off with a light shrug. "I thought it might get her mind off of things."

I look at him for too long after that, and wonder why, exactly, Jake has to keep doing this—has to keep having these moments of saying or doing exactly the right thing, throwing my perception of him all off-kilter. Moments like these make me want more from him than I have ever wanted from any guy—or even just another person, period.

It scares me, makes me itch to either run away screaming

or push him up against the nearest tree and kiss him until I can't breathe.

Jake catches me staring and wrinkles his nose. "What?"

"Nothing," I say quickly.

To keep him from asking more questions, I swipe the fedora off of his head and shove it onto my own. He laughs, trying to steal it back, and we end up wrestling for it until Laney turns around and gives us a pointed look, one hand on her hip.

"Sorry," I gasp out, breathless from laughing so hard, "sorry. Please, continue with, uh, paying your respects. Ignore us."

"We'll behave now," Jake assures her in a low, growly voice. A voice that makes me blush. He stands close to me, shoulder pressed against mine. I blush harder.

Laney finishes up, kissing her fingertips and brushing them across the metal slat affixed to the tree trunk. We get back on the road, and the three of us sing along to the Beach Boys at the top of our lungs until we hit the Pacific Coast Highway, and then keep singing, even after that.

According to the atlas, it would've been faster to take the interstate up from Cholame and cross the Bay Bridge into San Francisco, but Jake said if we were going to be driving for so long anyway, we might as well take the scenic route. It's a good call—what passes by outside our windows more than makes up for the time difference. The farther up Highway 1 you go, the more the scenery changes. The beaches down south are like the ones you see on television. Rippled golden sand and sparkling water and palm trees everywhere. I heard once that most of California's palm trees aren't even natural, just transplanted for the sake of tourists' expectations. Up north the water still sparkles, but everything feels a little more wild, with dramatic jagged cliffs and lots of brush. I like it better. You can sort of pretend it hasn't been touched by mankind.

Eventually we turn off the interstate and drive into San Francisco. When we reach the city limits, Jake pulls out a folded-up piece of paper from his sun visor and hands it to me. There are directions written on it in his scratched-out scrawl.

"She doesn't live too far from here," he says.

Laney pops her head up from the backseat. "Who, exactly, is this 'she'?"

"Her name's Carmen."

"And how do we know she's not some crazy psycho who'll kidnap us?"

"She used to date my brother."

"That doesn't answer my question."

Jake reaches one hand around to slap her shoulder playfully. "Carmen's cool, I swear. I've known her since we were kids. She's sort of like my surrogate older sister, you know? We still write and everything."

I have a hard time imagining Jake sitting at a desk, pounding out a letter to a pen pal. Not to mention his handwriting sucks.

"She does know we're coming, right?" I ask.

"Well..." He hems and haws a bit. "Not exactly."

Laney immediately smacks the back of his head. "Jake! You mean we're showing up unannounced? That is so rude!"

"What if she isn't there? What are we going to do?" I smack him once, too, for good measure. "What is *wrong* with you?"

"Can we please stop with the abuse?" he says. He rubs a hand through his hair. "She'll be there, okay? I promise. Relax."

We follow Jake's barely legible directions and end up in front of a beige apartment building with a terra-cotta roof. He parks on the side of the street, and we get out of the van and walk up to the building entrance. Jake squints at the intercom box before pressing the buzzer next to a label that says Delgado.

A minute or so passes, but no one responds.

"I am going to kill you," I tell Jake. It's sweltering out here, and we're all going to die of heatstroke while we wait. Why couldn't he have called?

He rolls his eyes and presses the buzzer three more times in quick succession, then takes a few steps back. Seconds later, a window on the third floor above us opens, and a girl's head peeks out, her long black ponytail dangling over one shoulder.

"I already told you, I'm not gonna subscribe to your stupid magazine!" she yells.

"We're not selling anything," Jake calls back. "We just came to see my favorite *chula* this side of the Mississippi."

The girl pauses and shields her eyes to get a better look. "Jacob? That you?"

"In the flesh," he confirms with a broad grin.

She covers her mouth with both hands and emits something between a laugh and a squeal.

"Hang on a second," she says, then disappears from the window and reappears moments later, something in her hand catching the afternoon light and flashing gold. "The damn buzzer's broken. Let me throw you a key."

Jake steps back and holds his hands above his head. She tosses the key down, and with a quick dive to the left, he's able to snatch it out of the air. After unlocking the door, he steps aside so that Laney and I can pass through first, and then follows us up the three flights of stairs.

By the time we've reached the top, we're all huffing a little. I try to catch my breath so I can ask which apartment is hers when one of the doors swings open. Out comes Carmen, sporting an old yellow polo and ratty jeans with holes at the knees. Both are covered in red paint. There's a lopsided smear of it on her right cheek. Even so, she's stunning, with her sleek black hair, smooth olive skin and wide-set dark brown eyes.

"*Vato!*" she cries, making a beeline for Jake. She grabs him in a ferocious hug.

Laney and I trade silent looks. I know she has to be thinking the same thing as me: here's another piece of the puzzle that is the eternal mystery of Jacob Tolan.

"I'm sorry, I'm such a mess—painting the living room—I had no idea—" Carmen releases Jake and wipes her palms off on her jeans. "What are you even doing here, Jake? Where's your brother?"

"Eli's back in Michigan. Someone has to man the fort, I guess," he says. He glances over at Laney and me for a brief moment and then back to Carmen. "We've been road tripping."

"Oh." She gives him a studied look. "Any reason?"

"I have an aunt with a beach house in Santa Barbara," Laney lies smoothly. "We thought it'd be fun. You only graduate high school once, right?"

Jake's eyes dart to mine, surprised, and I half shrug, because it's not like I had any idea Laney would say that. Her cover story is pretty brilliant, actually, simple in explanation, a touch of believable detail in mentioning the fictional aunt's beach house, and a subtle implication that we're all eighteen and thus legal adults with the graduation bit. Laney is a natural actress.

This explanation seems to satisfy Carmen, because she turns to Laney and nods, then swats Jake on the arm in a sisterly kind of way.

"Don't be so rude!" she chastises. "Introduce me!"

"These are my…friends," he says hesitantly. "Laney, Harper, this is Carmen Delgado, Carmen, this is Laney and Harper."

"Pleased to meet you," Laney says. "And, not to be rude, honestly, but please, *please* tell me you have air-conditioning."

Carmen laughs. "I do. Come in, come in."

She shepherds us into her apartment. It's small but cozy, with polished wooden floors and enough windows to utilize the natural sunlight. The furniture in the living room is covered with plastic, and two paint cans sit open on the floor, next to a large foam roller and set of smaller brushes. Half of the walls are colored bright red, the other half still pale cream.

"Sorry about the disaster area. I'm redecorating," explains Carmen apologetically.

I notice a black cat on the floor batting its paws at the bunched-up plastic draped over the couch. Another gray one eyes us curiously from its perch on the couch's arm.

"Your cats seem to be enjoying it," I remark.

"They're menaces," Carmen says with a good-natured eye roll. The black cat takes a flying leap and begins to wrestle with a ball of yarn on the floor. Carmen sits on the couch, scratching the gray tabby's back as he purrs loudly.

"The red suits you. I like it," Jake says. He flops down beside Carmen, the plastic squeaking underneath him.

"Me too," she agrees. She pats him on the knee and looks to Laney. "If you want a snack to cool down, I have Popsicles in the freezer, right down the hall. Feel free to help yourself."

Laney, never one to turn down such an offer, scurries straight to the kitchen. I settle into the armchair across from the couch. Carmen's cat sits on her lap as she snakes its tail through her fingers.

"How's your ma?" Jake asks.

"You know her. Nag nag nag. She thinks it's crazy I haven't married and popped out any kids yet." She laughs. "So how's Eli doing? He never calls anymore."

Jake shrugs. "He's fine. Busy running the store."

"And what about you?" Her tone goes softer, more serious. "You sure everything's okay?"

"Yes," he says, "but—"

"Oh, here we go!"

"—we could use a place to crash. Just for a night or two."

"What kind of trouble you in, Jacob? And be straight with me, or I'll call your brother and find out."

"You can't call Eli."

"Why not?"

"You just can't!"

"He even know you're here?" When Jake doesn't respond, Carmen presses the heels of her hands to her temples. "He doesn't even know, does he? I know you think he's a jerk—"

Jake snorts indignantly. "Only because he *is*—"

"—but that's a crap-ass move, leaving him in the dark. What are you *doing* here?"

I step forward. "It's my fault."

Both of them quit arguing and turn to stare at me like they've just realized I'm in the room.

"He's here because of me," I tell Carmen. "Actually, not me. He's here because of my sister."

And that is when I tell her everything. Well, not *everything*—but I explain how June died. Her dreams of California. The ashes. It's weird how easily the story spills out of me; starting is the hardest part, but once I have, I don't even have to think about it.

Carmen listens without saying a word the whole way through, and when I'm done, she comes over and puts her arms around me gently, which is a little embarrassing. And then she hugs Jake, and hugs me again. When all of this hugging business is finished, she steps back and tilts her head at us both.

"You can stay here. Of course you can stay here," she says. "And I think my friend Tina can help you out. Her man Charlie works at a marina in Sausalito. She owes me one ever since

I did hair and makeup for her, three bridesmaids and a flower girl at her wedding, no charge. I can call in a favor."

My eyes go wide. "Seriously?" Could it really be that easy?

"Of course. It's nothing," she says with a smile, and then I look at Jake and he's smiling, and I'm smiling back, and I feel like I might cry, even.

All this time, part of me has doubted our ability to pull this off. But now it looks like we're really going to. My sister is going to get the goodbye she deserves.

"Now I gotta clean up the spare room," Carmen says with a sigh. "I've been using it to store all my junk. There's no space to hardly breathe in there."

"I'll help," I volunteer. I feel such a rush of gratitude toward her that I would do anything she asked. I would scrub her toilets, change her kitty litter, become her indentured servant. Whatever she needs.

Carmen smiles. "That's sweet, but I got it." She turns to cuff Jake upside the head. "You know, a heads-up would've been nice. Christ." She glances upward and makes the sign of the cross over herself on her way out of the room.

Just as she leaves, Laney reappears, sucking on a half-eaten cherry Popsicle. She pulls it out of her mouth and looks at us curiously.

"Did I miss anything?"

fifteen

Carmen is basically made of awesome. I figure Eli Tolan must be the biggest idiot alive to have ever let her go. She's gorgeous, funny, smart and makes a mean quesadilla.

The two of us sit outside on her balcony eating from paper plates while Laney takes a shower and Jake works on painting the living-room wall. There's a nice view of the neighborhood from here. The cool night air smells a little salty, like the ocean. I wonder how far we are from the bay.

I look over at Carmen, her profile silhouetted by the moonlight. "Can I ask you something?"

"Sure," she says.

"What was it like, growing up with Jake and Eli?"

I want to know more about the Tolans. I want to know what Jake won't tell me—about his past, why his mom isn't around, what really happened to make him so...hardened. People aren't born that way; I know I wasn't. If anyone knows, Carmen does.

"The Tolan brothers," she says wistfully. She shakes her head with a little startled laugh, like she's remembering something she hasn't thought about in ages. "Well, I lived next door. They were good kids, you know? Eli and I, we dated for a while. He was so different. I really cared about him. Broke my fucking heart when it ended."

"Why didn't it work out?" I ask.

"We were young. I guess I thought I could save him. I was sixteen. What did I know?" Her smile is thin. "He was always talking about leaving—he wanted to go to New York and be a starving artist or something. Me, I love California. I'll never leave. I know they'd lived in a lot of other places before then. Their mother…" She stops, uncertain. "Has he talked about her?"

I look down at my feet. "I don't know the whole story, but I get the impression she was…unstable."

Carmen drags one manicured hand through her thick hair. She puts her elbows on her knees and clasps her hands, pressing her mouth to her fists, staring somewhere into the distance in front of her.

"She loved those boys," she says firmly. "But she couldn't take care of them. She never could. It was always them having to fend for themselves. Eli hated her for that, he really did. They lived here for a few years, and then as soon as Eli graduated school, he split for good, and their mom dragged Jake all over the place. He wrote me letters all the time. Mostly about music. Bands and songs he liked, that kind of thing. I had no clue what was really going on."

I want to push for more, but I know if I'm patient, if I wait, she'll tell me the rest. I can see in her eyes that it's hard for her. She twists the silver ring on her thumb around and around and around, evading my gaze.

"She left," she says finally, in a voice so quiet I have to strain to hear it at all. "One day she just walked out and didn't come back. Jake was alone for over a month before anyone realized. She'd done that before a few times—taken off and not told anyone, then showed up days later. I think he thought she would come back eventually."

"So that's how he ended up with his brother."

"Eli's been taking care of him for the last three or four years, yeah."

"And their mother?"

Carmen sighs, a sad, heavy sound. In the moment she takes to pause, I hear the cacophony of crickets below us, buzzing in the humid evening air, filling her silence.

"People like that... People who don't want to be found? They're usually really good at staying lost."

I fall asleep thinking about mothers. About what it would feel like if mine just up and left without warning. I don't know what would be worse: being an orphan by accident or being abandoned by choice. My mom is far from perfect—she tried too hard with June and not enough with me. But at least she cares, in her own dysfunctional way. At least she was *there*. I don't appreciate that the way that I should.

I wake up in the morning before anybody else and decide to fix breakfast for everyone. Mom used to make eggs Benedict all the time. I've never made it on my own, but I've seen her do it, so it can't be too hard. Carmen's kitchen is well stocked. I pull out the ingredients I recognize and turn on the stove.

Of course, me being me, I somehow end up burning my hand on the stove pan before I've even cracked a single egg.

"Dammit!" Frustrated, I throw the pan down, suck on the stretch of skin between my thumb and index finger. It hurts like a bitch.

"Is this a bad time?"

I whirl around to see Jake lingering in the doorway, shoulder pressed against the frame, arms crossed and mouth curved in that patented half grin. He looks sleepy and rumpled and I didn't realize anyone could make bedhead look so sexy.

"Apparently all my hours logged watching the Food Network were in vain," I pout, shaking out my hand.

Jake comes forward, takes hold of my wrist in order to inspect the burn mark. The skin there is already blooming an angry red.

"Here." He turns on the faucet and guides my hand under the tap. "Stay put."

"Yes, sir," I retort mockingly, and then twist my head around to watch him as he sets the pan back on the stove. "What are you doing?"

"Finishing what you started," he teases.

He surveys the array of ingredients assembled on the counter: eggs, ham slices, ground pepper, four English muffins, yogurt, mustard and low-fat mayo.

"Um…" He glances over at me, baffled. "What exactly were you planning on making?"

"Eggs Benedict," I sigh. At his look, I shrug. "What? My mom used to make it all the time. I thought I could wing it."

"Yeah…ambitious though you may be, we're gonna go a little old-school and try French toast instead."

He puts everything away except the eggs and the jar of mayo. He rummages through the refrigerator and pulls out a half gallon of milk, a stick of butter and maple syrup, then kicks the door shut with one socked foot.

I raise my eyebrows. "You use mayonnaise to make French toast?"

"The mayo is for you. It'll help the burn."

I keep my hand under the cold water as he works. He cracks an egg into a wide bowl, whisks it up with a fork and lets pieces of bread soak in it for a while.

"You make French toast a lot?" I ask.

"Nah. But cooking's kind of like riding a bike, or having sex. You never really forget." At least he has the decency to look sheepish after catching his slip on the last part.

"Where'd you even learn how to make it?"

He starts to slice some fruit on the counter, avoiding my gaze. "You know, you grow up.... Ma's always busy scrounging up money and teaching the neighborhood henna class.... Good old Dad's never around, because he's looking for ways to illegally fund his drug habit, and even when he *is* there, he's not really since he's using.... Eventually the prospect of mac-and-cheese every night loses its charm."

"I'm sorry," I say. "If it matters."

"It does." He sets the knife down and wipes his hands off with a dishcloth. "Look, I've learned that the only way to prevent being a product of your environment is to at least be honest about what that means—your sister taught me that."

"What do you mean?"

"She's the reason I graduated," he says. "Honestly, I always planned to drop out. It's not like I ever cared about school. No one in my family ever expected any different. And then the school set me up for tutoring with June, and... I don't know. Somehow she convinced me to try. Said pulling up my grades and passing would piss off the administration more than anything else." He smiles a little to himself. "She made me promise to get my shit together—no drinking, no getting in trouble, no blowing off school. So I did. Because she believed I could do it."

"Wow," I say carefully, "that's really..." Sad? Weird? No. Not weird. It's exactly the kind of thing June would do. The kind of thing that made me both proud to be her sister and ashamed that I was never able to be so naturally *good* the way she was. "I mean, I'm glad," I tell him. "That she could help you."

Jake drops the dishcloth and leans on his elbows against the counter next to me. "I'm really sorry she died," he says. He tucks his chin into his chest. "If it matters."

It does, but I don't know how to tell him that without feeling like I'm putting too much on the table. Which is stupid, because it's not like he hasn't seen me vulnerable. Hell, he's seen me naked. And if I was a better person—if I was June—I would recognize this vulnerable moment of his, this olive branch he's holding out, and extend one of my own.

Except I'm not June. I'm just me.

I look at the running water and say, "My hand is numb."

He reaches across my shoulder and turns off the faucet. For a few seconds we stay that way, his front pressed against my back. His entire body brushes mine, and I can feel the heat of his skin radiating through his thin cotton shirt; his mouth is in my hair. I shiver.

When I turn to face him, Jake's crowded me so close to the sink that I have to lift my chin to look him in the eyes. That boyish vulnerability has been replaced by a heated look. I think about how it felt to kiss him before, and I want to kiss him so badly, those kisses that were so consuming. Melting everything else away.

"You know what's really weird," I finally say, when the silence is too much. "Mix CDs."

And now he's just confused. "Mix CDs?" he says skeptically.

"Think about it. With technology and everything, compact discs are going to be, like, vintage soon, right? The way vinyl is now. Like, if I ever have kids, they're going to look at CDs and think, 'What is this crap, geez, how clunky.' By then everyone will have the fiftieth edition of iPods—or maybe they'll just have music downloaded directly into their brains, like with microchips, or something. And I'll be the old lady in the corner going, 'Back when I was a kid, we had mix tapes, and floppy disks, and gas didn't cost twenty bucks a gallon, and oh, yeah, MTV actually played music videos, if you can believe it.' And they'll probably say, 'Oh, Mom, you and your *stories*, we're jetting to the oxygen bar, see you later,' and take off in their flying cars. You know there'll be flying cars, it's only a matter of time."

Jake tilts his head to one side. "You're rambling."

"I know," I say. "I do that when I'm nervous."

"And when you're drunk."

"You'd know better than me on that one."

"Yeah," he says, and laughs. "Well. Personally speaking, mix CDs will never go out of style. I like having something tangible, you know? And making mixes is a craft. Like storytelling. It has to flow. I mean, you can't follow up a Sam Cooke ballad with Black Sabbath. It's gotta build, have the right climax and ending. Like a book."

I remember the first time I listened to the CD he gave June, how that was exactly what I'd thought.

Jake reaches for the mayonnaise jar and unscrews the lid. "You don't have to be nervous. It'll all work out."

"It will?" What is he referring to? The two of us?

"Sure," he says. "Later today we'll go to Sausalito and meet up with this Charlie guy, and after that, it'll be smooth sailing. Terrible pun intended."

The final stage of the plan. Of course.

Jake gently smears some mayonnaise over the burn mark and wraps it with saran wrap. His grip on my hand lingers; our mouths are really close together. "Good as new," he murmurs.

And then we make out.

Except not really. We could. I want to, and I'm pretty sure he wants to, too, but kissing him will change this from a fluke to a habit, and the last thing I need is a bad habit. Couldn't I just start biting my nails or something? Or maybe I'll just start smoking on a more regular basis. Surely emphysema or lung cancer or whatever horrible disease I'd be inflicted with would be a preferable fate to making out with Jake and then having to talk about our *feelings*.

"I should…" I untangle our hands and gesture past him.

He steps back, and I start to rush out of the kitchen. Except then I see an open shoebox sitting on the table, and when I pause to look inside, I realize it's full of my Polaroids.

Jake notices me looking. "I brought those in last night. Didn't want them to get all bent." He pauses, wiping his hands off with a dishcloth, and smiles a little. "You know, they're really good."

"You looked at them?" I'm sort of embarrassed. The only person who ever looks at my photographs is Laney, and even then she never really has anything to say about them except that she thinks they're good. I love Laney, but I don't exactly hold her opinion on art too high.

"You're really talented," he says. "Have you thought about doing something with your photography? I mean, really doing something. You could, if you wanted."

"That would be, like, impossible."

"Not any more impossible than being the person who names nail polish colors," he teases.

Later, while I'm in the shower, I think about it. Could Jake be right? Am I good enough to even attempt photography as a real career? I feel like he wouldn't just say that if he didn't mean it—he has no reason to give me false praise. And I do want to. I guess I always assumed there was just no way, so why even try? Better to make myself want something else within reach.

But what else is there? I don't have any passions. I'm not particularly good at anything else. Why should I have to settle? Maybe…maybe Jake isn't so off base. Maybe it's okay for me to want something more.

When I finally emerge from the bathroom, Carmen and Laney are at the kitchen table, polishing off the French toast. I've barely sat down before Carmen is on her feet, downing the last of her coffee and reaching for her purse. She explains she has to get to the salon for a morning appointment, and that she's booked most of the day, but she's written out directions to the marina in Sausalito on the back of an old grocery list and stuck it on the front of the fridge. She wishes us luck and ruffles Jake's hair before she leaves.

"And then there were three," Laney intones solemnly. Jake and I roll our eyes at the same time.

There are a few hours to kill, so we decide to burn off our nervous energy by surprising Carmen with a second coat of paint on her walls. Jake and I grab the foam rollers as Laney commandeers the stereo.

"I'm tired of listening to nothing but old white guys," she says.

She puts in a Dr. Dre album and raps along through the first two songs flawlessly, taking a small brush and detailing the wall corner, head bopping in time to the beat. We work all through the entire first loop of the CD, then take a break for lemonade and a bag of sugar cookies and television watching. Laney flips it over to some old movie on one of the cable channels.

"I want to find the Rock Hudson to my Doris Day," she proclaims with a heavy sigh.

"Rock Hudson was gay," I remind her.

"Fine. The William Powell to my Myrna Loy. The Bogie to my Bacall. The—"

"I'm getting more cookies," Jake says, and abruptly gets off the couch. The plastic sheet makes a weird puckering sound when he peels himself off of it.

I watch him leave the room, and Laney watches me watch

him. "And here I thought you two resolved all that unresolved sexual tension," she says.

I turn up the volume on the television. "There's no tension. I have about fifty million other things on my mind that rank much higher in importance than Jacob Tolan."

"Sorry. I know. It's just easier to fixate on your boy drama than deal with my own."

"And how is that going? The dealing?"

"Not so well," she says lightly. "I'm sort of completely and totally plagued by this all-consuming panic that I only manage to keep at bay by indulging in some hard-core denial." She leans her cheek against my shoulder, exhaling a deep breath. "I hate this."

I look down at her. "You know I'm behind you, whatever you choose to do." I keep my voice neutral. "You do have options."

"No good ones." She sighs. "I don't know what I want to do yet."

"That's okay. It's a pretty big decision." Bigger than I can wrap my mind around.

Laney is quiet for a while, long enough that I think I should say something more, even though I don't know what—I'm no good at pretending to be wise. I can't dispense any advice because I have no clue what I would do if I was in her place.

"Life is so unfair," she says bluntly. It's the kind of thing you say when you're six years old, but even now it still holds true. It doesn't matter how much you complain, it's always going to be true.

I pat the top of her head in consolation. "Don't I know it."

"Before we go out there, we got a few ground rules to cover." Captain Charlie is a formidable man, built like a rugged linebacker with his broad shoulders and tree trunk of a neck. He narrows his eyes at us, a seemingly permanent scowl in place, as the wooden boards of the dock creak beneath our feet. "First off, what you're doing's illegal. Usually you gotta get a permit to do a scattering. Since I've been told that ain't possible, it's gonna be like this: I don't want to know your names, and when we get out there, I'm gonna go into the cabin and you do whatever you do and I ain't gonna have any knowledge of it. The second you step foot off this boat, I never seen you before in my life. Understood?"

Jake, Laney and I trade looks and nod.

"Got it," I confirm.

"All right, then. All aboard, ladies and gent."

Charlie's boat is old but solid. He revs it up, messes around with some rope ties and pushes off into the ocean. Jake stands at the railing while I sit on a bench in the bow deck, clutching the urn to my chest, shivering even though it's not that cold. Laney settles beside me. She holds on to my hand, her warm fingers entwined with mine, and says nothing.

With every lurch of the boat I think about how in my arms June's ashes are shifting around in the vase. I've been holding them ever since we got into Joplin for the short drive to Sausalito. When we crossed the Golden Gate Bridge, I stared out the window and wondered if this was right. If this was where she'd want to be laid to rest.

I tried my best. That has to count for something.

Wind whips at us like ghosts on all sides. Despite that, Jake manages to slide a cigarette out from behind his ear and light it. He turns to me and holds it out. An offering. I shake my head no. I'm done with the smoking. Done with all of the stupid things I've been doing just to prove a point no one but me cares about to begin with.

The water sparkles dark blue as the sun begins to sink onto the horizon and make everything shimmer. Soon enough we hit the bay, and then there's the Golden Gate Bridge, not too far off, red and striking and sprawling. This is a beautiful place. This is a good place to spread the ashes. Peaceful and pretty—like the front of a postcard.

Charlie comes around from the stern and calls out, "I'm pulling up!" The engine putters and dies, cutting off and leaving only the sound of the waves as they slap up against the side of the boat. He ducks into the cabin and out of sight.

Laney's hands move to the lid of the urn. Mine tighten around it instinctively, and she looks at me and asks, "Are you ready?"

I'm not sure, but I nod anyway. I grip the urn's sides as she works at the lid, which is sealed tight, and after some twisting, there's a loud *pop* and the release of air as it gives.

"Here," Laney says softly, helping me stand. We join Jake on the deck. Our side of the boat faces the bridge. "We can leave you alone. Come on, Jake."

She starts to reach for him, but I shake my head. "No. Don't. I want you here for this." I pause and glance at Jake. "Both of you."

He frowns a little. "Are you sure you want us to be part of this?"

"You already are. We came this far together, didn't we?"

I didn't get here alone. I don't want to do this alone.

I turn to Laney and gesture to the open urn with my chin. Understanding, she steps forward and scoops out a handful of ashes. She keeps her hand half-inside the urn, biting down on her lower lip.

"I guess I should say something," she says shakily. She looks down into the urn. "June, I know we weren't super-tight, really, but you meant so much to Harper. I was always a little jealous of her, because I never—I never had a sister. You were the closest thing, really. It sucks that you're gone, but I hope you're happier. Wherever you are."

With that, she opens her palm, and the ashes spill out and into the water. She brushes tears off her cheeks and backs away from the railing.

"Guess that means I'm up next, huh?" Jake pinches the bridge of his nose briefly, then reaches into the urn. His eyes stay on me the whole time, like he's scared I'll change my mind and jerk the urn away from under his nose. He bends over the railing with the fistful of ash, bows his head.

"Say something," Laney urges.

"Uh—" He coughs, clears his throat and fidgets nervously. Finally he takes a deep breath and says, "June, you...you helped me out a lot. I can only hope I've returned the favor. You were a good friend, and I'll miss you. Every day I'll miss you."

He scatters the ashes slowly, and after he's done, he just stares down into the ocean, head bowed. He sniffs like he's trying not to cry, and runs his hands through his hair, before he finally turns his back to the water.

And then it's my turn. I realize I should've prepared for this better, should've thought of something to say, a profound and meaningful last goodbye. Why hadn't I stopped to think about it? It's my own fault, really. June's ashes are gritty against my skin, fragments of hard bone among powdered dust. Pieces of her that withstood the flames of a furnace, that couldn't be destroyed. I let them fill my palm and close my eyes.

There is so much I could say—and even more that I will never be able to formulate into words, ever.

All I can think of is how when I was six, I jumped out of a tree in our backyard with paper wings taped to my back and sprained my ankle. June was only eight, but she didn't freak out. She just held my hand while I cried my eyes out, the whole time until Mom found us. And she told me when

I was suspended in the air for just a moment, I looked like a bird flying out of its cage.

Maybe that was what she wanted all along. To be set free.

"I'm sorry," I say. "For everything I did. For everything I didn't. I wish you were here. I know it's not enough, but I guess this is the closest I'm going to get, to saving you."

I lean over the railing and let the breeze blow the ashes out of my hand, and then I overturn the urn and pour the rest into the ocean, where it forms a cloud beneath the surface. As the cloud slowly dissipates, I drop the urn completely, watch as it fills with water and sinks to the bottom. Jake pulls out a single carnation from inside his jacket and hands it to me. I let it flutter down into the ocean, floating on the waves.

And that's it. Everything that was left of my sister is gone.

Except not, because I have sixteen years' worth of memories, and they mean more than bone and ash ever could.

I'm gripping the steel rail so hard I think I'll fall over if I let go. But I don't have to worry about that, because Laney and Jake flank me on both sides, ease me down onto the deck. They hold me up with their weight and their arms. Laney buries her face in my neck, her tears wet against my skin, and Jake tucks his chin on top of my head. They wrap themselves around me so close and so tight it's like we're all one person.

And I'm not alone.

I gaze out at the glittering sea, the breathtaking sky above it, and think of birds and the moment before the fall, and how my sister as a child had been strong enough for the both of us, and I wonder when exactly that changed. I don't know when, but it did. Jake was right—I'm strong in a way June never was. Because I know that I want to be here. Even with the pain. Even with the ugliness. I've seen the other side—marching side by side down city streets with people who all believe they can change the world and the view of the sunset from Fridgehenge and Tom Waits lyrics and doing the waltz and kisses so hot they melt into each other and best friends who hold your hand and stretching out underneath a sky draped with stars and everything else. There is so much beauty in just *existing*. In being alive.

I don't want to miss a second.

I only cry a little, after, at the beach next to the marina. When Charlie drops us off at the docks, I shake his hand and thank him profusely. He squeezes back and says, "Don't mention it, kid," which maybe is him being humble, or maybe him wanting me to take it literally. It's probably a safer bet to assume the latter.

Jake says he wants to see the sun set over the water, so we walk over to the nearest beach and sit on the sand. It's there that the tears gather behind my eyes and spill over. It isn't even that I'm sad. I mean, I *am* sad, but this feels like a release, like someone has lifted this leaden weight off of my chest and I can finally breathe again.

"Look," Laney says. She stands up and jogs closer to the shore, then runs a few steps and turns three perfect cartwheels, all in a row. When she lands, she raises her arms over her head showily and cries, "Ta-*da*!"

I smile and wipe the tears away with my fist. Jake shrugs off his jacket, drapes it over my shaking shoulders.

"Thanks," I say, snuggling into it. It's still warm with his body heat, and it smells like him, too.

"So what do you want to do now?" he asks quietly.

I hug my legs up to my chest, rest my chin on my knees and look out toward the water, where Laney is doing a handstand. "Go back home, I guess. Hope my mother won't kill me on the spot. What about you?"

"I've got the Oleo waiting for me," he says. "That's pretty

much the extent of my future plans. I like to keep my options open."

"What about college?"

"What about it?"

"Aren't you planning on going?"

He laughs like I've just suggested he join the Ringling Brothers. "Me? College? Uh, I don't think so."

"Why not?" I ask. "You're a smart guy, Jake. I mean, yeah, sure, maybe you don't have to shoot for Ivy League, but you could always get into the community college—"

"Yeah, maybe," he says curtly, and I can tell by his tone that this is one subject I shouldn't push.

As the last rays of dusk disappear behind the horizon, I ease myself between Jake's legs, tangle my hands in his hair and meet his mouth with mine. We kiss, slow and languid. It's not like before; there's no desperation here. After a while I settle my head against his chest and listen to the waves, to his heart beating.

He feels so alive. And I feel alive, too, like—really, really *alive*. I don't know why but realizing that makes the tears well up all over again.

We walk back to Joplin in the dark. Jake holds on to my right hand, and Laney grasps my left, and on the ride back to Carmen's, there is no music, just the wind rushing in through the open windows. The silence seems louder, somehow.

That night, I sleep for what feels like forever. And it's a deeper, more restful sleep than I've had since—well, it's been a while. When I wake up, I feel sated, my limbs heavy and warm. I don't know what time it is, but sunlight is streaming in through the window, bright and yellow. Laney isn't on her side of the bed, so I assume it has to be way late, since no one sleeps more than she does. I stretch my body out like a cat and let myself lie there for a while, enjoying the feeling.

Eventually I drag myself out to the kitchen. I expect to see Jake and Laney eating breakfast, but instead I'm met with Jake and Carmen. They're sitting at the kitchen table, no food in sight, speaking in hushed tones, and as soon as they see me in the doorway, they both fall silent.

"Sorry, I didn't mean to interrupt." I cover a long yawn. "Carmen, don't you work today?"

"Someone's covering my appointments," she explains. She glances at Jake and then at me. "I'll, uh, be in my room. Let you two talk."

She exits the kitchen quickly, and I turn to Jake with my eyebrows raised. "That was...weird. So where's Laney?"

"In the bathroom, packing," he says. He isn't smiling.

"Oh. We're driving back today?"

"No. You and Laney are flying back to Michigan today."

For a second I think I've misheard him, but I look at his expression and realize he's serious. My stomach plummets to my feet. "What? How—"

"I called your parents this morning. They already bought the plane tickets," he says. "Carmen's going to drive you to the airport. Your flight leaves around four."

I feel like someone just sucker punched me in the gut. It takes a while for me to do anything other than gape at him, stunned. Finally I find my voice long enough to choke out, "Why? Why would you do that?"

Jake pushes back his chair and walks over to me. "You said I was hiding something," he says. "You were right."

"What are you talking about?"

Something in his expression is scaring me. Rattling me down to my bones.

"The last time I saw June—it was the day before...before

everything. She was helping me study for finals, and I ended up taking one of her notebooks home by mistake. I was going to give it back to her the next day, and then..."

He trails off, like he can't bear to say it, and he doesn't have to, because of course I know what happened. Why he didn't have the chance.

"Anyway," he says, "I found this in it."

Suddenly he shoves something into my hands. I look down. It's an envelope—slightly bent from being pressed in pages, a crisp white except for my name, written along the back in careful, pretty cursive. *Harper.*

It's June's handwriting.

"I should've given it to you earlier," he continues. "I meant to, at the wake. It's why I went. But when we talked outside, it didn't seem right. I even went back to find you, upstairs, and that's when I overheard you and Laney talking about California. I thought maybe...maybe coming out here, it'd be a good way to do it, I guess."

I can't speak. I can't breathe. The envelope is heavy in my hands as I run my thumb across where she'd put the pen down and etched out my name. "And you waited until now to tell me?"

"I meant to say something earlier. A million times I meant to, I just... There was never a good time."

"Never a good time," I echo, my voice hollow in my own ears. "That's bullshit and you know it."

"I knew you'd be mad."

"Shut up. You don't know anything." Least of all me.

"I knew June," he says, and it hits me harder than anything, because I don't want it to be true.

He has to be wrong about that, too. Because he didn't know June. None of us knew June. If we had we wouldn't be here right now.

"So what? Were you, like, in love with her?" My voice shakes as it rises. "Did you fuck her, too?"

"Not everything is about sex, Harper."

"That is so not an answer." I reach out and shove his shoulders, hard. He rocks back on his heels but doesn't move. Shoving him feels good, being angry feels good, easier, easier than being sad, than having my heart crushed, so I hold on to that and push him again, harder, until he stumbles back a step. "Tell me, goddammit! Be honest with me, for once in your life!"

I am beyond mad. I am beyond furious. I can't believe I was such an idiot, to think Jake was different, to trust him with my secrets, with my body. With my *heart*.

"No!" he says vehemently. "Of course not. I told you already, nothing happened."

"But you wanted to, didn't you?" I ask. "Did you—did you only want me because I was the closest you could get, or something?"

He looks so betrayed and disgusted that for the briefest of seconds my anger falters. "I can't believe you'd think that. After everything."

"What am I supposed to think? Seriously, tell me. Because I really don't know."

"You're nothing like your sister," he tells me. "She meant a lot to me, okay? It's true. But the things I like about you have nothing to do with her. You—you are so strong and stubborn it drives me crazy. You're the one going through all this and you still put Laney first every time, instead of throwing yourself the pity party we both know you deserve. You call me out on my shit, and I like that, because sometimes I need someone to call me out on my shit. And you *get* Johnny Cash, and you take these incredible photos, and everything about you makes me hurt, in a good way, and it blows my mind that someone can be so amazing and not even see it."

I'm shaking too hard to answer. Is that how he really sees me?

"If I wanted a replacement for June, it could never be you," he says. "The only thing you have in common with her is the fact that she didn't treat me like I was stupid, and she wasn't scared of me, either. I was never in love with her. We were friends, and that's it. But she treated me like I was a decent person. Like I mattered."

"Well, isn't that great for you," I snap.

"You don't know what it's like! You have Laney, and your family, and you hate them for having these expectations, but at least they want things for you. Do you know what I would give for that? No one in my life ever expected anything from me except for me to screw up. But June did. She was the first person to believe I could be somebody, and I needed that."

"You *needed* that?" I mimic spitefully. "Well, you knew what *I* needed. You knew how I felt, how it killed me that she didn't say anything. You *knew.* And still, you had this the whole time. You're nothing but a coward. You were too scared to give me this, you're too scared to write your own music, you're too scared to get off your ass and do something with your life. Other people didn't push you? No one there to pat you on the back or hold your hand? Boo-fucking-hoo. That's just an excuse for you being a fucking coward."

I punctuate the last sentence with a vicious jab of the envelope to his chest. There are tears now, running down my face faster than I can wipe them away. I don't even try.

Jake starts forward, his eyes like liquid, but I back away with my hand held up to ward off whatever he's thinking of trying.

"I hate you!" I'm screaming at him, seriously screaming, the words clawing out of my throat like a wild animal. "Get the fuck away from me! I fucking hate you! You piece of shit!"

His arms drop to his sides. "I know."

He can't know, he can't possibly know. I hate him, I hate

him so much, and it's more real than anything I've felt in a long time.

"I'm going to go," he says, his voice hoarse and tight. "I left her notebook on the table for you. I'm—I'm sorry. I know it doesn't mean anything, but I am. I'm really sorry."

He leaves, and I don't dare breathe again until I hear the front door slam. I hold on to the kitchen table to keep myself from falling over, and when the tears stop, I only stand there, body trembling from head to toe.

Jake's right. Sorry isn't enough.

Not this time.

sixteen

June is over. July dawns bright and relentlessly hot; there's no escaping it.

Being home again is a shock to the system. Not because I'm returning to chaos—quite the opposite. Everything is shockingly mundane. Even the stupid puppy calendar I stare down every morning in the kitchen is a constant reminder that life goes on, the white squares filled with my mother's doctor appointments and knitting club meetings and the birthdays of family friends. No sign of June anywhere.

I spend my days sealed inside air-conditioning, sucking on ice cubes and watching reruns of *M*A*S*H*. I wish Laney was around so we could analyze in detail the plain-as-day homoerotic subtext between Hawkeye and B.J., and work on our tans at the park, and drive to Duncan's for late-night sundaes. Unfortunately for us, though our return home was met initially with relief and joy from our parents, it didn't take long for that rush of goodwill to sour into a full month's grounding for us both.

I know that as far as punishments go, I got off with a light sentence. Being under house arrest isn't too bad. It gives me a convenient excuse not to interact with anyone, which is good, since I don't even want to think about when—or if—I'll see Jake face-to-face again. The worst is worrying about Laney. Mom disconnected my internet and confiscated my cell phone, but I did manage to find the internet cord and connect while she was running errands. I sent Laney an email asking what was going on, in the vaguest terms possible, since I don't know if her parents are monitoring her account.

Her response was only one line: *Everything's okay. I'll talk to you when I can. xoxo.*

I miss her the most when I sit alone on the roof, observing the kids down the street as they lick ice cream cones and wage war with water balloons. This is ice cream weather, run-around-in-sprinklers weather, weather meant to be enjoyed with friends.

For my mother, it's gardening weather. She's returned to work part-time, easing back into her schedule, and spends her afternoons and evenings digging around in the backyard with cotton gloves and a trowel in hand. I helped her out one weekend with the weeding—there was a lot to be done, and I found it oddly satisfying, ripping each one out by its roots. We worked side by side for hours on our hands and knees, sometimes talking, sometimes not. She never pushed, but I could tell that when I did talk, she listened intently. Maybe that was why I felt okay with letting some details slip—I told her about Laney and me visiting the arch, Fridgehenge, the Arizona stars, the way the water looked in California when I saw the ocean for the first time.

I didn't mention Jake. Some things are better kept to myself.

A few things changed during my absence. Aunt Helen moved out, and though she occasionally stops by for dinner, she seems to be consciously holding her tongue. There's no more booze in the house; I even made sure by checking all the hiding spots, like my mom's shoe closet and inside bottles of vitamin water. And Mom seems different—she isn't totally together, and sometimes she still cries, but she isn't the broken mess I remember. She's trying. I've decided that I need to try, too.

And it isn't like Mom is the only one who ever gets sad, either. Once the garden was cleared of all the weeds and new soil had been put in, she started coming home from work with a new box of flowers from the greenhouse every day. On the day she brought home carnations, I cried in the shower for an hour, feeling foolish and brokenhearted, and missing June more than ever.

Today, it's daisies. Daisies, at least, don't inspire any emotional meltdowns.

"Aren't they gorgeous?" she gushes as I hand her a tall, frosted glass of lemonade. "They complement the magnolias perfectly."

I stand back to better admire the row of deep pink flowers, the tips of their petals tinged with white.

"You know, I'm not a big fan of pink," I say, "but in this case, yes. I approve."

I sit back down on the porch steps, arms folded over my knees. Mom stands up, brushes the dirt off her jeans and joins me. I don't mean to but I can't help but stare at her. I'm still getting used to this new incarnation of my mother, this woman who is trying to be so careful with me, who isn't falling apart, and while she isn't completely together, she's rebuilding herself, day by day. She's so much stronger than I ever gave her credit for.

I thought she'd be angry with me when she found out what I'd done with June's ashes. My father was. He didn't say it to my face, but he called me the day after I came home, and he came by that night to take me out to dinner. He wanted to know what had happened. I supplied him with evasive answers over Chinese, never saying more than I absolutely had to. I could tell he was frustrated by my reticence, but he didn't call me out on it. Our awkward silences hung heavy with all the things we didn't dare say.

When he took me home, he walked me to the door, and before I opened it he asked me if I was okay. I told him yes without knowing if it was an honest answer or not; I knew it was what he wanted to hear. He didn't ask again. He waited until I'd gone upstairs to talk to Mom in the foyer. I sat on the floor at the top of the steps, hidden behind the banister like a little kid as I listened to the two of them talk.

"I can't believe what she did. I had a right, you know," he said, and the anger in his voice was more emotion than I'd heard from him in a long time. "She was my daughter."

I knew from the way he said "daughter" he meant June, not me, and that he meant what I had done with her ashes. It was something I hadn't considered much—what, exactly, I was taking away from him by stealing the urn. It was another thing to feel bad about, on top of everything else.

"I know," Mom said to him. "She was mine, too." Neither of them spoke for a moment, but I knew what they must be thinking. That this was a pain the two of them shared that no one else could touch. Not even me. And they would share it for the rest of their lives, even if they weren't together. I couldn't think of a more terrible thing to bind two people.

"I wish I'd known," he said. "I would have stopped her. You should have stopped her."

I expected the conversation to escalate into another one of their arguments, but all Mom said was, "It's over. What's done is done. You're going to have to let it go."

Now she sits beside me with her eyes to the sky, wistful. "It's a beautiful day," she says.

I look at her for a long time. "Did you read the letter?"

I know the question will ruin the moment, but I have to know. And when my mother's eyes meet mine, I know. She did.

I haven't. I almost did, on the plane ride—but I couldn't bring myself to tear open the envelope while crammed in a seat in coach, with Laney nodded off in the seat next to me. I did flip through the rest of her notebook; nothing was there except for calculus notes. I did notice they stopped a few days before she died. Maybe she'd made up her mind by then, and decided it wasn't worth the effort.

I held on to the letter until Mom and I got home. When she threw her car keys onto the kitchen counter with a sigh and just stared at them, rubbing her temples, I slid the envelope next to the key ring and said, "June wrote this," before walking out of the room.

We haven't discussed it since.

"I think you should read it," she says.

"Why? It won't change anything. It won't change what she did."

I thought taking her to California would fix things. Would allow me to make peace with what she did. But I know now that it isn't that easy. Nothing is. I understand June a little better, I think, but I feel like some part of me is going to be angry at her for the rest of my life. And angry at myself.

I stare down at my shoes; they're covered with rich black soil. "Do you think I'll ever be able to forgive her?"

"I don't know, baby. That's up to you, isn't it?"

I fight back the tears welling up behind my eyes. When did I turn into such a fucking faucet? It's ridiculous.

"Hey." Mom reaches out and touches the side of my face. I try to turn away, embarrassed, but she makes me look at her. She's got little lines by her eyes, and lines by her mouth. Laugh lines? Frown lines? I'm not sure. "I love you. You know that, right? I love you."

I nod, put my hand over hers and draw it away, but I keep holding it. It feels weird, being this openly affectionate when we never really have before. But at the same time it's sort of nice, too. I figure I should enjoy the maternal affection while it lasts.

Mom turns toward the garden again, her head tilted to one side appraisingly. "It's a little late in the season to be planting. You think it's too late for the daisies to make it?"

I look at them, that splash of bright color, the stems that extend into the thick soil. Held down by the roots.

"Nah." I shake my head and smile a little. "It's not too late."

On the Fourth of July, Mom goes out with Aunt Helen to meet up with their knitting group for a barbecue. She offers to let me shed the ball and chain and tag along, but I opt instead to sit on the roof with a tuna sandwich and watch the kids across the street play with sparklers on their front lawn. Soon enough their parents will probably be carting them off to the park by the lake, where the whole town always gathers to see the fireworks.

I have the letter with me. Mom must have sneaked into my room while I was sleeping, because this morning I woke up to find it placed on my nightstand. I keep turning it over in my hands, fingering the torn edge of the envelope, but I'm too scared to open it. I know it's stupid to be so freaked out by a piece of paper. I know I should get over myself and just read it already. But before I can talk myself into opening it, I'm interrupted.

"Hey, stranger."

Laney's voice makes me jump about a mile high. I turn to

see her head popping through the window, and I surreptitiously slide the envelope out of sight.

"You know, you really shouldn't sneak up on someone perched precariously on a rooftop," I point out.

"Whatever. If you fell you'd survive. You'd probably break a leg, maybe crack some ribs, but you'd survive." She climbs through the window and pushes me to one side. "Move over."

I scoot over to make room as she settles in beside me. She hands me a Popsicle, then unwraps her own and sticks it in her mouth.

"So what is this? Your parents let you out on parole?" I ask. I peel off the wrapper of my Popsicle—it's one of those triple-flavor tiered ones: red, white and blue. Very patriotic.

"More like I'm AWOL," she confesses. "They're having dinner at the steak house, then they'll be at the fireworks display and probably go out for drinks afterward, so I've got a few hours. I figured I'd make the most of my one night of freedom." She glances down at her Popsicle. "Hey, what flavor do you think the white is supposed to be? The red's obviously cherry, and the blue is blueberry, but they never say what the white is."

"White lemon, maybe?" I guess. We sit there eating for a little while, and then I look right at her, unable to hide my worry. "Laney. How are you? What happened? Did you—?"

It takes her a minute to answer the unspoken question. She shrugs and says, "I'm not pregnant."

"What? How—"

"I lost it."

I freeze. "You did?"

"It didn't look like anything. It was just...like, like I had really bad cramps, and I bled a little, and I sort of completely freaked, but I snuck out and took the bus to the free clinic on the west side, and they told me it happens a lot. They said some women don't even notice when it happens."

"Oh," I say. "Laney, I'm…" Sorry? Glad? No. Relieved, mostly, but also sad—sad that this had to happen in the first place.

Laney seems to understand. "Yeah, I know," she says. "It happened the day after we got back. My parents don't have a clue." She goes quiet for a moment. "I just keep thinking—what if this is karma? What if I'm being punished?"

I stare at her, incredulous. "Punished? For *what*?"

"For slutting around. For not wanting it."

"You're looking at this the wrong way. Aren't you the one who's always saying everything happens for a reason? Maybe this was supposed to happen. Like, it was fate or something."

"Do you really believe that?"

"I don't know," I say. "But it doesn't really matter what I think, does it?"

Laney considers this as she sucks on her Popsicle and watches the kids below, screaming and chasing each other in dizzying circles with their sparklers in hand.

"Have you talked to Jake?" she asks.

The question makes my stomach twist; I was wondering when I'd be forced to have this conversation. "No. And I don't plan to," I tell her. "Why? Have you?"

"Only once," she admits. "He called and asked if I still needed any money, so I explained to him why I didn't. And then I told him off for what he did to you." She pauses. "I may have at some point referred to him as a douche nozzle."

I can't help but laugh. "You did not! A *douche nozzle*? I don't even know what that is!"

Laney starts giggling, too, and it's like it's contagious, because soon enough we're falling all over ourselves with laughter.

"You know," she says breathlessly, a few minutes later when

we've composed ourselves, "I get why you're mad, and don't get me wrong, I'm totally on your side. I'll hate him till the day I die if you want. But I think he's pretty broken up over this. I'm not saying he was, like, crying tears of man pain over the phone, but he sounded upset."

I don't look at her as I lick the melted Popsicle juice off of my sticky fingers. "Good. He should be."

"All right, I've said my piece, so I'm staying out of this, forever and ever amen." She raises her hands in a conceding gesture before biting off the rest of her Popsicle. "Hey, I meant to ask you—have you decided what you're going to do with all those pictures you took? You must have a ton."

"Yeah," I say. "I mean, no, I haven't really thought about it."

Laney licks her Popsicle stick clean and squints at it. "Say, what do you call a piece of wood with nothing to do?"

I think for a moment. "Board?"

"Got it in one!" she exclaims, and when she holds up her hand, I roll my eyes but indulge her with a high five anyway. She looks up at the sky and says, "Too bad we can't see the fireworks from here."

That makes me think of something. "Hey," I say, "I've got an idea."

We scramble through the window and down the stairs, out the front door, and I pay one of the kids across the street two dollars for two of his sparkler sticks. I have my heavy black funeral dress in one hand and my mom's lighter in the other. Laney stares at me like I'm crazy as I spread the dress out on the driveway.

"What are you doing?" she asks, but she says it like she already knows the answer.

"Making our own fireworks."

I light the end of the sparkler, then press the tip into the heap of fabric on the asphalt. It takes a few tries with both the sparkler and the lighter, but the material is flammable, and soon enough the dress goes up in flames. After a minute or so of watching it burn, Laney rushes to grab the hose. She douses the remaining flames, until all that's left is charred remnants of the dress.

It's not all gone. That's just science—matter can be neither created nor destroyed. The same way pieces of June survived in the dust of her ashes, the way those pieces are settling into the ocean floor right now. The dress and the memories that go along with it will last forever. Or until everyone who remembers dies, too.

Laney drops the hose and looks at me. "Harper. How are you doing? I mean, really?"

I think about it and say, "Better," and as I speak the word I realize it's true.

I still go to bed sad, and wake up sad, and it still hurts like hell, but there are moments during the day when it hurts less. Sometimes I can think of June and not want to burst into tears or put my fist through a wall. Sometimes I'm close to happy and it doesn't even hurt. Much. I'll never be the way I was before, but maybe that's okay. Life goes on, I'm going on, even without her. Not every day hurts. Not every breath hurts.

Maybe that's all we can really ask for.

All of the pictures taken en route to California are still inside Carmen's shoebox. I shoved it far under my bed the same night I came back to Grand Lake, and since then I've mostly forgotten about them. But the day after Laney reminds me of their existence, I get down on my hands and knees and slide the box back out from underneath the bed.

The photos aren't the only thing I haven't sorted through—my duffel bag remains halfway unpacked. I probably would've finished if I hadn't discovered Jake's CBGB T-shirt buried among my things. Yup, somehow I mistakenly ended up with his shirt. Seeing it made my heart hurt, and I was torn between setting it on fire in the front yard like I did the dress or curling up on the bed and sleeping with it like a little kid's blanket.

I was too pissed off to do the latter, and feeling too maudlin to do the former, so I settled for tossing my duffel in my closet and leaving it there, untouched.

Now I sit on top of my bed with the shoebox in front of me. I pull off the lid and turn it over onto the bedspread, scraps of celluloid spilling out everywhere. I pluck a photo out of the pile at random—it's a candid of Jake and Laney pretending to duel with beef jerky ropes at some gas station in Texas. Or maybe it was Arizona, I can't remember for sure.

What am I supposed to do with these? Keeping them stashed away in a shoebox doesn't seem right. I could put them in an album, except I don't have any that are empty, and I'd probably have to buy a special one to fit Polaroids. I'm mulling over my options when I turn my head and see the answer staring me in the face.

The wall closest to my bed. My white and empty and begging-for-decoration wall, the only blank one in my room. The others are covered in film posters and other pictures I've taken and liked well enough to showcase. My closet door is proudly decorated with patches of orange and green paper—all of the detention and tardy slips I've accumulated over the years, badges of my insubordination. It was Laney's idea.

Just as I'm working out the arrangement in my head, the doorbell rings. It can't be Mom, since she's at work, so really there are only two viable options: It's either Aunt Helen, dropping by for one of her cherished surprise visits, or Laney, having managed to liberate herself once more. All the way down the stairs, I cross my fingers for it to be Option Number Two.

Turns out, it's neither. I open the door to see…no one.

There's no car or person in sight. At first I assume some stupid brat on the block decided it'd be fun to play a game of Ding Dong Ditch, but then I glance down and see it.

A mix CD.

It's sitting on the doormat, in a clear case. I bend over and pick it up, and I can make out the words written across the silver disc—Saving June.

Back in my room, I set it on top of my stereo, then pace back and forth for so long I make a dark trail on the carpet. What is this supposed to mean? It has to be from Jake, obviously, being his modus operandi and all. No one else would've done this. No one else would've known what I'd said, that evening on the boat.

Finally I decide to stop torturing myself and listen to the damn CD.

Every song on it is something we listened to at some point during the trip. The Bruce Springsteen jam he blasted when he picked me up, the Beatles song I cried along to in Oklahoma, the Doors song that played when we—while we—

Listening to that one brings back a slew of memories. The feel of his mouth on mine, the way our bodies stuck together with sweat in the afterglow. God, even just thinking about it, alone in my room, makes me blush.

It isn't fair. It isn't fair that Jake had to ruin everything by giving me that letter, or that June had to ruin everything by writing it in the first place, by choosing to end her life, by not caring what that did to everyone else's. It is so unfair, and I am so, so mad at them, but even so, I still love them both, against my better judgment. It'd be so much easier if I could hate them—but I can't.

It's like that Crosby, Stills and Nash song Jake sang to me on the hood of his van; my love for June and Jake is an anchor, bound with unbreakable chains. Weighing me down, but at the same time…keeping me grounded. Keeping me here. Tying me to the world. It hurts, but it's supposed to, because that's what it means to be alive. And that's comforting, actually. The realization that I'm not some robot devoid of emotions. That I still have the ability to feel things this brutally, this immediate and sharp.

When the room plunges into silence, I think at first the CD has finished, but then static crackles, and Jake's voice comes out of the speakers.

"Uh, hi, Harper. Didn't expect this, did you? Well, you told me I was too chicken-shit to write my own songs. You're not entirely wrong about that. But I don't back down from a challenge, so here's my best shot. I know it probably sucks, but… I hope you don't hate it."

There's another silence, and then some rustling like he's moving around, followed by the strum of a guitar.

"We left behind this small town
But we couldn't leave behind the ghosts
As we headed for the coast, yeah, and you know
There was something in the way she told me
How my hair looked stupid, and
How she couldn't hold her tequila, and
How she was broken and beautiful and
Still standing, and how was I supposed to know
All along we were saving June
Saving June, yeah
She had flowers in her hair and one powerful glare
My modern day Rubik's Cube, she made me feel
Like maybe we could have it all
But you can never have it all
And now I've gone and lost
All the things that they always sang about
All the things that I still dream about

Now I'm counting up the days, counting all the ways
I never said what I meant, but it's too late 'cause
June is over and so are we
And I'm the one left, with nothing to save."

The song is just Jake and his acoustic guitar, open and aching and unguarded. It's beautiful. It makes me want to laugh and cry at the same time, but I do neither. I just sit on my bed and listen to the CD on a loop until I've finished sticking each and every Polaroid to my wall.

Until I've picked up my sister's letter and finally read the last words she ever wrote, words intended for me.

Until I've figured out exactly what I want—what I need—to do.

The writing in June's letter is sloppy compared to her usual perfect script, like maybe her hand was shaking while she wrote the words. I imagine her sitting down, plotting this out in a notebook, her final message, the grace notes of her life's composition. The moment that must have cemented her decision. I'll never know what she was thinking. What, exactly, drove her to that point.

The closest I'll come to knowing is through her note.

Harper,
I know you will not understand this. I don't expect you to. I don't feel the need to justify why I'm doing what I am to anyone except myself, but I do want you to know a few things.

1. I love you and Mom and Dad, and I know you all love me. I'm sorry for the hurt this will cause you.
2. Trust me that it's better this way. It's the only way I can

be free of this. I'm so sad I can't think. I'm scared all the time. Nothing helps. I don't see the point. I can't explain it. The bastards have ground me down. Maybe I'm crazy. I don't know I don't know I don't know.

I should've tried harder. I'm sorry. I'm sorry I can't be strong like you. I think you were right before, about real love not existing. At least not the love I needed. But that's my fault. Not yours.

Tell whoever finds me that I'm sorry. I tried my hardest not to leave a mess.

I feel like I should say more, but there's nothing else.

I love you.

I'm sorry.

Love,

June

P.S.—I'm not scared anymore.

seventeen

Twenty-four minutes. That is how long it takes to get from the bus stop closest to my house to the Oleo Strut. Fourteen minutes on the bus, six minutes of walking time and four minutes of stopping every fifteen feet and willing myself not to ditch out on this.

At least the heat helps, in the sense that I finally reason to myself that if I don't get out of the sun, I'm going to fall over and die of heatstroke, and that'll be of help to no one.

"Well, hello, hello," Eli greets the second I walk into the Oleo. He's taping a blue flyer advertising a Journey cover band to the inside of the window. "Hey, weren't you in here a while ago with that blond girl? The one who thought she was Nancy Drew?"

"Maybe," I answer evasively.

He waggles his eyebrows—much like Jake used to waggle his. Must be a genetic trait. "Hope you're not here for a follow-up interrogation."

"Don't worry, I'll spare you," I assure him. I take a deep breath. "Is your brother around?"

"Ah," he says with a knowing smirk, and I'd be embarrassed if I wasn't so annoyed. Apparently also a Tolan family trait: the ability to bug the crap out of me with a single look.

Eli makes up for it a little by informing me that Jake is out back and allowing me to cut through the exit in the stockroom rather than walk all the way around the building. I push open the heavy door and find Jake hosing down Joplin, a bucket of soapy water at his feet. My heart warms a little at the sight of the familiar black van. It's stupid, it's just a piece of machinery, metal and bolts and rubber, but I've missed it.

Jake is wearing black jeans, as usual, and a shabby dark gray wife beater. No fedora today. Other than the fact that the bruise below his eye has faded, he looks exactly the same, even though so much has changed. But of course he wouldn't look any different. It's only been a few weeks.

I wait for a few seconds, and then I say, "Joplin's looking good."

The idea was to have a smooth, cool opening line, something that would give me the upper hand, but in this case, the element of surprise does not work in my favor. When Jake turns in the direction of my voice, the hose turns with him— and douses my entire front.

"Shit!" He jerks the nozzle away, shuts off the spray of water and looks at me, shocked. "Shit, I'm sorry, I didn't mean to—"

"It's okay," I say quickly. I wipe the cold water off of my face with one hand and pull the bottom of my drenched shirt away from my middle. "Uh, I actually needed the cool-down anyway."

"Oh." He stares at me with his mouth open, like he's trying to decide what to say. Finally he clears his throat and says, "Um. Do you want to come inside? I can get you a towel—and…and I wanted to show you something. If you don't mind."

This isn't how I pictured my first time in Jake's room, but

here I am: standing in the middle of it, dripping water all over his hardwood floor. He goes to the bathroom for a towel as I survey his space. It's pretty much what I imagined it to be; the walls are layered ceiling-to-floor in posters of old rock stars and punk bands, with a few jazz artists thrown in for good measure, signed flyers from local shows and newspaper clippings from various protests.

I'm reading about two guys who scaled a skyscraper in Manhattan to raise awareness for global warming when Jake reenters the room. He wordlessly hands me a blue towel.

"Thanks," I say, patting off my face. We look at each for a while, both silent. I realize he's waiting for me to make the first move. I'm not sure where to start—but I figure there's no point in beating around the bush. "I read June's letter."

"Oh." He blinks a few times, but doesn't move. "Did it help?"

"Yes," I say, "and no. It said all of the right things—and none of the right things. Does that make sense?"

"Yes," he says, without hesitation, and I know he's telling the truth, because Jake never thinks twice about telling me when I'm not making sense.

The look on his face draws me by the anchor chain between us closer to him. I'm swept a step forward, my heart so tight in my chest it could burst.

"I really miss her," I say. My voice cracks a little around the edges.

"I know."

"And you."

"What?"

"You. I miss you."

His mouth hangs open, and then he smiles sadly, in a way that makes my insides ache, with longing and hurt and everything else standing between us.

"I…miss you, too," he says.

It's what I want to hear, but—

"I'm still pissed," I tell him.

"I know."

"Good." All of that was hard enough to say out loud that I have to look away for a minute. Eventually I meet his eyes again and say, "So what did you want to show me?"

Jake goes to the vinyl record player sitting on top of his dresser, turns it on and sets the needle. He holds up the record cover—it's the autographed Jimi Hendrix album.

"I wanted you to hear it," he explains. "Listening to Jimi Hendrix on vinyl is something I think every person should experience at least once in their life." He sits down on the floor with his back against his bed, and I lower myself down next to him, close enough so that our hips and thighs touch. The contact sparks something inside of me, hot and breathtaking, thrumming.

We listen to the music in mutual appreciative silence. Jimi makes the guitar come alive, makes it wail and scream and rage and sing, each soaring riff searing through me. This is the kind of music that changes people, the kind of music that changes the world.

The same kind of music that changed me.

I close my eyes, soaking it in, and when I open them again, Jake is looking at me funny. His mouth slants to one side like he doesn't know whether or not it's okay to smile.

"I'm sorry," he says, "I just— I didn't expect you to show up. Ever. I mean, I'm glad you did. You just caught me off guard, is all."

"I wasn't going to," I say. "But I listened to your CD."

A lengthy pause. "What did you think?"

"It sucks."

"Really?" His mouth turns down in disappointment. "You didn't like the music?"

"No, the music was great. And your song at the end, I loved it. I did. It's just—you told me that the art of the mix CD is like a book. That it has to have the exciting hook in the beginning and the right closer that wraps everything up the way it needs to be. Your song was amazing, but there's a problem. It's not an ending."

"Not sure I follow you."

I take his hand in mine. He looks down at our interlocked fingers and then back up at me. His eyes are this unreal shade of green. I remember, the first time I saw him in the garden, how that was the first thing I noticed, before I knew anything else about him.

"*June is over and so are we,*" I say. "I don't want that to be how things end."

"You don't?"

I meant it when I said I was still mad. There's no instant fix for this. But I care about Jake, and that means something, right? Maybe it's a mistake, maybe I'll get hurt in the end. But maybe not. I loved June. I still love her, and that will never change, but for the first time in my life, I truly, truly don't want to be her. I don't want to be so scared all the time. So alone. I want to believe something can be worth it. Worth the pain. Worth the risk.

Deciding to kiss Jake is like standing on the edge of a pool, staring down and wanting to take the leap, but fearing how cold the water will be.

I hold my breath and jump.

★ ★ ★ ★ ★

Saving June

THE SOUNDTRACKS

NOLITE TE BASTARDES CARBORUNDORUM

———

1) "Start Me Up," The Rolling Stones

2) "O Sweet Nothing," Velvet Underground

3) "Nights in White Satin," The Moody Blues

4) "Stairway to Heaven," Led Zeppelin

5) "Gloomy Sunday," Billie Holiday

6) "Where Is My Mind," The Pixies

7) "Asking for It," Hole

8) "Boom Swagger Boom," Murder City Devils

9) "Train in Vain," The Clash

10) "Under Pressure," Queen, featuring David Bowie

11) "If Six Was Nine," The Jimi Hendrix Experience

12) "American Girl," Tom Petty

13) "Tangled Up in Blue," Bob Dylan

14) "Don't Know Much About History," Sam Cooke

15) "Michelangelo," Emmylou Harris

16) "Bang Bang (My Baby Shot Me Down)," Nancy Sinatra

17) "God," John Lennon

18) "Where Did You Sleep Last Night," Nirvana

19) "The Sounds of Silence," Simon & Garfunkel

JAKE'S "SAY MY NAME" MIX

———

1) "Me and Bobby McGee," Janis Joplin

2) "Come on Eileen," Dexy's Midnight Runners

3) "Demon John," Jeff Buckley

4) "Stephanie Says," Velvet Underground

5) "Daniel," Elton John

6) "Layla," Eric Clapton

7) "A Boy Named Sue," Johnny Cash

8) "Ruby Tuesday," The Rolling Stones

9) "Peggy Sue," Buddy Holly

10) "Joey," Concrete Blonde

11) "Charlotte Sometimes," The Cure

12) "Jacqueline," Franz Ferdinand

13) "Gloria," Patti Smith

14) "Deanna," Nick Cave

15) "Allison," Elvis Costello

16) "Clementine," Elliott Smith

17) "Hey Jude," The Beatles

SAVING JUNE

———

1) "Going to California," Led Zeppelin

2) "This Time Tomorrow," The Kinks

3) "Thunder Road," Bruce Springsteen

4) "Take a Chance on Me," ABBA

5) "Falling Is Like This," Ani DiFranco

6) "Let It Be," The Beatles

7) "Southern Cross," Crosby, Stills and Nash

8) "You Can't Always Get What You Want," The Rolling Stones

9) "Never Argue With a German If You're Tired
or European," Jefferson Airplane

10) "Rebel Girl," Bikini Kill

11) "Touch Me," The Doors

12) "California Love," Tupac, featuring Dr. Dre

13) "God Only Knows," The Beach Boys

14) "On the Radio," Regina Spektor

15) "Fix You," Coldplay

16) "I Am Trying to Break Your Heart (Wilco Cover)," Nickel Creek

17) "Chelsea Hotel No. 2," Leonard Cohen

18) "The Book of Love," Magnetic Fields

19) "3 Rounds and a Sound," Blind Pilot

BONUS TRACK: "Saving June," Jake Tolan

ACKNOWLEDGMENTS

First I need to thank my agent and biggest advocate, Diana Fox, for having enough confidence in me and my writing for the both of us. I couldn't ask for better. I'd also like to thank my wonderful editor, Natashya Wilson, for falling so in love with my story and wanting to share it with the world. And thank you to everyone else at Harlequin Teen for making that happen.

To my earliest supporters—Lisa Rowe, Joanne Ferlas, Bridget Clark, Nell Gram, Gabrielle Rajerison, Ann Finstad, Erin Whipple, Rebekah Ross, thank you for your general awesomeness and love. Kim Montelibano Heil, you helped give me the push do this. Anna Genoese, you are the coolest and smartest person I know, and I respect your opinion more than anything. Thanks for never telling me I suck, even when I do. Olivia Castellanos, this book would not exist without you, period. Thank you for being the first person to ever read it, thank you for being on the receiving end of so many emails and phone calls throughout this entire process, and thank you even more for never doubting this could happen. Your friendship means the world to me.

My fifth-grade teacher, Eric Schweinzger—thank you for sharing my essays out loud in class, giving me glowing praise on my silly short stories, and basically helping a kid who wasn't that great at much feel like maybe she could be pretty good at this one thing, if nothing else.

Mom, thank you for raising me on such awesome music, and for everything else. And I do mean everything. Your support is beyond words, and I love you.

Turn the page for a sneak peek at
SPEECHLESS
by Hannah Harrington,
now available from Harlequin TEEN.

IN WHICH NATIONAL GEOGRAPHIC INADVERTENTLY CHANGES MY LIFE

Keeping secrets isn't my specialty. It never has been, ever since kindergarten when I found out Becky Swanson had a crush on Tommy Barnes, and I managed to circulate that fact to the entire class, including Tommy himself, within our fifteen-minute recess—a pretty impressive feat, in retrospect. That was ten years ago, and it still may hold the record for my personal best.

The secret I have right now is so, so much juicier than that. I'm just about ready to burst at the seams.

"Will you stop the teasing already?" Kristen says. We're in her bedroom where I'm helping her decide on an outfit for tonight—a drawn-out process when your wardrobe is as massive as hers. "It's annoying. Just tell me."

Kristen is not a patient person. I realize I've been pushing it by alluding to my newfound information over the past twenty minutes without actually divulging anything. Of course I'm going to tell her; she's my best friend, and I can't keep it to myself much longer without truly pissing her off. A pissed-off Kristen is not a fun Kristen. Still, it's rare for me to have the upper hand with her, so I can't help but hold it over her head just a little.

"I don't know," I say innocently. "I'm not sure you can handle it…"

She turns around from where she's digging through her closet and chucks a black leather sandal at me. I shield my face with both hands, laughing as the shoe bounces off one arm and onto the mattress. Kristen props a hand on her narrow hip and cocks her head at me, her glossy, shoulder-length blond hair swaying with the motion.

"You're building this up way too much," she says. She yanks out a shimmery red top from her closet before facing me again. "I bet whatever it is, it's completely lame."

"Well, in that case, I'll keep it to myself." When she glares at me, I just smile in return and say, "Don't wear that. That baby-doll cut looks like something out of the maternity section."

She hangs the top back up and comes over to the bed, flopping down on her stomach next to me. "Spill," she whines, the previous iciness dissolving into borderline desperation. This is as close as Kristen ever gets to groveling. "Otherwise I'm uninviting you from the party."

The threat can't be real—Kristen knows I've been looking forward to her New Year's Eve party for over a month now. She even helped concoct the cover story necessary to convince my mother to let me come over to her house despite the grounding I received after my parents saw my latest report card. Like I'm ever going to need geometry in real life anyway.

Even though Kristen can be…*touchy,* she wouldn't uninvite me from the party over something like this—but I decide it's better to cave already than to test her on it.

"Okay, okay," I relent. "I'll tell you."

She breaks into a grin and scoots closer to me. I like having her attention like this; Kristen is easily bored, so when I do get her full focus, it makes me feel like I'm doing something right. She is, after all, one of—if not *the*—most popular girls in the sophomore class, if you keep track of that sort of thing, which I do. She's used to people fawning all over her to get on her good side. I've been on her good side for almost two years now, and I intend to stay there.

I'd better make this good.

"So I met up with Megan today because she wanted me to help her pick out new shoes, right?" I start. "She also wanted to bitch to me about Owen, because he totally blew her off last weekend and they've been fighting a lot, and she's wondering if she should break up with him."

Kristen's mouth tugs into a frown. "Um, yawn. I already know this."

"I'm not done yet," I assure her. "Anyway, so Megan brings along Tessa Schauer, which...whatever. She's annoying, but I can deal. We shop for a while and everything's fine, and then I remember I need to call my mom about picking stuff up from the dry cleaner's, except I'm an idiot who didn't charge my phone and the battery's dead. I ask Tessa if I can borrow hers since she's right there, and she hands it off and walks away. I call my mom, and then I'm about to give it back, but I decided to look through the pictures on the phone because I'm nosy like that, and..." I pause for a moment, just to draw out the anticipation.

"And...?" Kristen prompts. She's totally hanging on to every word.

"And," I say, "the first one I see? It's of Tessa. With Owen. Looking very...shall we say...*friendly*."

Her eyes widen. "*How* friendly?" she asks.

I dig my phone out of my pocket and toss it at her. "Look for yourself."

I watch in amusement as she fumbles with my phone, scrolling through my text messages. "Shut up," she gasps, looking back up at me. "You forwarded the pictures to yourself?"

"Duh."

"Won't Tessa know?"

I'm a little insulted by the question, to be honest. Of course I thought ahead. I'm not an amateur. "I deleted the sent texts," I explain. "She'll have no idea."

"That is…" Kristen pauses, and then grins up at me. "Totally brilliant."

I take the phone back and look at the screen, where the high-angled self-portrait of Tessa and Owen midkiss stares back at me. So tacky. Not just the picture, or how Owen's mouth is open so wide I can actually see his tongue entering Tessa's mouth (gross, gross, gross), but making out with your alleged best friend's boyfriend behind her back? That's just classless. I would never in a million years hook up with Kristen's boyfriend, Warren Snyder, while she's dating him. Okay, I would never hook up with him, period, because he's a sleaze, but that's beside the point. The point is, some things are sacred.

"She's a shitty friend," I tell Kristen. "I can't believe she did that to Megan." There's no way Megan will forgive her when she finds out. She's dated Owen for over a year, and Tessa's been her best friend for longer than that. An entire friendship down the drain, all because Tessa couldn't keep her hands off Owen. No boy is worth that. Not even Brendon Ryan, whom I would do a number of immoral and insane things for, and who is quite possibly the love of my life, even if he doesn't know it yet. We've been caught in a wildly passionate, completely one-sided affair since freshman year.

"Tessa Schauer is a slutty bitch. I hope Megan kicks her ass," Kristen says. "When are you going to tell her?"

"Tonight, probably." Megan and Tessa will both be at the party, so I'll have to find a way to corner Megan alone and break the news. Tessa will know it's me, even if I erased my tracks, but whatever. Who cares? Snooping on someone's phone is a far more minor offense than slutting around with your best friend's boyfriend. No one will have sympathy for her.

Kristen rolls off the bed and stands in front of her full-length mirror, fiddling with the ends of her perfect hair. "You know, you could have some fun with this," she muses.

I sit up. "How?"

"If you tell Tessa you know about her and Owen, I bet she'd do just about *anything* to keep you from sharing that with Megan."

"Like blackmail?" I frown. "I don't know..."

"I'm just saying," Kristen says, "I know for a *fact* that she has a fake ID. She was attention-whoring like crazy, showing it off to everyone who would listen in Econ last week. Maybe you could convince her to hook up the two of us with our own."

Interesting idea. Except—

"What would we do with a fake ID?" I ask. Buying booze is the obvious answer, but while Kristen might pass for twenty-one with the right push-up bra and a pair of heels, there's no way I could. I am much less...*developed* than her.

"Well, I could go to Rave with Warren, for starters," she says. "You only have to be eighteen to get in."

Rave is this nightclub in Westfield, the next town over. Warren turned eighteen last month and went there to celebrate, and wouldn't shut up about it for two weeks. I have to admit, it would be interesting to see what all the fuss is about.

And if it's important to Kristen, then it's important to me.

"I'll see what I can do," I tell her, and by the way Kristen smiles at me, I know that was exactly what she wanted to hear.

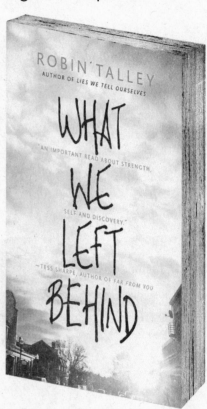

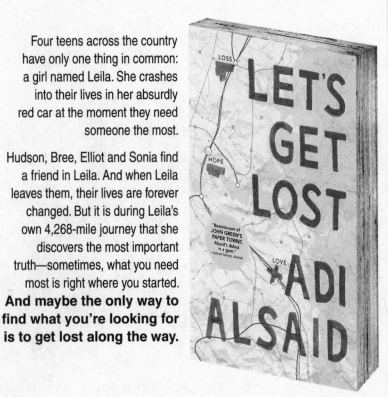

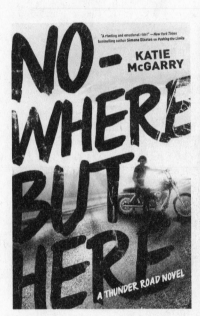

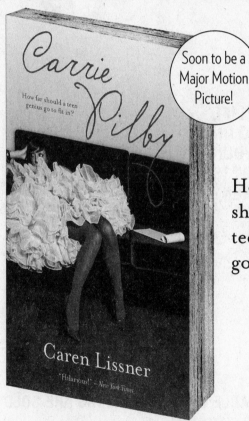